THE CASABLANCA QUARTET

I. WAR
&
II. PEACE

THE CASABLANCA QUARTET

I. WAR
1942–1946

&

II. PEACE
1948–1952

Based on true stories

JOSH SHOEMAKE

Opium Books

The main character of this novel is Casablanca in the years between 1942 and 1956. It is a life of its own, through which other lives move, changing it in ways both subtle and significant, only to return again like memories, strengthening the connections between them until patterns emerge, melodies and refrains, a discovered symphony — a life.

Like the city of Casablanca itself, those characters are based on real people, now mostly forgotten, and here reimagined. The facts of their lives and deaths, to the extent that they are still known, have been respected to the best of my ability.

PERSONS REPRESENTED

Victor Tessier (b. 1925) – French pilot

Franklin Sidney Felton (b. 1914) – American vice-consul (COI/OSS/CIA)

Arkady Zubov (b. 1910) – major in the NKVD, Soviet secret police

Camille Morin (b. 1923) – French girl from Dakar
Madame Morin (b. 1902) – her mother

Tommy August (b. 1918) – American Navy pilot
Lucy August (b. 1922) – his wife

Mike "Mag" Magursky (b. 1918) – American Army supply sergeant
Lieutenant Stec (b. 1907) – his superior

Josephine Baker (b. 1906) – American singer, dancer, actress

Abdelwahed Chaoui (b. 1911) – actor, producer, journalist, businessman, Nationalist
Zina Chaoui (b. 1916) – his wife
Touria Chaoui (b. 1936) – their daughter, pilot, Nationalist
Salah Chaoui (b. 1944) – their son

Ahmed Touil (b. 1922) – driver, resistant, cop

Aziza Benayiche (b. 1911) – Jewish businesswoman, owner of clothing shop
Suzanne Benayiche (b. 1934) – her daughter

Fadila (b. 1928) – a prostitute
Jean Bart (b. 1922) – her *patronne*

Jacques Lemaigre-Dubreuil (b. 1894) – industrialist, politician, writer
Simon Castet (b. 1928) – male model, friend of Lemaigre-Dubreuil

Albert Forestier (b. 1929) – journalist, soldier, policeman

François Avival (b. 1920) – manager of La Gironde, former boxer
Antoine "Tony" Méléro (b. 1929) – policeman
Congos (b. 1928) – policeman
Jean "the Gypsy" (b. 1928) – policeman

Rémy, Jean "le Footballeur", Omar "le Sheik", Michel "le Juif", Andre "El Negro", François, and other members of the Red Hand.

Captain Fillette (b. 1909) – director of Action Service of the SDECE, French foreign intelligence agency

Saadia Taibi (b. 1934) – nurse, resistant
Zaïm (b. 1908) – resistant

Directeur Martin (b. 1905) – French director of the flight school at Tit Mellil
Lieutenant Noguera (b. 1922) – French pilot, instructor at Tit Mellil

Haj Alaoui (b. 1906) – businessman connected to the Sultan
Hajja Aliya Alaoui (b. 1912) – his wife, a philanthropist
Haj Driss Alaoui (b. 1930) – their son, a businessman
Hajja Hiba Alaoui (b. 1916) – her sister

Major Sartout (b. 1907) – French police officer in Affaires Indigènes, newspaper director
Antoine Mazzella (b. 1916) – French newspaper editor

Mohamed Zerktouni (b. 1927) – resistant

L WAR
1942-1946
JOSH SHOEMAKE
F-AIUL
THE CASABLANCA QUARTET

THE CASABLANCA QUARTET

I. WAR

1942–1946

Based on true stories

JOSH SHOEMAKE

Opium Books

WAR

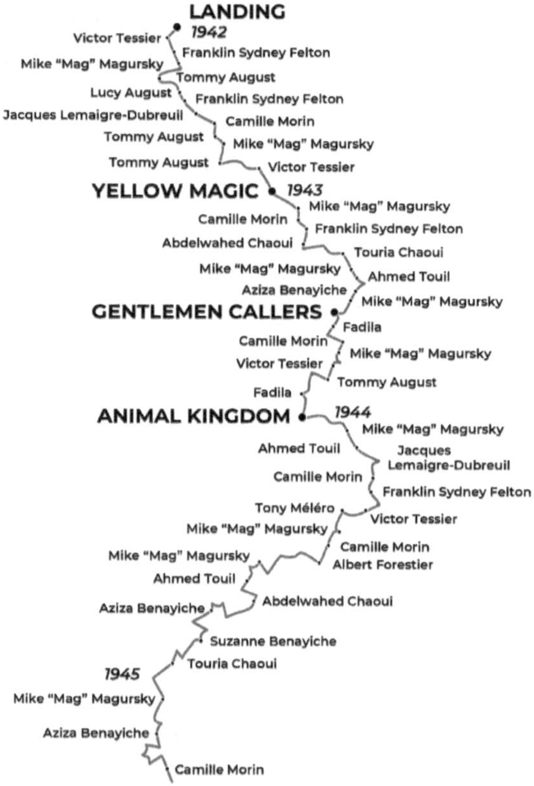

LANDING *1942*

Victor Tessier

Franklin Sydney Felton

Mike "Mag" Magursky

Tommy August

Lucy August

Franklin Sydney Felton

Jacques Lemaigre-Dubreuil

Camille Morin

Tommy August

Mike "Mag" Magursky

Tommy August

Victor Tessier

YELLOW MAGIC *1943*

Mike "Mag" Magursky

Camille Morin

Franklin Sydney Felton

Abdelwahed Chaoui

Touria Chaoui

Mike "Mag" Magursky

Ahmed Touil

Aziza Benayiche

Mike "Mag" Magursky

GENTLEMEN CALLERS

Fadila

Camille Morin

Victor Tessier

Mike "Mag" Magursky

Tommy August

Fadila

ANIMAL KINGDOM *1944*

Mike "Mag" Magursky

Ahmed Touil

Jacques Lemaigre-Dubreuil

Camille Morin

Franklin Sydney Felton

Tony Méléro

Victor Tessier

Mike "Mag" Magursky

Camille Morin

Mike "Mag" Magursky

Albert Forestier

Ahmed Touil

Aziza Benayiche

Abdelwahed Chaoui

Suzanne Benayiche

Touria Chaoui

1945

Mike "Mag" Magursky

Aziza Benayiche

Camille Morin

PEACE
THE ANGLE OF ATTACK
1948
Abdelwahed Chaoui
Touria Chaoui
Zina Chaoui
Salah Chaoui
Tony Méléro
Abdelwahed Chaoui
1949
Albert Forestier
Touria Chaoui
Franklin Sydney Felton
Camille Morin
Jacques Lemaigre-Dubreuil
Fadila
Suzanne Benayiche
Touria Chaoui
Tony Méléro
BLUESHIFT
1950
1951
Abdelwahed Chaoui
Touria Chaoui
Victor Tessier
Victor Tessier
Abdelwahed Chaoui
Suzanne Benayiche
Victor Tessier
Touria Chaoui
Fadila
Suzanne Benayiche
Touria Chaoui
HANDS
Abdelwahed Chaoui
Tony Méléro
1952
Aziza Benayiche
Touria Chaoui
Hajja Aliya Alaoui
Tommy August
Camille Morin
Lucy August
Victor Tessier
Albert Forestier
Tony Méléro
Albert Forestier
Suzanne Benayiche
Aziza Benayiche
Abdelwahed Chaoui
Suzanne Benayiche
Albert Forestier
Hajja Aliya Alaoui
Touria Chaoui

RESISTANCE

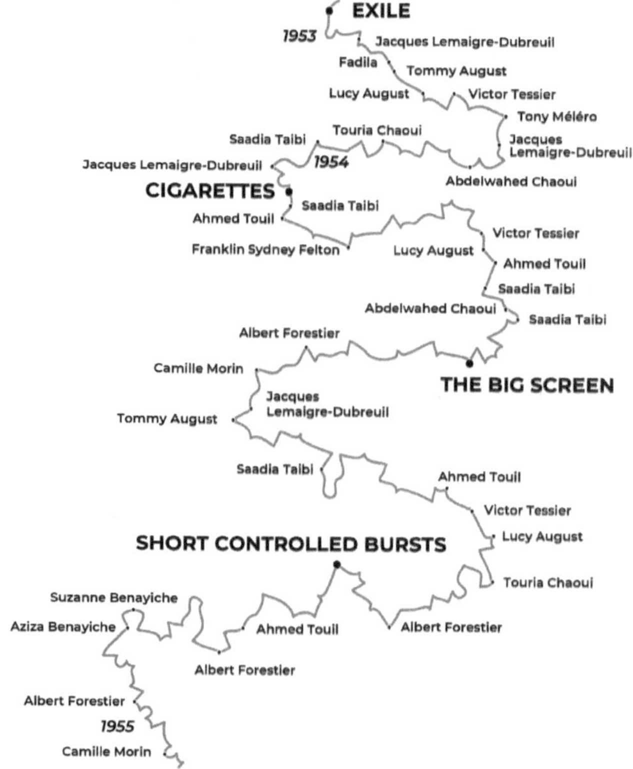
EXILE
1953
Jacques Lemaigre-Dubreuil
Fadila
Tommy August
Lucy August
Victor Tessier
Tony Méléro
Touria Chaoui
Saadia Taibi
Jacques Lemaigre-Dubreuil
Jacques Lemaigre-Dubreuil
1954
Abdelwahed Chaoui
CIGARETTES
Saadia Taibi
Ahmed Touil
Victor Tessier
Franklin Sydney Felton
Lucy August
Ahmed Touil
Saadia Taibi
Abdelwahed Chaoui
Saadia Taibi
Albert Forestier
Camille Morin
THE BIG SCREEN
Jacques
Lemaigre-Dubreuil
Tommy August
Saadia Taibi
Ahmed Touil
Victor Tessier
SHORT CONTROLLED BURSTS
Lucy August
Touria Chaoui
Suzanne Benayiche
Aziza Benayiche
Ahmed Touil
Albert Forestier
Albert Forestier
Albert Forestier
1955
Camille Morin

FREEDOM
DJINNS
Lucy August
Tommy August
Victor Tessier
Suzanne Benayiche
Touria Chaoui
Victor Tessier
Hajja Aliya Alaoui
Touria Chaoui
Tony Méléro
Jacques Lemaigre-Dubreuil
INVISIBLE LINES
Touria Chaoui
Aziza Benayiche
Tony Méléro
Saadia Taibi
Hajja Aliya Alaoui
Victor Tessier
Mike "Mag" Magursky
Aziza Benayiche
Ahmed Touil
Touria Chaoui
Mike "Mag" Magursky
Fadila
Tony Méléro
1956
THE BIRDCAGE
Ahmed Touil
Mike "Mag" Magursky
Touria Chaoui
Fadila
Suzanne Benayiche
Tommy August
Aziza Benayiche
Lucy August
Suzanne Benayiche
Tony Méléro
Hajja Aliya Alaoui
Tommy August
Touria Chaoui
INDEPENDENCE DAY
Salah Chaoui
Tony Méléro
Saadia Taibi
Abdelwahed Chaoui
Aziza Benayiche
Fadila
Victor Tessier
Mike "Mag" Magursky

CASABLANCA 1950

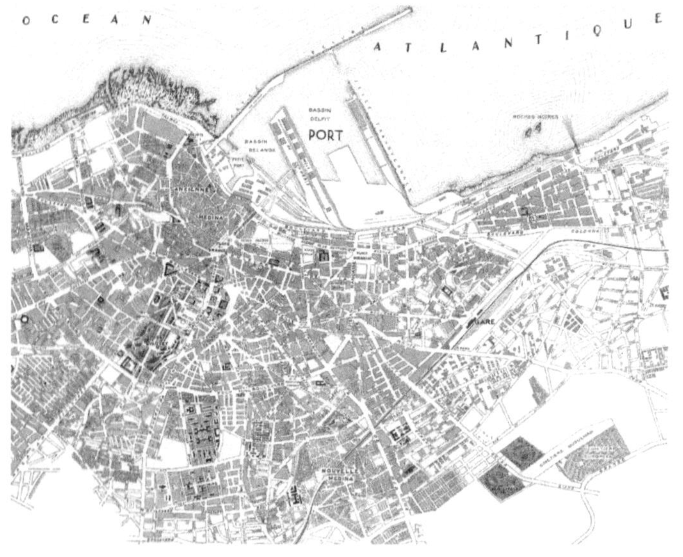

LANDING
November 7–10, 1942

High above the Place de France, a paper flier fell like a piece of giant confetti, twisting and turning down through the darkness before sticking flat to the damp pavement. It was eleven o'clock at night on Saturday, November 7, and across the square within the cavernous Cinema Vox, Victor Tessier sat deep in the second balcony beside a new girl. For weeks rumors of attacks from the air or sea against Vichy forces in French North Africa had brought nightly blackouts to Casablanca, and restless couples had packed the movie houses. Since Tuesday, Victor had escorted three other girls to see *La Maison dans la Dune*. One had finally conceded a kiss, but the moment had been little more than a pantomime of the passion onscreen, where Colette Darfeuil devoured cigarettes and slithered into the arms of lovers as if she might shed her dress at any instant. Victor blindly reached towards the girl, surprising her cool thigh for an instant before she gave him her hand, which now lay between his fingers like a dead sparrow. Her indifference struck him as perverse, and furiously he thought again of how the movie was more alive than anything in Casablanca, where life was always the same, the girls were always the same, and even this movie was always the same, and always would be. Colette Darfeuil would never touch her lover on the cheek any differently, would always light her cigarettes at the same precise moments, with that precise lighter, and Victor would never really find out what happened next – not next, but *next*.

Around eleven-thirty the film cut, and onscreen a

sentence was projected: *All sailors, soldiers and merchant marines, return to your quarters.* Like Victor, many of the men in the theater were uniformed, although few with much pride. Groaning, they began streaming down the aisles. "We have to go," he said to the girl.

"But I want to see how it ends," she complained. Victor hesitated for a moment, then snatched up his leather pea coat, grabbed her by the elbow, and dragged her along towards the exit, where they stepped out into a damp alleyway. This is how it ends.

Out in the Place de France, drunken soldiers shouted and stopped traffic. Victor guided the girl towards Boulevard de la Gare, having promised to walk her home before returning to the military offices on Place Lyautey. He didn't know where she lived. They were just walking, quickly, as if she had missed curfew. This invented urgency seemed to unite them again. Patiently he kept his hand at the small of her back. The night was dense and misty and smelled of the dank green Atlantic.

Rue Colbert was quieter, and finally he got up the nerve to slice into her path, meeting her lips with a kiss. False alarms of attacks had occurred before, but even false alarms were exciting. The girl returned the kiss until two Moroccans in hooded djellabahs shuffled past like ghosts, muttering in Arabic. A car rolled by, and in the milky glow of its headlights, he saw her smeared lips. Were the rest of her lips smudged over his face? He dragged a fist across his mouth. The sky rumbled, and through a gap in the clouds, Cassiopeia fell as the Great Bear rose. The blackouts revealed the stars, and he made her look at them, his scrawny chest pressed against her bony back, his arm stabbing at the constellations.

Astronomy was the only subject at school he'd ever cared anything about, apart from some philosophy. The stars were proof of other worlds. Other possibilities.

Victor Tessier was slim and strong, with pale blue eyes and a handsome face that eventually struck one as asymmetrical. He was perfect, but something was off, and his long lashes made him look even younger than seventeen. He had lied about his age to join the army after expulsion from an English boarding school. The headmaster had called it insubordination. He had called it *other possibilities*. His parents, wealthy French exporters residing for years in Casablanca, had agreed with the headmaster. They had felt he needed structure, which as far as Victor was concerned was just another word for defeat. But he was forming his own plan. He would become a pilot, because the pilots in the movies were the steely ones, and because up above the clouds you could see the whole universe.

The sky roared, airplanes massing behind the weather. He pictured American carriers anchored off the coast in the mist. He wondered how many there might be, and if the French would choose to fight their old Allies. He walked awkwardly with the girl along narrow side streets flanked by Art Deco buildings with white façades glowing like tombstones. Then the fliers began to fall, specks appearing out of the clouds, twirling down until just overhead they grew alarmingly large before rocking gently to the ground. Victor ignored the fear in his belly to whistle a line of jagged classical music. Finally it had begun.

Rue de l'Horloge was dark and deserted. He stopped and wrapped his arms around the girl's waist, hastily moved a hand up to a breast, kissed the back of her neck. She was warm and malleable and let him linger, so beside the Jardin d'Été, black palms overhead, he led her into a broad shopping arcade with stained-glass ceilings and kissed her even harder. Never had he been closer.

But the girl drew back, doubtful of the shadowy spot. It was only then that they noticed the two French soldiers deeper into the passageway, beating one another with slow, bloody punches, with a silent, brutal force, as if enacting an archaic ritual. One soldier's arm hung at his side, broken. The other's face had been pummeled into a dark smear. Circling one another, they grunted as a knee or a fist was landed. Neither fell, although both looked half dead. Navy, Victor saw from their uniforms, enlisted men. Then the one-armed man reared back and delivered a vicious blow to the other man's temple, loosing his eye from its socket.

The girl gasped and pulled Victor close, her eyes still on the fighters. The wounded man held a hand to his face, softly moaning, but continuing to circle his adversary. "Let's go," Victor murmured. His stomach had melted, and he couldn't stand to look. The girl, however, was transfixed. She still wanted to see how it ended. "Kiss me, Victor," she whispered. "Kiss me!"

His heart ricocheted, but she insisted, devouring his mouth as she pulled him against the wall, wrapping a bare leg around his waist. He was dizzy with terror, or desire, and finally it seemed then that everything was possible.

○

1   No nation is more closely linked, by both history and deep friendship, to the people of France than the United States of America. Americans are now fighting not only for their own future, but to restore the liberties and democratic principles of all who live under the tricolored flag. We have come to liberate you from conquerors who only want to deprive you, forever, of your rights to sovereignty, freedom of religion, and the freedom to live your lives in peace. We have come only to destroy your enemies – we do not wish to harm you. We have come with the promise that we will leave as soon as Germany and Italy are no longer threats. I appeal to your sense of reality, as well as your idealism. Do nothing to prevent the accomplishment of this great plan. Help us, and hasten the dawn of a day of universal peace.

2

Near midnight the telephone rang behind the bar of the Hotel Transatlantique. Nobody answered. The city's new international crowd was busy flinging itself at another Saturday night. Girls shimmied between tables of uniformed French, Germans, Poles, Japanese, and others of indeterminate provenance. Franklin Sidney Felton, twenty-eight, surveyed this menagerie from the corner table he shared with Dave King and Staff Reid, the other American vice-consuls. His eyes lingered again on Arkady Zubov, the Soviet military attaché whom everyone knew was NKVD. Arkady sat alone at his table scribbling in his little notebook, oblivious to temptation or intrigue, occasionally sipping his cup of coffee, which he prolonged with the small pitcher of hot water he always ordered on the side. Diluted pleasures. Arkady never howled at the moon. Franklin considered going over to continue their earlier conversation, but he was still too annoyed. No, not annoyed, just bored.

Smoke hovered beneath the chandeliers. Waiters in white jackets sailed through sweeping up glasses and setting down others midstride. "Freddie and Walter are in full splendor tonight," Staff murmured. Freddie, the French actor, and Walter, the Austrian middleweight boxing champ, had fought together with Franco in Spain. They were intimate friends of Teddie Auer, head of the Casablanca German Armistice Commission, and known for their questionable gossip. Freddie danced over to the Americans' table. "*Bonsoir* Frank-leen," he cried. "I need to talk to you.

Very important." Felton smiled and waved, having discovered that friendliness, in great quantities, could make almost everyone go away. This was a strategy. Let them underestimate him. Out of the corner of his eye, he registered King's familiar scowl. Then Staff, spared the wrath of the noble elder, spotted Captain Park, a dull conniver in British SIS, and gamely jogged off to take another crack at him.

"See about another bottle of champagne while you're up?" Franklin called out, a few seconds too late. Never mind. He should probably keep his head tonight. The plan was about to be put into action. Secretly the three Americans were founding members of the OSS, reporting directly to the president, who had tasked them with studying Vichy French naval defense installations. If the United States decided to enter the war in Europe, then securing a supply route through Africa's largest Atlantic port, just two hundred miles southwest of the Strait of Gibraltar, would be critical. So upon arriving that summer they had commandeered a villa in Anfa, the leafy hillside neighborhood coveted by the officers of the GAC, and had set about throwing informative weekly champagne parties while cultivating official reputations as playboys of little consequence. Let them underestimate him.

Again he glanced over at dull Arkady. Was he a friend? For several months the two men had spent Sunday afternoons together, cycling off into the forests or down the beach road to birdwatch – sanderlings, plovers, the migratory patterns over Morocco brought even rarer species too. A connection had formed across these ornithological Sundays, and in many ways Felton felt closer to the Soviet than to his fellow Americans, whose backgrounds were so similar to his own: Groton after a Park Avenue childhood, then Columbia – not the ideal choice for an aspiring diplomat, but then he disdained the careerism of men from Harvard and Yale. This conviction had been confirmed by his time with Dave King and Staff Reid, who possessed little feeling for the real Morocco and thought only of the next move on the chess board they called life. They were one-dimensional men, whereas moving silently through the trees with Arkady, across grasslands still untouched by so-called progress, or crouched in a hollow with his binoculars, Franklin knew for certain that he had been put on earth to glimpse the extraordinary. They would win the war, and undercover he would happily fight the fascists, but after victory he intended to travel south into Africa towards undiscovered places, where he would write poetry and learn to live among the natives. Howl at the moon.

Arkady's uniform was simple and undecorated, a sad declaration. Earlier when they had greeted one another, the Russian had claimed that the previous week, after pulling off the road at the Merja Zerga lagoon on a trip back down from Tangier, he had spotted the slender-billed curlew. Even now, with Staff mouthing something from across the room, the story ate at Franklin. The slender-billed curlew bred in the marshes of the Siberian taiga and was practically extinct. It was known to winter around the Mediterranean, true, and Arkady was an admittedly accomplished birder, but his gut told him that the Russian had made a false sighting, illegitimately adding the bird to his list.

"*The slender-billed curlew?*" he had asked, smiling intensely. "You're sure it wasn't a sandpiper? Or a whimbrel?"

"The head pattern was similar to a whimbrel's, but the central crown stripe was unmistakable, and the overall pattern was more vivid."

The Soviet's joyless description had turned the smile into a smirk. "Those distinctions are tough to see in the field, Arkady, even with binoculars."

"But then it called out. *Coor-lee! Coor-lee!* Not dissimilar to the Eurasian curlew, but higher-pitched and more melodic." Shaking his head, Franklin had walked off, and then the bar had filled up, and he hadn't gotten the chance to revisit the subject.

Now Staff was signaling from the bar, the phone cupped in his hand.

So it's tonight, Franklin thought, somewhat surprised.

○

"They represent a perfect picture of the mixture of race and characteristics in that wild conglomeration called the United States of America. We can only congratulate ourselves on the selection of this group who will give us no trouble. In view of the fact that they are totally lacking in method, organization and discipline, the danger presented by their arrival in North Africa may be considered nil. It would be merely a waste of paper to describe their personal idiosyncrasies and characteristics."

— Intercepted German cable from the Casablanca German Armistice Commission to Berlin regarding the vice-consuls — Fall 1942[2]

<hr>

2   Robert Murphy – *Diplomat Among Warriors* – Doubleday, 1964

3

A week earlier the largest flotilla in history had been zig-zagging across the Atlantic. Among the hundred ships was the *Buenos Aires*, a former luxury liner that had been converted into a troop transport, which meant stripped of anything that might have been mistaken for luxury. Bunks were stacked five men high, and the latrine consisted of two long parallel troughs, one for washing, the other for everything else. The bunkroom below the waterline, which they called torpedo heaven, was home-sweet-home to the army's Port Battalion. The German U-boats prowling the ocean's depths would get them first, depriving America of one supremely rancorous group of men, and Philadelphia of a good portion of its longshoreman's union. Stacked atop one another, the boys had been grumbling since Norfolk. The stench had grown powerful, but they had begun to inhabit the stench, and it no longer seemed so bad. At night they held off dreams to listen through the boat's now familiar creaks for unrecognizable sounds.

Scuttlebutt was they were headed for France, or England, or Senegal. In early November, after a week at sea, the officers announced that it would be Casablanca, which wasn't especially enlightening. Supply Sergeant Mike Magursky gave odds on that being a city in Morocco, which was soon confirmed. He made a bit from the vigorish and was now dealing ice cream for cigarettes to the destroyer boys whenever they puttered around with the mail, none of which was ever addressed to Mag. Washington jokers had been put in charge of the planning of this thing. The *Buenos Aires* lacked toilet

11

paper but was overstocked with ice cream, which meant that for a price there were cigarettes aplenty for the stevedores now residing in torpedo heaven. The toilet paper they did without. They were green, the ocean was endless, and early in the morning when some finally slept, Berkovich would shout from his dreams, "Stop crying! Stop crying!" Nobody ever dared ask who was crying about what.

Nous sommes des soldats américains, nous sommes vos amis. They chanted it on deck while doing their morning jumping jacks until the nonsensical words came as easily as breathing. Officers barked orders, their ranks generally corresponding to their power within the ILU, the longshoreman's union. Afternoons meant paint-chipping duty, hammers and chisels clanging against the ship's sides. The pretty paint they'd applied in Norfolk was flammable, it had been determined, and needed to come off. So at least in battle they wouldn't burn to death. They'd just drown.

And then one night the ship's vibrations slowed, as if it were now feeling its way through the water like a sleepwalker through darkness. The men were again packed around Mag's bunk playing blackjack by the light of candles and Zippos, which had so inconvenienced Berkovich, one of Mag's four bunkmates, that since setting sail he'd been transformed from a friendly kid from Columbus into an obstreperous loner with bags under his eyes. Which partially explained his hit on seventeen, saving the house a push. Mag was the house and reached out across the mattress to rake a pile of cigarettes towards his chest. After giving a cut to Lieutenant Stec, a fellow Polack proving to be an even bigger bastard than he'd been as an ILU officer back on Chatham Street, Mag would have a few more cartons before the end of the night.

The boys ribbed Berkovich, and Spillane glanced down at the kid's dog tags and said, "Hey, you're marked as a Jew." Berkovich grabbed Spillane by the hair and told him to go fuck himself. His father had been Jewish, but he'd been raised in Columbus by his good Christian mother. Spillane held a Zippo to Berkovich's neck, and the men squeezed in to examine the dog tag, where there was, in fact, an "H" for Hebrew stamped below Berkovich's name and serial number. He'd never noticed it before. "Ah hell," Berkovich said. "They fuck you every which way."

The men laughed. "Hey Berkovich. You'll be missing us when the Krauts get you."

"Better a Kraut than Delilah," Berkovich growled, and the men roared. That morning Spillane had failed another "short-arm inspection", a painful legacy of the famous Delilah from the Norfolk girlie trailer, who'd felled several dozen men.

"Quit your pissin'," Mag growled, dealing another round. "Only action Port Battalion's gonna see is right here. Now you's in or you's out?"

○

A mile across the ocean from the *Buenos Aires* on the aircraft carrier USS *Ranger*, the Red Ripper squadron sat around the captain's table studying flashcards. Tommy

August flipped one over and said: "H-75? Or ME-109?" Breezy hesitated. "Better soak this in, Breezy," Tommy insisted. He was taller than the others and built like a quarterback. "Once we're up there cooking with gas, I won't be making formal introductions."

So they started again, flipping over cards, each printed with the silhouette and armament details of an enemy plane. Among them was the crafty single-engine French Dewoitine 520 fighter, with its four small-caliber machine guns, and – rankling Lieutenant Tommy August the most – American-built Curtiss Hawks and Douglas bombers, delivered to the French before they had thrown in with the Nazis.

Onboard intelligence officers had laid out stacks of material: surveillance photographs, maps, Baedeker guides, copies of *National Geographic*. The boys were cramming for their big exam, and after dinner every night they filled up on coffee and convened in the staff room, where plane-quizzing went late. Here they projected the pictures onto a screen, and the first night it took Wilson seventy-three seconds to identify the first slide, a P-36. The second night improved, and within a few days each of the men could recognize any enemy aircraft faster than they could blink.

They studied detailed maps until they saw Casablanca in their dreams, every rock and tree in the target areas, especially the likely emplacements of anti-aircraft guns. Enemy fuel storage, bridges, telegraph wires, and radio stations were not to be touched. Most importantly, they were to avoid provoking the local Arab population by damaging the Sultan's palace or any mosques. This was all assuming they actually ended up fighting. They were not to engage until the French engaged first, which in the opinion of the Red Rippers, none of whom had flown a single combat mission in their lives, the French would regret pretty quick. Their commanders might not have permitted practice flights out over the Atlantic for fear the squadron would crash the air power of the U.S. Navy directly into the sea, but the Red Rippers had mastered their flashcards and now had some swagger, so they broke for the night after forming a tight circle to chant the squadron toast: "Here's to the Red Rippers, a bunch of hell-raising, Bologna-slinging, two-fisted, he-man bastards!"

Back down in the hold, Tommy August was still grinning as he kicked off his boots and lay down in bed. They were good men, the best sort of Americans, brave and optimistic, and he was proud of the squadron, who'd been together since AvCad training in Corpus Christi. After those intense months Tommy now felt vastly more capable than the twenty-four-year-old Chicago kid who'd arrived like some foreigner deep in the heart of Texas. Lucy had loved to sing that song into his ear. The radio those months had hardly played anything else. Oh Lucy.

He slipped the pages of her last letter from his pocket and brought it close to his face, attempting to read it again in the dim blue light cast from the bulb over the door of the hold. She'd been taking long walks out at Mustang Island, remembering the day they'd sailed Daddy's dinghy across the bay. The water was cold now, but she'd gone for a swim. She was still his mermaid, and afterwards she'd sat on the sand for hours, looking out at the Gulf of Mexico, scanning the horizon with the fiercest concentration until something told her that her eyes had found the straightest path towards Tommy August out on the sea, to those freckles and that dimple on her man's perfect chin. He smiled, slipped the letter back into his pocket, and closed his eyes. Within seconds he was asleep, dreaming not of the rocks and trees of Casablanca, but of a blonde Texas mermaid stretched out on a beach in a red bathing suit.

On deck the next morning somebody spotted a seagull.

4

"Turn on the radio," Staff murmured from the back seat. It was now half past midnight, and the three vice-consuls were speeding up Boulevard de Paris towards the consulate in Franklin's Parma wine Pontiac Torpedo. Shadows raced through the streets, and everywhere the fliers fell, tumbling onto the passing sidewalks, stunned by the headlights before whipping up over the windshield. The mist still hung heavy, which was worrisome, and the wipers flicked slowly back and forth.

Nothing would be on the radio, Franklin knew, not yet, but he twisted the knob, and stifled laughter when Josephine Baker's voice filled the car, singing her old hit, *J'ai deux amours*. Unfortunately there was no time to stop by the Clinique Mers Sultan, where the world's sexiest woman and potentially Franklin's lover had been laid up for seventeen months with an infection she wouldn't discuss. Franklin said nothing, but left the radio on, knowing King was too proud to suggest they turn it off. He was no fan of Joe's and had discouraged her friendship with Franklin, even if her clinic room had become a principal meeting point for undercover Free French, men with aliases like Mister Monday and the Slug. Everybody wanted to meet Josephine Baker, and so the lobby traffic never aroused suspicion. Felton visited often and figured he might be in love. He was capable of such daring. Because whenever they were finally alone, Joe would draw him close, kiss his cheeks, and call him her baby. "The others just see a little black tramp from Saint Louis," she had said, "but you see your mama." That was probably just her way of talking, but he had kissed her back, imagining what his father would have said of that *mama*.

When the clinic room was bustling, he liked to watch as she played hostess from bed wearing nothing but a bathrobe. Sometimes a white mouse would pop up from between her breasts. She tended to keep several of them beneath the robe, letting them run freely over her, sometimes fishing one out by the neck for an animated conversation. When Felton had finally presented Arkady, the mouse Joe called Flaky had squirmed out of her grasp and hopped down to the floor, but Arkady had quickly scooped it up, so she had given him Flaky, which he had carried awkwardly out into the sunshine. Arkady came another couple of times but never mentioned Flaky, and Joe found him a bore, which of course he was.

The clock tower of the Hotel de Ville had gone dark, but the windows of the consulate blazed. "Here we go," King grunted, wrenching open his door as Franklin skidded to a stop. Inside the phones hadn't stopped ringing since the appearance of the first flier, and Consul-General Earle Russell was politely annoyed. Almost every call had been for his three vice-consuls, whose activities had been kept a secret from everyone in the State Department, including the Secretary of State himself. Along with the consul-generals in Tangier, Oran, Algiers and Tunis, Russell had also just discovered that their headquarters had been linked by wireless transmitters secretly installed by Franklin and Reid. "Gentlemen do not read each other's mail," Russell liked to say. He was an old-school diplomat, but then his own staff had been spying from his own consulate, and now he could only pace officiously from desk to desk, putting off questions he couldn't answer. Pearl Harbor had changed everything. That's what a tired diplomat like Russell couldn't see.

"You might want to take this," Rebecca called out. She stood at her desk with a phone in each hand and a third crooked under her chin, a hip hitched to the side. "It's Crusoe." Hearing the name, the other two vice-consuls peeled off in opposite directions, leaving Franklin to relieve Rebecca of one phone, which she replaced by silencing another.

"*Monsieur King?*" said the voice on the other end of the line.

"Monsieur Felton, actually," Franklin said, watching Rebecca's slim hips shift as she juggled receivers. Danger was an aphrodisiac. Ordinary Americans didn't get enough of it. "We, ah, met briefly in Algiers, Mister… Crusoe." The Frenchman ran the largest cooking oil empire in Europe, had powerful connections within the French military, and had helped plan the invasion from Algiers. He had also chosen his own codename – *Crusoe*. Naturally the Americans had shared nothing of their plans with him. Crusoe was compromised by his perception of his own power.

"This is a disaster! You have not given us enough time." The line crackled. Franklin thought with some pride of the superior connection in the secret radio room up under the roof. "General Giraud was not made *au courant*, and he is furious! Pétain will have his head, and the French navy will defend itself. What happened to Dakar for next month?"

"Dakar was a decoy."

"You cannot strike at French territory like this,

Monsieur Felton. You know this! You must stop this preposterous invasion immediately!"

"I'll see what I can do," Felton cheerily replied, and hung up the phone.

"And how is our friend Crusoe?" Rebecca asked.

"Worried about his future," Felton said with a grin. Typically French. Russians weren't nearly as predictable, he thought darkly, then leapt two steps at a time up to the top floor of the consulate, down a quiet corridor into the guest quarters, where he entered the closet and crouched through a low opening. The little attic room was almost pitch dark, and suffocating. Staff, codename Lincoln, was crouched over his radio set, twisting dials and cursing the antenna. Yankee in Algiers was coming and going, and the Stork in Tangier had drowned in static.

"I'll go stroke her a bit," Franklin said, and ducked back out through the closet into the guest quarters, where he flung open the French doors and stepped onto the balcony, making a clatter, but it no longer mattered. Now they were running the show. Outside the mist was clearing, and bigger gaps had appeared between the clouds. "Trust us, you French bastards," he said out towards the Hotel de Ville. "You can't imagine what's coming."

The antenna was on the rooftop. Franklin climbed up the precarious balcony railing, and with the city sleeping restlessly beneath his feet, he sang out, "*Coor-lee! Coor-lee!*"

5

At four that morning, onboard the *Savoie*, which was anchored at port, a bang sounded at a door. Camille Morin jolted up in bed, clutching the blanket to her chest. Perhaps she had dreamed it. In the silence she waited, and then the noise came again, startling her again. Was Maman still asleep? She glanced towards the next bed, but the darkness was complete. "*Oui?*" she said, hardly more than a whisper.

"Madame, we have orders to disembark immediately. Please put on your life jacket and proceed directly to the bridge. Do not bring anything else." Camille could hear banging down the corridor now, the order being repeated.

"Maman?" They had arrived the previous morning from Dakar, refugees from the Allied invasion expected there by the end of December. Camille and her mother had experienced the previous, failed British attack of 1940, and Camille's uncle, a naval engineer who had supported them since the death of Camille's father, had insisted that this time they would be safer in Casablanca. So he had secured them passage on Transat's *Savoie*.

"Maman," she said louder, pushing the blankets down her legs and shivering in the nightgown, "a man says we have to go." Now she heard sirens. A lamp flicked on, and she was surprised to see her mother already on her feet. "We are not animals, Camille," Maman said. "We do not traipse about ports in nightgowns."

Camille nodded, suppressing a flash of unacceptable rage. She slipped out of bed and tiptoed over to the closet, where they had hung the dresses bought in town

21

that day. It wasn't like Maman to splurge, but the two dresses had fit Camille so perfectly that they hadn't been able to resist. As Maman said, she was already nineteen and would soon be married, and with her would go a young lady's trousseau. The word made Camille feel as if she had gone blank. The feeling was familiar. She didn't know anyone with a trousseau.

"The pink brassiere, please," Maman said. "The white blouse, and then the blue suit." Camille slipped the items from their hangers, whispering *the white blouse, the blue suit*, as she laid them out on the bed for Maman.

The sirens still blared, but the corridor had gone silent. So when the banging came again, she gasped. The door rattled as if it was about to break open. "Evacuate this cabin immediately! We are about to come under attack!" Then heavy boots pounded along a metal floor. Camille slipped out of her nightgown and into the pink flowered dress which the shopgirl had said flattered her figure so remarkably. "Let me see," Maman said. Camille made one quick turn and put a trembling fist to her mouth. Maman nodded, pinning back her hair in the mirror, and Camille noticed that her mother's new jacket was missing a button. Two white threads peeked out of the blue wool like a bug's antennae, but she kept quiet. Maman would have been displeased, and Camille's life had been structured to avoid Maman's displeasure.

They detached two new orange lifejackets from the wall and awkwardly lowered them over their heads. Briefly they discussed packing a bag, but Maman felt certain that they would be back in their beds within the hour. "Well," she sighed, brushing Camille's dark curly hair from her forehead, "we have done our best." Then they slipped on their shoes, took one last look in the mirror, and opened the door.

Out on deck two soldiers crossly prodded them along to the gangplank and down into a sea of passengers moving away from the port towards shore. The *Savoie*, the *Lipari*, and the *Porthos* had all arrived the previous morning and had now disembarked thousands of civilians into the night. Many stumbled along with blankets still wrapped around their shoulders. Only the soldiers, Camille, and her mother were dressed. The two women struggled to keep close to one another. The crowd's panic was catching, and as Camille hurried along, her fear grew wild, as if it wanted to break through her skin, or make her cry. She gripped her mother's hand and glanced up at the sky. The day's clouds had vanished, and stars shone.

Soldiers ran back and forth, some out to the ships again, perhaps to set sail, others across the pier towards the giant silhouette of the battleship *Jean Bart*, still under construction, but with functioning anti-aircraft batteries. A voice called out at the edge of the pier, and Camille glanced over at a tiny Navy chaplain running back and forth, his arms beating the air, his black cassock billowing behind him like a tiny sail. "My children, you are going to die!" he shouted at passing soldiers. "Make your act of contrition, and I shall give you absolution!" Camille shivered and held her mother's hand tighter. Off to the left, from the bridge of the destroyer *Tempête*, a voice shouted through a bullhorn, drowning out the chaplain: "*Nom de Dieu!* We're not going to die!"

"Stay close, Camille," Maman said, breathing heavily. She wasn't as accustomed to walking as she had once been. *We're not going to die*, Camille whispered. *Nom de Dieu.*

Most of the passengers had already been corralled into empty grain silos, but these were already too crowded. A frantic seaman, no older than Camille, told them to keep moving, quickly please, they would be sheltered in the warehouses further up the pier. "He wasn't very convincing," Maman said, gasping for breath, and Camille realized her mother was scared, which somehow made her feel stronger. Bodies pushed into them, and then they heard airplanes. The sound of their engines dipped then roared, as if circling, invisibly swooping, searching for Camille.

The dark warehouse was filled with rows of stacked plastic drums of cooking oil. The women moved up into a row behind others until they could walk no further. Through gaps in the drums, they saw people shuffling down other rows. The corrugated roof of the warehouse rattled. The planes were closer now, swarming. Maman sunk down to the floor beside a drum to rest. "Just be glad we're not wearing nightgowns," she whispered, glaring at a disheveled nearby family to emphasize her point. Camille leaned against the drum and ran her fingers through a patch of slick oil coating the hard plastic.

Then there was gunfire, close and dense, powerful blasts that shook the oil drums in their stacks. The *Jean Bart* had taken aim. Afterwards the sky was quiet again, but then came a long, slow whine, then another, and the bombs began to explode. Screams filled the warehouse, and bodies pressed against Camille again as she tried to lift her mother from the ground. "Help me," she whispered, frightened even of her own voice, but no one did. The others were fighting for the exits, clambering over her mother's legs, terrified by the explosions outside, but more terrified of being trapped inside. Camille got her mother up and pushed her along the oil drums, which swayed precariously as the crowd swelled past them. She glanced up towards the roof and saw the tops of the columns waving like the heads of palm trees. Her mother was too winded to speak. They ran as fast as they could.

Somebody shouted something about the Red Cross, and Camille felt an oil drum reach out and brush her arm, then draw back quickly, like a cold hand. Then overhead she saw a drum come off the stack and hurtle through the air to topple a stack in the next row, then the next. Beside her another came down at an angle, splashing open like a water balloon as it hit the cement floor, showering her with oil. Somebody was groaning. She ran blindly, feeling the oil slide down her arms and legs, grabbing at her dress to lift the hem and wipe her eyes, blinking, then wiping them again. Outside everybody was running towards the city, explosions here and there. Camille realized that she was no longer clutching her mother's hand. She stopped and turned in a full circle, looking everywhere as others hurtled past. *Maman?* Her mother was nowhere in sight. A bomb fell, splitting a dock in half. Camille covered her face with her arms, then turned back towards the city and ran, the oil slick on her legs. She ripped open the clasp of her lifejacket and tossed it over her head, and then she ran even faster.

6

Tommy August glided over fields of wheat and grapes and oranges, surprisingly abundant. Green trees grew from soil as dark as coffee. White waves crawled towards the shore and sunk soundlessly into white beaches. Off the coast, maneuvering American battleships pressed flat circles onto the water, pumping shells towards the French coastal batteries. The Dauntless bombers still dove over the port, snuffing out any orange slashes shooting up from the jetties. Dull explosions sounded in the distance, mere vibrations beneath the pleasant hum of Tommy's engine. Ever since boyhood he'd been able to see with his ears. Before turning eleven he'd played the wind instruments, and then he'd played the brass. After the Navy he wanted to become a composer, and crossing the Atlantic he'd entertained the men by pressing his ear to the deck and announcing the exact revolutions per minute of the ship's engines. At first they'd had Breezy run up to the bridge to check, but then they hadn't bothered. Tommy was as good as a tachometer.

The morning flight had gone like clockwork, and now the Red Rippers banked south over a village of square mud huts and cactus fences. Dirt roads disappeared into the horizon, lined by pale, dusty eucalyptus trees. Two boys prodding a donkey along with a stick squinted into the sun and waved. Tommy waved back. The radios were silent. The war was being played with toys on some other planet while he casually floated along in his own perfect vacuum.

Keeping formation, they came in high over the city again and headed southwest for the airbase at Cazès.

Soon hangars appeared, their metal roofs rusted, just as in the photographs provided by the spy planes, and then the green runways, some French planes off to the side. Vichy didn't appear to be making any effort to get them off the ground. Then, along the perimeter fence, three smoke rings appeared, AA batteries firing blindly. Tommy couldn't localize the flak. His spine tingled as he inhaled deeply and spoke into the radio, "Batter up."

A few seconds passed, and then the radio crackled: "Play ball." He let out his breath. The Rippers scattered into pairs and dove to streak low across the runways, strafing the anti-aircraft guns, which were thickening the air with lead and smoke. Two German Heinkel bombers and a Junkers transport were being wheeled out onto the runway. A group of German officers appeared at the door of a hangar, cowering as if huddling from a rainstorm, their heads craned up to the sky. The French guns still fired wildly, every miss swelling the Rippers' confidence, and they raced in at less than fifty meters to pepper the field with bullets. The Frenchmen might have had better luck tossing rocks.

A German staff car appeared beside the hangar and stopped. Eight of the officers piled in before the car peeled off, its doors flapping like wings as the lucky passengers struggled to pull them shut. The remaining men disappeared back into the hangar, and Tommy was diving again when a striped-nose Dewoitine appeared at his starboard. *Cripes*, he thought. Pulling up hard he noticed two P-36s floating overhead. The Dewoitine was closer, so he turned and bore down, but he overshot the Vichyman, who neatly pivoted and stuck to his tail. Something cracked against his fuselage. A hit, but it didn't feel serious. Kicking the rudder into a quick turn that put his nose towards the Dewoitine, he impatiently unleashed a burst of the .50-calibers from a reckless distance. Miraculously, the Dewoitine's tail jerked up, and it drifted towards starboard until its right wing detached and fluttered off like a leaf. The nose then pitched and dove for the ground. Tommy was so excited that he stuck right to the Dewoitine's tail until it hit the runway, bounced, and plowed through a fence. The pilot hadn't ejected, and Tommy couldn't spot him as he flew over, nearly clipping the wreckage. He pulled up to get his bearings again and realized he'd lost his wingmate Breezy.

"Where are you, Breezy?" Breezy didn't respond, so Tommy looped around, eventually spotting a Wildcat streaking in across the field not more than ten feet above the ground. Two P-36s were at his tail. Tommy saw that it was Breezy, who shouted into the radio, "Tommy boy, get these bastards off my tail, and make it quick!"

Tommy dove out of the sun and spun in at an angle, landing just level with one of the P-36s, which attempted to shake free with predictable Immelmanns, but Tommy was glued to him and fired a burst, grazing the engine, which bloomed into smoke. The pilot flipped over to eject, and Tommy waved as he passed. The Frenchman waved back, his face contorted in anger. Then Tommy turned to scout for Breezy, who had managed to circle around on his Frenchman and chase him off. Those P-36s were no match for the Wildcats, which could turn on a dime.

Afterwards they joined up and flew west at altitude, out past the beaches and up the coast. Further north at

Fedala the troop transports were dropping landing boats, which left behind white squiggles as they moved out towards the rendezvous circles, where they would wait until all boats had assembled before swarming ashore like minnows.

○

The *Buenos Aires* had puttered towards shore at Fedala in an attempt to drop its landing boats and was now taking heavy fire from coastal batteries. Men crowded the decks struggling to disembark down cargo nets. Climbing towards the landing boats, they fell through the nets and into the water. Many couldn't swim, and although they wore life jackets, they panicked and thrashed about, their heads bobbing beneath the water. There were not enough boats, two had already overturned, and one had been sunk by a shell that had skipped across the water's surface like a pebble. The water was so perilous that some of the landing boats had rashly headed for land, only to be ripped apart by machine guns as they lurched up onto the beaches and dropped their ramps. A few men had made it across the beach into the first dense tangle of bushes, but they lay flat and dug into the sand, too terrified to return fire.

The Port Battalion had been ordered to fight. Lieutenant Stec had rushed back and forth screaming at them to move, but having never expected to take fire, they were dragging their heels. "Get down in that hold Sergeant Magursky! Rally those men up here and into those boats!" Mag hadn't moved. He'd smoked the last of his cigarette, delaying orders. Then, as he stubbed the butt beneath his boot heel, a shell had ripped into the hold and exploded, killing at least six men. The fire quickly spread towards the livestock pens – so much for that paint chipping – where a dozen frightened pigs broke loose and mauled the wounded men, some of whom were unconscious. They ate Paddy Spillane, who had taken mortar shrapnel in the chest. He'd been so scared the night before that in the latrine he'd cut off his trigger finger to keep from having to fight.

Now Mag stood at the bow and eyed the churning water. Men were fighting for places in the boats, but there were no places left. *I'm not gonna be lunch for some fuggin pig*, he thought, and jumped into the ocean.

○

According to the latest news from North Africa, severe fighting is in progress in Morocco.

Off Casablanca naval engagements are taking place.

Our troops are striving to stem disembarkations at Safi and Fedala.

Algiers is encircled by troops coming from the east and west.

Fighting is going on between Arzeu and Oran.
– *Vichy French radio communiqué*[3]

---

[3]   Reuters – 11/08/1942

Tommy and the Red Rippers had returned to the carrier for refueling. Now they were being slingshot into the sky again. American casualties had been light, although a radio gunner had been killed by anti-aircraft fire coming from the Ahl Fass cemetery, which they'd had on their maps. Again the flight deck officer raised his flag and let it fall. Tommy released the brakes, and the plane lurched forward, its tail wagging like a salamander's until he got the rudder adjusted and straightened her out. The faster he went, the straighter he got, and in an instant the roar of the flight deck was behind him, and he had hurtled back into the void.

The dive bombers had done good work, supported by the pounding of the U.S. naval guns. Near the port two French destroyers lay on their sides like beached whales, the red bands of their funnels keeled into the water. The bombers still pounded the port, taking sharp angles at the *Jean Bart*, whose guns were talking down the whole of its length. The batteries at the Jetée Transversale and the El Hank racecourse had been silenced, and hell was being indiscriminately rained on the tombstones of the Ahl Fass cemetery.

For the moment the sky was clear of Vichy planes, so Tommy gave the others a rendezvous at Saddle Rock, out past Cazès. The landscape here was dried pale and featureless. A Dewoitine burned on an expanse of cracked clay. Another was crumpled like a kite in the branches of a wiry tree. Soaring above it all, Tommy thought of that cold March birthday – seven, eight? – when his father had taken him to Lincoln Park to fly his present, a kite. He remembered the thrill of finally coaxing it into the air, the tug of the string at his fingers. Scampering across the grass, he had let out string until the kite drifted into a giant ash and snatched him backwards. A cold wind was coming off Lake Michigan. They had stared up into the branches. Tommy yanked at the string, impatient to regain control of the kite, but his father had warned that if he pulled too hard, he might rip the fabric, and if the string broke, the kite would be lost forever. So Tommy had edged around the trunk of the ash for what felt like hours, desperately attempting to communicate with the green diamond through his fingers, feeling for the exact angle that would set it free. But the kite would not budge, and he had grown disconsolate, until it seemed that he was the kite, and there was a boy in the tree who controlled the string, and him. Finally, as the sun dipped low, his father had forced the string from his fingers and had carried him out of the park, leaving behind the new kite, as well as the boy in the tree.

"Get to Cazès. The bombers are gassing up." Wilson was on the radio.

"We're coming," Tommy shouted, and the four Wildcats dropped altitude to head for the base. So the French were sending up bombers with no fighters left to cover them? Vichy's disorganization was unbelievable. In a flash the airfield came up on them, and they went down in pairs. The bombers were hard to miss. Tommy pulled the trigger at five hundred yards, which wasn't much more than a blink at four hundred miles per hour. One bomber exploded up under him, lashing his wings with debris. He pulled up hard and flew clear, out past the airfield, where below him a shepherd placidly moved down a scribbled path in the midst of a few dozen sheep.

Only then did he realize he'd been hit. Smoke filled the cockpit. The oil cooler, he knew. Either he would have to find a spot to land or bail out. "I'm unloading my guns over the desert there, Breezy.

Stay clear." He dropped the guns, which helped keep altitude and removed at least that danger from a crash landing. "There's a promising field below me," Wilson said.

"I can't see it from here. Drag it for me, Wilson." Wilson went down to investigate. The radio crackled: "You can't land here, Tommy. You've got cows everywhere. Big rocks, too." Tommy's engine spluttered, jolted and died.

"The hell I can't. My engine just conked. I'm going down."

The plane now glided so slowly that Tommy feared he'd drop out of the sky. The rudder steadied it, however, and he floated down towards the field until his wheels touched, but then the flaps weren't working, and he raced along until the left wheel hit a rock and came off.

Watch that cow, Tommy!

"Damn the cows," he muttered, scraping along on a wheel and a wingtip until he hit a ditch, stubbed his nose into the ground, and pitched his tail into the air before crashing back to earth.

You okay, Tommy?

○

Much later that night Mag stumbled along a beach. His clothes were soaked through, his rations sat at the bottom of the ocean, and he'd lost his gun, but at least he hadn't been hit in the day's fighting. Men groaned from various dark hollows. Others wandered shell-shocked through the dunes, calling out "George!" in terror whenever they glimpsed movement, then hearing "Patton!" with relief, the sign and countersign, the only two words that still had any meaning.

Sporadic gunfire sent him back down to the sand. For a while he'd holed up with a kid from Massachusetts named Slider, but Slider had gotten skittish after sunset. George. George. George. They'd seen a shadow twitch, but the shadow wasn't talking, so Slider had chucked a grenade, covering them both in what turned out to be donkey parts. That was the point at which Mag ended their friendship.

Frogs moaned from the trees, fuggin spooky frogs. They made the pit of your stomach feel like it was covered in cold moss, but maybe that was just hunger. The lighthouse beam swept the beach every ten seconds. Mag was trying to stay hidden between the sweeps, but the oblivious Arabs down by the water's edge didn't seem too concerned. They gathered up life jackets, canteens, maybe a gun or two, anything they could carry.

The beam swept past. Mag puffed, lifted himself to his feet, and lumbered towards the dunes.

"George!"

"Patton!"

7

To every noble Arab: Greetings and peace of Allah be upon you. The bearer of this letter is an officer of the United States of America and a faithful friend of all Arab nations. We beg of you to treat him well, guard his life from every harm, supply his needs of food and drink, and guide him to the nearest American encampment. You will be generously rewarded in money for all your services. Peace and mercy of Allah be upon you.[4]

○

Tommy felt an itch at his hairline and scratched it. His fingers came away bloody. He slipped a handkerchief from his pocket and wiped the fingers. He couldn't get blood on his uniform, or on the plane. Shutting his eyes for a moment, he focused on the steps of the routine. Grab your escape kit, your charts, your passport, your pistol, your fifty-dollar bill, and the letter in Arabic to be used in case of capture. He couldn't be captured. Checking off each item in his mind brought him greater clarity. He was in control. He held the string and was master of the kite. Pushing out of the cockpit, he lowered himself to solid ground for the first time in two weeks.

Across the field he noticed two Moroccan Spahis, French colonial troops, approaching on horseback. Their crossed bandoliers flashed in the sunlight, and

---

4   John W. Lambert – *Wildcats Over Casablanca* – 1943, Little, Brown, and Company

their brown capes snapped in the breeze. Panic made him dizzy. He wasn't made to be a prisoner. He couldn't abandon the Red Rippers. He took off running but collapsed immediately, eating a mouthful of dust.

When he opened his eyes, one of the Spahis had blocked out the sun. He wore sandals cut from an old tire, and a long dagger was slipped through the belt of his bandolier. Beneath his soiled turban the Moroccan was chuckling, and Tommy noticed that the man held his pistol, and that his own wrists had been bound with rough twine. The pain in his head was still worse than that in his wrists.

"*Anglais,*" the man said.

Tommy shook his head: "*Officier américain,*" he grunted, awkwardly moving his bound hands towards his pocket. With two fingers he slipped out his passport and the letter in Arabic. Surely the Spahis would get him to a boat once they saw the letter. America and Morocco were united in the fight against Vichy. But the Spahi ignored the letter, shoving it into a fold in his robes while examining the passport. The two men repeatedly opened and closed the little booklet until one announced: "*Prisonnier!*"

"You can't do that!" Tommy shouted as they dragged him to his feet. "American! Officer!" They laughed. Probably didn't even speak English, and all he knew of French were musical terms and a few lines from Bizet librettos. His head pounded, and reeling on his feet he watched as if in a dream as they emptied his kit, haggling with one another over each new inessential item: fish hooks, goggles, a fountain pen, and his shark knife, which they fought over for several minutes. Then they found the flare pistol and cried out in excitement, mistaking it for a high-caliber revolver. The one who appeared to be in charge barked at the other and proudly holstered the flare gun in his belt. None of this mattered, at least not to Tommy. He could make no sense of their language, and the more he tried to explain his situation in English and French libretto, the less attention they paid him. For a moment he wondered if he might be dead, but that was a ridiculous thought. Maybe he was seriously hurt.

American shells occasionally whistled overhead. One screamed into the field, and cows mooed out from the point of impact, like shock waves in slow motion. Like the cows, Tommy knew they needed to move. Those American destroyers wouldn't be letting up anytime soon, he thought proudly. The Spahis seemed to understand this themselves and attached a longer rope to his tied wrists before mounting their decrepit Arab horses. "*Officier!*" Tommy insisted, but the Spahis just laughed as if he'd mooed like a cow on a leash. They set off, and as he shuffled along behind them, his only consolation was the knowledge that these two ignorant Moroccans would regret how they had humiliated him. The Americans would liberate Casablanca if it wasn't liberated already, and the Spahis would realize their mistake. Keep the faith, Tommy August. The world revolved according to divine principles. Keep faith.

Miles passed. The Spahis sang romantic Arabic songs that brought tears to their eyes, and briefly Tommy lost himself in the music, unwanted thoughts blooming in the syncopated gaps in the rhythm. Soon enough he would be reported missing, and in Chicago his mother would be receiving one of those Navy telegrams. But not Lucy. He would marry her as soon as he set foot again in America, so that they would never again lose contact. He would marry her, and that would keep them close even when they were worlds apart. For a moment he felt almost happy, and the song of the Spahis was briefly beautiful. But then he remembered that he was their prisoner, and then it wasn't even music. It was just wailing, or barking at the moon.

Get ahold of yourself Tommy August. He took a deep breath and shuffled along, smelling the dank, matted fur of the horses. Through a gap in the eucalyptus trees, the ocean appeared. Four American bombers circled above before heading back out to sea. He raised his face to the sky, but they couldn't possibly have seen him. The road approached the coast, and he saw beaches and a few blue-hulled fishing boats drifting obliviously on the water. The two overturned French destroyers with their submerged funnels lay like prehistoric ruins. The Spahis took no particular interest in any of this: the planes, the boats, the war. The sun dipped lower over the Atlantic and turned gold. The air smelled of salt, smoke, and mud. God, it was so beautiful, the most beautiful place he'd ever seen.

But boredom came again. Vaguely he sensed his dragging feet, but now his thoughts were consumed almost solely with the pain of his bound wrists. The appearance of the city's outskirts distracted him from the pain. Here the streets were lined with white villas set amidst gardens of jasmine and oleander. There were few signs of battle, just occasional concrete blocks behind which the French had belatedly set up machine guns, and military trucks haphazardly abandoned.

Some troops milled around, camping on street corners or wandering along streets – Frenchmen, but also Senegalese infantrymen, whose own country had been colonized by the French. They wore red fezzes and camped along the railroad tracks in a series of squalid-looking tents, squatting beside smoky fires that reeked of garbage and spoiled fish. On bridges clusters of guards stood smoking or playing cards, ignoring the shells still occasionally whizzing overhead. Tommy was astonished that nobody paid him and the Spahis any attention.

Cars drove past. French policemen waved at traffic. A pack of Moroccan boys appeared and tagged along behind them, calling out *"Américain, Américain!"* Tommy grinned at the kids, hoping for a friend, but a Spahi savagely swung his dagger, and the boys ran off shrieking. Closer to the center broad avenues were lined with tall, white Art Deco buildings spooled out in grand vistas, a legacy of the French Resident-General Lyautey, Tommy knew from his drilling, the man who had sought to make of Casablanca his own little Paris. Tommy had never been to France, although he was likely to get there soon enough, and Casablanca corresponded with the Paris he had imagined, cafés furled around corners, shaded by awnings, and geometric gardens bursting with flowers and trees heavy with leaves, even in early November. Up ahead an elegant Italianate clock tower sat on a broad square.

Across the square the Spahis dismounted in front of a large building that appeared governmental. The edge of the sun dipped below its roof, and pink shot up into the sky as if the city had been punctured.

"So what happens now, fellas?" Tommy drawled, but the Spahis had become anxious, and in any case were still ignoring him. He wished they would at least sing again, but they waited in awful silence until a young French corporal came out of the building in a crisp khaki uniform and boots so polished they caught the fading sun. The Spahis said something in French, and the corporal sniffed. "Lieutenant," he said, sneering at Tommy while cutting the twine at his wrists with a pocketknife. "You are now our prisoner of war."

The corporal was now in control, and a tear rolled down Tommy's face, or at least that's how it felt. Probably it was just blood. Probably it was just that he wanted more than anything to hold Lucy in his arms.

○

Victor Tessier had been charged with guarding their American prisoner. Nobody else had known what to do with the pilot, and then somebody had mentioned that Victor had studied in England. The officers mostly resented their unexpected visitor, but Victor was glad to meet finally a real pilot, even if he had called him Vic, which he hated because it made him sound like a kid. He hadn't been able to dress the wound on the man's head, but in the basement he had found him a thin blanket and a flimsy mattress. Now Lieutenant August slept beneath a desk among the bare legs of secretaries who had never given Victor the time of day. These same secretaries now wanted to know everything Victor could tell them about the handsome American pilot. They were a giddy contrast to the sullen officers who loafed on the edges of their desks draining wine bottles and debating the French predicament. Gunfire rattled the windows. The men took turns opening and closing the blackout shutters that sealed off the room from its little balcony, updating one another on whatever distant fighting could be glimpsed. They were bitter and argued over what should have been done. This was all about to end, but Victor had already known it was ending as he had walked to the offices flush with his first real sexual conquest.

Leaning against a wall, he kept watch over the American for hours, his body slowly melding into the architecture until at the edge of sleep it snapped back alive. A few officers slept crumpled in corners, empty bottles of wine overturned at their fingers. At one point the American awakened and stared up at him, shivering blankly. Victor shrugged off his leather pea coat and brought it over to cover him. The pilot thanked him and miserably prodded his wound. Victor glanced around at the sleeping officers and suggested they go out to the balcony for some fresh air. Silently they cracked open the blackout shutters and slipped outside. Below were the gardens of the Place Lyautey, fragrant beneath the stars. Together they looked up at the sky, Victor proudly pointing out the Seven Sisters, the brightest cluster of them all, four hundred light years away.

"How do you know so much about the stars, Vic?" Lieutenant August asked after a while. Victor replied that he'd studied them in school. And that he wanted to be a pilot like Lieutenant August. That he wanted to fly close to the stars. The American asked him how old he was.

"Eighteen," Victor said. He could have been. This whole situation was all made up. He knew that much. Even the officers didn't know what they were doing. Victor could be eighteen.

Distant sirens rang. A transport plane puttered across the sky, lights blinking. More of those German bastards fleeing, but he didn't mention it. The planes made a music, Lieutenant August said, and Victor agreed, although he added that he preferred Stravinsky.

"What do you know about Stravinsky?" the American asked, suddenly wide awake.

"*Rite of Spring*," Victor murmured. "In London I stole a recording by the Philharmonic-Symphony Orchestra of New York."

Lieutenant August grinned and shook his head. Pleased, Victor considered saying something more about himself, but then the sirens of the ambulances parked down in the square came to life, stopping any chance of conversation. Fighter planes roared across the sky, and empty cylinders clattered against the roof. Lieutenant August waved his arms in the air and whooped with joy, embarrassing Victor. "Bravo!" the American shouted, as if he'd just heard a symphony, getting some hostile looks from the officers who had now joined them on the balcony. Lieutenant August blushed and checked himself, then announced to Victor that he'd better go lie down again.

○

AT ALLIED HEADQUARTERS IN NORTH AFRICA

Violent hostilities have been renewed in Casablanca after the French turned down an armistice proposal offered by Major Gen. George S. Patton Jr., commander of American forces in the Morocco area.

General Patton went ashore in the Casablanca area and presented an ultimatum that was turned down by the local commander. General Patton returned to his ship under a flag of truce and hostilities were resumed with great violence.[5]

○

The kid Vic was sixteen, maybe seventeen, and Tommy was sorry to have made him lie about his age. He wanted to be a pilot someday, and Tommy liked his spirit. A bit odd, maybe, but he'd been kind. Light was beginning to creep through the blackout shutters, and he could make out Vic now crouched asleep against the wall. Again he fingered the bump on his head and rolled onto his side, hoping to find a more comfortable position. Vic's coat was warm, but something in its pocket dug into his ribs. He reached into the pocket and felt a stack of cards, as well as an instant nostalgia for his nightly quiz sessions with the Rippers. Hiding the movement beneath the blanket, he pulled out the cards. They

---

5   United Press – 11/10/1942

were photographic postcards, eight of them, numbered inconsecutively and entitled *Femme Marocaine dans son Intérieur.* In each photograph a disrobed Moroccan woman, or several, wore spangled headdresses or heavy silver jewelry. Some were completely naked, lounging on embroidered Arab couches or rattan mats. Others wore sheer kaftans through which you could see their breasts. Three dark beauties, waists covered by licks of silk, drank tea and leered. Another was heavily tattooed. Tommy whistled softly through his teeth. He wasn't so lonely then. Vic and he shared a secret. From the beginning he'd sensed that he could count on the kid, and so he slipped the postcards back into the pocket so as not to embarrass him again in front of the others.

Later Vic woke him with a tray of bread and butter and some watery barley coffee, which the kid explained was all they got since rationing. Somebody turned on a radio, but two stations now crowded the same frequency, one broadcast from the USS *Texas,* repeating demands for the French to lay down their arms, then playing both the French and American national anthems, the other Radio Maroc, warning its listeners to ignore its new competitor, which was broadcasting unauthorized propaganda. Around noon the offices filled up again. That morning five hundred sailors had been killed on the *Jean Bart,* and the mood was glum. Officers frantically sent codes over the telegraph, but they were no longer even taking care to hide their codebooks, which lay open on their desks and could have been read by Tommy or anyone else. By then he knew there was no need to bother. He would be free soon enough.

He dozed again beneath the desk and woke much

later to an upside-down smile from Vic, who announced that an armistice had been signed. "That's some damned fine news, Vic!" Tommy cried, wriggling out from under the desk. "I guess we can officially be friends." He took another cup of barley coffee, which now tasted as fine as Maxwell House. The atmosphere in the building had been transformed, and formerly surly officers crowded around him, slapping him on the back and trying out their English. Almost everybody seemed relieved, and genuinely happy.

In the excitement Vic disappeared, but later Tommy noticed him beckoning from the doorway. They went out into the corridor. "There are some Americans here," Vic whispered. "They say they've come to get you." Tommy chuckled and clumsily hopped down the staircase two steps at a time. At the entrance standing beneath a portrait of Marshal Pétain were some of the last faces he'd expected to see: Breezy and a few other Navy fliers, also shot down and looking even worse for the wear than Tommy, but all of them beaming.

"Man, it's good to see you boys!" he cried, leaping into their arms. "I have to admit I've been missing you a bit. Take a load off and let me grab a couple things. I'll be right back." Upstairs the Frenchmen had fallen silent around the radio, where the news told of Germans rolling into Vichy France in retaliation for France's surrender to the Americans. Hitler would control the entire country now, and Tommy felt sorry for them then. He looked around for Vic, but the kid had vanished, so Tommy decided he'd stop by later to say goodbye.

In the crowded streets people cheered the bedraggled Americans. French soldiers were trying to maintain order. Boys called out for cigarettes. Moroccan women ululated. Some advanced American Army units rolled past in trucks, stirring up tattered fliers, which still littered the streets. A French flag went up a pole, and then up another pole, the Stars and Stripes. A French soldier muttered. In a crowd of dancing natives, Tommy caught sight of his two Spahis and cried out to them, hoping to get his pistol back, but they were swept on by the dancers, their faces ecstatically grinning. Tommy chuckled and thought of their song. Maybe those two hadn't been such bad fellas after all. Night was approaching, and only then did he realize he was still wearing Vic's coat.

○

CASABLANCA YIELDS – RESISTANCE TO AMERICAN FORCES VIRTUALLY AT AN END IN COLONIES

Casablanca, the chief port of French Morocco, surrendered today to the American forces, marking the end of all effective resistance to the occupation of North Africa, designed eventually to liberate France.

There were battles still to be fought, but Morocco and Algeria were temporarily under the Stars and Stripes, to be held in trust until the day of victory, when they can be restored to French rule and the Tricolor.

So, in less than four days, with a minimum of

bloodshed, the first American campaign against the European Axis, under the command of American Lieut. Gen. Dwight D. Eisenhower, has come to a decisive conclusion. And, by a bold and well planned stroke, the war has reached a turning point where, for the first time, Reichsfuehrer Hitler is forced into defensive action that stretches his forces in a way that he had neither planned nor timed.[6]

---

6   *The New York Times* – 11/12/1942

YELLOW MAGIC
1943

This is the Armed Forces Radio Service. It's eight o'clock. If you're not working, you're in trouble, but! The radio blared across the port, where Mag had propped himself against a pylon to watch the battalion unload another Liberty Ship. "That's getting fuggin old," he said to nobody in particular. "But!"

It was January, and for two solid months the Port Battalion had been working dawn to dusk. The Navy had dredged the port, and the wrecks of French destroyers and cruisers had been towed out into the ocean. Now American supply ships occupied the piers. The only remaining sign of the French Navy was the carcass of the *Jean Bart*, which had been too big to move.

Announcements kept breaking into the radio broadcast. Special visitors were expected over the coming days, and Lord Patton himself would be holding an inspection, so the docks needed to be cleared. Mag had heard about enough from Patton. Over the past weeks the general's Gestapo had twice fined him ten dollars, once for failing to appear in proper uniform, the other for what they'd called unconventional grooming. Mag had tried to explain that Barbasol shaving cream was all that was keeping him and his men from frying like bacon under the African sun, but Patton's goons hadn't listened. You lathered, you shaved, you washed your goddamn face. Barbasol wasn't sun cream.

He lit a cigarette. The battalion had cracked the hatch of the next ship and were now removing its planks. Then some private would drop through the square opening into the hold and check for any surprises. Most often the ships were filled with cartons of rations on wooden pallets wrapped in cargo nets like cocoons. They fed the tens of thousands of soldiers in Morocco and off at the front in Tunisia, and the one and only rule of Mag's battalion was that you never pilfered anything meant for enlisted men. Occasionally, however, you'd find a pallet of whiskey or frozen meat or some other delicacy reserved for officers. That stuff was fair game. You redirected a few cases here or there, and since nobody in the entire military had any idea of what the endless stream of Liberty Ships actually contained, nobody was ever the wiser. For example, the six tons of women's silk stockings they'd recently unloaded, which some Washington genius had figured might be useful in bartering with the native women. The only woman Mag had seen in weeks was a Red Cross bruiser named Jocelyne who looked as if she could whup the whole battalion with her right arm tied behind her back. Mag didn't figure she wore silk stockings. Then again, who knew. He had never understood women, which suited him just fine.

You only had to look off towards the battalion's barbed-wire encampment, a sodden field of sagging pup tents and open latrines, to understand how they justified their pilferage. At night, with muscles cramped from long days of heavy lifting, for a warm meal they were obliged to build fires beneath oil drums filled with murky water. Once the water bubbled, they dropped in their C-rations, let them swim for a few minutes, then fished them out with sticks. Many grumbled that they would have done better out on the jetty rocks with the branches the Moroccans used in the mornings to bring up gleaming fish. Those Moroccans had it figured, Mag felt. They just sat around without the slightest intention of doing anything else all day, except maybe eating those fish.

He stubbed out his cigarette on the pier and shifted his solid weight on the pylon. Lieutenant Stec had appeared out of an officer's tent, but that was alright. Stec had been accounted for, repeatedly, although today he seemed on edge. The bastard was making a beeline across the tarmac. Mag took the pack of Luckys from his chest pocket and shook one out. "Sergeant!" Stec barked. Mag did a reasonable approximation of a salute as the lieutenant started in on his routine, patting his pockets with this bewildered look on his face until Mag held out the cigarette, and Stec said, "Oh, why not," leaning into the Zippo Mag had already flicked. Fuggin Stec.

"The beagle is sniffing around the water dish," the lieutenant continued, his lips curling grotesquely towards the filter. "It better not shit the lawn." Mag nodded. Most of the time you couldn't understand a word the guy said. Even back in Philly, Stec had been ninety percent incomprehensible, which in part explained how he'd risen to the position of secretary in the ILU. Since being given the Army codebook, however, he'd more or less been permanently speaking gobbledygook.

"Need to give this hellhole some structure, Sergeant," he continued. "Looks like a tornado came through a gypsy refugee camp. And you know damn well how I feel about gypsies...." They looked out across the piers together. Forklifts moved pallets from one pile to another. This pile alone would take days, because they still hadn't managed to locate the Liberty Ship containing the rest of the forklifts. A tall column of cartons tumbled over, and helmets went bouncing off like basketballs. A private covered from head to toe in Barbasol jumped down off a ship and waved Mag over: "You'd better come see this, Sergeant!"

"Find anything interesting?" Stec murmured. "First time I notice that watch you're wearing, Sergeant. A Gallet Flying Officer, eh? When did those come in?"

"A gift from my ma," Mag growled. "I'll send over a case of gin tonight."

"What the horse thinks he knows," the lieutenant said, patting Mag on the cheek, "the rider knows better." Then he strode back off towards the officers' tents, trailing delicate puffs of smoke. Mag scowled but held his tongue. For years on the docks of Philly, he'd been humiliated by Stec and his cronies. He'd worked ungodly hours unloading meat, stabbing hooks into heavy carcasses until his own flesh permanently stunk, advertising your slavish existence to everyone. Want to escape the docks and move up in the longshoreman's union? Fat chance. Stec and his gang had rigged the game. You were nothing but meat to them. You'd be slaving until you were dead, and then they'd stab a hook into your carcass and sell it off. That had started to change in Casablanca, however. Mag had found an angle, and though Stec might still become a problem, anything was better than the way it had been.

Down in the hold of the Liberty Ship, Slick Bambelli had cracked open a pallet of cigarettes. Mag thudded down the ladder into the ship's bowels and waited for his eyes to adjust to the gloom. Then he saw Slick holding out a carton with this stupid grin on his face. "Aw hell," Mag groaned. "You know we don't touch cigarettes. You want a pack, go buy it at the commissary."

And that was the problem, Mag was well aware, which was why he'd been asked to haul his ass down there. On Sunday night, Slick had gone into debt on a busted flush, and since then he'd been picking up lunch shifts in an attempt to pay off Mag and finally buy himself some Luckys. His eyes were bloodshot. For days he'd been in a foul mood.

"We got six pallets of some fancy perfume back here," Berkovich cried from deep in the hold.

"Box them up and lose the papers," Mag said. "I'll organize the rest."

"Personal delivery, right Mag?" Slick said, grinning madly. "Ha!"

"Shut the fug up, Slick. Ya owe me money."

"I'm gonna pay you, Sergeant, you know I'm good. My head's just pounding, and I thought maybe you could let me move a few of these cigs, then I could pay you back, double the interest. Yeah, *double the interest*. Or maybe I could loan a pack off you. The guys haven't really wanted to…." Mag let the numbskull talk as he climbed the ladder back up to the main deck. Then he turned and spit back down into the hold.

Half an hour later they had winched a heavy pallet of ammunition up clear of the ship when the cargo net slipped and the load teetered before collapsing back down into the hole, puncturing Slick Bambelli's lung. He hadn't properly looped the fourth corner onto the hook and never saw it coming.

They carried him across the tarmac on a stretcher.

Mag watched from his post against the pylon. So Slick wouldn't be sent off to the front anytime soon, lucky bastard. The front was Mag's biggest nightmare, because even if Casablanca was a hellhole, it was his hellhole. On the front you were just cannon fodder in some general's wet dream.

Later that afternoon as they cracked open the next ship, Mag wandered over to the western end of the port to watch the fishing boats coming in. Their blue hulls curled up out of the sea, and briefly he wished he'd learned to fish, wished he'd learned to do a lot of things. The Moroccans unloaded their nets without speaking. They'd been doing this for centuries. Word was the French ships sunk by the Americans had made for good fishing, although that kind of living, hauling up catches fed on the eyeballs of French sailors, had its own problems. He wondered what went on in the Moroccans' minds as they sat out there all day tossing on the waves. He almost never wondered this about himself. A man might hear many voices inside, but if you knew what was good for you, you only listened to one.

All around him rows of drums and crates had been deposited without rhyme or reason. At least not to anyone but Mag, who had organized it all in his mind. He strolled along the rows smoking, keeping an eye on Stec back across the tarmac. Mag gave his men a generous cut, because he worried that one might try to deal directly with the lieutenant, leaving him right back where he'd started. But now Stec was getting berated by the colonel, and Mag figured he'd keep pacing the rows a while longer. Shit flowed in only one direction. That was the nature of shit. The trick, if you could manage it, was to get to where you could afford a plumber.

Now here sat five cages of fuggin pigeons. Hello pigeons. Coo coo coo. At some point somebody had been meant to load them onto a truck, but the trucks had been requisitioned by the brass, and so here were still five cages of fuggin pigeons. Signal Corps wasn't ready for them either, since apparently the birds needed a week or two of acclimation before they could fly messages back from the front. Nobody had mentioned whether a carrier pigeon could go for a week or two without food. Welcome to the shit show.

Coo coo. Mag stopped abruptly in front of the cages. Through them he'd glimpsed someone or something moving. Coo coo. He moved closer to the cage, and through the thin metal bars a girl came into focus. She wasn't Moroccan. Must be French. She wore a flowered dress made of good cotton, and a necklace that looked gold. The dress fitted her nicely. "How the hell'd you get in here?"

The girl jumped, and pigeons fluttered. "I hear the music from the radio," she murmured, her voice like some nervous little bird's. Not a pigeon. Maybe a sparrow, or a dove. He had no fuggin idea what a dove sounded like, but still. Yeah, the accent sounded French, so maybe she hadn't understood him.

"I mean how'd you get past the guard."

The girl's hands flew up to her chest. You couldn't help but notice the chest, and so Mag could guess the answer to his question. "Maman asked me to come to see if a boat is leaving," she said. "We landed here from Dakar. They made us get off the boats. Poor Maman just hates Casablanca."

"Well tell your ma there's no boats leaving from here, okay?" As the girl nodded, she hid her hands behind her back, as if hands were impolite. She had a small mouth she was trying to make even smaller, lips pursed into a little button.

"You at least got a place to stay?" Mag continued, wondering if he still smelled like meat.

"We lost our papers in the attack. But the Croix Rouge found us an apartment."

"Yeah, the Red Cross," Mag grunted. She nodded once and whispered something to herself. The pigeons fluttered on their roosts. "Who takes care of them?" she asked. "Do you?"

Mag laughed.

"I can help take care of them," she said quickly.

He glanced back towards the cargo ships and spotted Berkovich moving along rows of supplies, marking a clipboard. Mag waved him over, moving around to the girl's side of the cages. She wiggled as if her feet were stuck to the ground, then Berkovich came running up with a special spring in his step. Jesus. This was already a mistake.

"Young lady here appreciates our feathered friends," Mag mumbled, avoiding eye contact with either of them. "Signal Corps can't get its shit sorted, so she's gonna to take care of a few. God knows how she got through the gate, but help her carry a cage or something and show her out. Tell Spanky I'll stop by the gate and see him later."

The girl murmured like a sparrow or a dove and ducked her head to hide a smile. "You can't sell 'em, okay?" Mag said, and Berkovich laughed.

Later that afternoon overseeing scut work, Mag ended up having to help out with a hold full of fifty-five-gallon drums of high-octane aviation fuel, the worst kind of surprise. Five-hundred-pound bombs could be rolled, at least, but you had to be gentle with fuel. For hours the men dully struggled to move them, and when the sun finally set, they staggered off to their pup tents. Mag was exhausted too. He'd see about the six pallets of perfume in the morning, he decided, annoyed with himself. He couldn't afford to slip. He was building something here, and he needed to keep building or he'd be cannon fodder off in Tunisia or wherever the generals got hot and bothered about next.

Before turning in, he wandered over to the pigeon cages, shivering in the cold. All day the sun beat down, but as soon as it vanished, you missed it. The nights were frigid. At first he thought he'd walked down the wrong row, but that wasn't like him. He retraced his steps. This was the right place, but the pigeons were gone. All the cages, every last one.

○

PRESIDENT GUARDED AS 'A-1' AT PARLEY; CHURCHILL, 'B-1' IN CODE, IGNORED SECRECY

CASABLANCA, French Morocco – The President of the United States and the Prime Minister of Great Britain were just a couple of symbols – "A-

1" and "B-1" – for the ten days they conferred here. A-1, the President, lived at a villa called "No. 2" and B-1 stayed at a place called "No. 3"….

Strictest secrecy veiled the President's movements during his entire stay. No outsider saw his arrival, which was at an airport some distance from Casablanca. Mr. Roosevelt left his villa only four times….

Mr. Churchill's activities, however, worried Scotland Yard men detailed to protect him. He hurried from his plane, shook hands with crew members, then walked briskly across the airport to greet other arrivals. He often left his villa and he was seen frequently inspecting the area, riding in a jeep or visiting the bar at the conference hotel.

Sidi Mohammed, Sultan of French Morocco, presented to the President an inlaid wooden box filled with jewels, as well as a carved silver Arabian knife, after he had been entertained at dinner at Mr. Roosevelt's villa. Because of the secrecy, the President was unable to pay a formal call at Sidi Mohammed's palace, for etiquette would have required the calling out of hundreds of gaudily dressed Arabian soldiers and horses.[7]

---

7   United Press – 1/29/1943

2

"Let's walk just a little bit, baby. I like to hear the crickets chirping. Reminds me of Saint Louis."

"Actually I believe that's the Egyptian nightjar. Quite a common bird in Morocco, and what you're hearing is its distinctive *churring*."

"Oh, poor Franklin. Take my arm, and just listen to it sing."

She pulled him close in the cold night. They strolled up the sidewalk under the arcade of Rue Colbert, back towards the clinic from Josephine Baker's long-awaited return to the stage at the Liberty Club. Passing the Hotel Transatlantique he had proposed a celebratory drink, imagining a corner table and acquaintances he would casually acknowledge, but Joe hadn't wanted crowds. In the spotlight she still mastered her old tricks, but outside that narrow circle she knew she had faded. Franklin clutched her bony arm, feeling the faint tug of her ravaged body. Beneath the hood of her voluminous men's djellabah, her dark eyes sagged with fatigue. A curl of black hair stuck to her pale forehead. It seemed she could have lifted her legs and weighed no more on his arm. He was walking in the moonlight alongside a thrilling ghost.

"You were extraordinary tonight." The doctors had advised against it, but she had agreed to perform on condition that her audience be black servicemen. She had captivated them, the Bronze Venus, the most famous woman in France, maybe in the world, a black American girl up from nothing. She'd mugged and tapped and flung her legs in the air. They would probably be shouting encores for hours. "Those men had never seen anything like it."

She didn't answer. A wild dog hobbled along the gutter, its fur matted with neglect. Crossing Boulevard de Marseille, they turned towards Boulevard Général-Leclerc. Beneath a streetlamp French policemen loitered on the pavement, eyeing them suspiciously. The blackouts had been lifted, and the French had reestablished control, and their cops had returned to harassing Moroccans. He felt certain that he hated this, but there was nothing he could do about it. Secrets were his responsibility, and the wires that connected secrets to one another. The wires were America's real power. Those wires were the secret map of the future world.

Their footsteps echoed off the Art Deco façades of sleeping apartment buildings. Felton spoke again to break the rhythm: "I was told that Patton wants to meet you."

"Baby, I met him last month with the president. If he really wanted to see me, he could have come to the show."

"Somehow I can't imagine him in a room full of negroes." Felton sneered awkwardly. "Although I do hear that if you're invited for dinner, he gives you a pack of cigarettes and a roll of Life Savers for dessert."

"Well isn't that just elegant," Joe said, and when she laughed he felt as if he'd safely leapt through the closing doors of a Manhattan train. He felt he wanted to move to a one-room apartment in Harlem and learn how to play the saxophone.

"Apparently during his visit Roosevelt promised the Sultan independence once the war is won."

"Well he should have!" Joe cried. "People have a right to choose how they want to live. They should be free."

"Yes, it's just that some of the old guard are rather upset. They think it's foolhardy for the president to be making promises that directly challenge our French allies."

"The *old guard?* What does that make you? The *ancient guard?*"

"Well they're all Harvard men, you know, and of course I went to Columbia, although Groton –"

"You think I give a shit about any of that? You're the new guard, baby, okay? You guard me. Now why don't you take me over to the reserved quarter everybody talks about? Bousbir. I hear the belly dancers take off everything, and there's a girl with a whistling cunt. I'd like to see that."

Franklin felt himself blush but quickly found a line to hide inside: "I've heard it's not so much a whistling, but a *churring.*" Joe laughed, and those two beloved deep parentheses appeared on either side of her mouth. He was in love with a black woman. "It's all rather exploitative, don't you think?"

"Boring," Joe groaned, rolling her eyes. He couldn't get through. Even her truest emotions were pantomimes of pantomimes, and now she gave him that look that said he was her *poor* baby, not her *baby* baby. "A whistling cunt would probably do you some good, Franklin. I don't know that you're ready yet for a cunt that *churrs.*"

That stung, and he felt it would be manlier not to respond. They passed a café terrace and heard the sound of tiny *parchís* dice hopping across iron tables. He hadn't smoked any kif since before the show and wanted some now, but once Joe got an idea in her head, she was as impetuous as a child, and perfectly capable of dragging him along as she somehow located Bousbir and hired a dozen women for them both. She was alive. Maybe he wasn't. In any case, he didn't want it tonight, not touristy, vulgar Bousbir. He still wanted to bask in her success together. Then thankfully she spotted a lonesome fruit seller across the street with a cart full of lemons gleaming in the moonlight. "Oh, Franklin," she cried, tugging his arm, flush with a new obsession, and there was always another. "Buy me some of those beautiful lemons."

"Your stomach," he said a little bitterly.

"I don't *eat* them," she groaned. "I squeeze them onto my skin. It's a little trick I learned in Harlem, a whitener."

"But your skin is beautiful, Joe."

"Don't be a two-time bore, baby. Six lemons, eight if they're not very juicy." So Felton crossed the street and bought her lemons. Looking back from the cart, he couldn't see her face in the shadows beneath the hood. She had hung her djellabah on an invisible peg and had walked off into the night.

Later he flagged down a cab, but she still wanted to walk. "I don't get enough ex-er-cise. Gotta keep these legs in shape." Until that night she had been limited to morning strolls with her nurse, Marie, through Parc Murdoch, whose greenery shaded her window at the clinic. More than anything she liked to watch the children play in the sandboxes and on the jungle gyms. The children brought tears to her eyes. Recently the doctor had confirmed that she would never have her baby.

Near Parc Murdoch, they stopped outside two doors open to a meeting hall packed with standing Moroccan men. On a low stage actors performed. Joe dragged Franklin into the back of the rapt crowd. Nobody noticed that a woman was beneath her hood. "*Tartuffe*," Franklin whispered into her neck as she pressed into him. "Molière."

His Arabic still needed work, but he knew the play: an unwelcome houseguest connives to steal everything from his host, including family, wife, and house itself. The crowd roared with laughter. The actors were all men, including Elmire, wife of Orgone, mustachioed and flamboyant in an elegant dress and heels. "Oh my!" Joe purred to Franklin's cheek. "He looks just like Errol Flynn. We should meet him."

Beside the entrance stood several French policemen, dispatched by the authorities to arrest any subversives, Felton supposed. They laughed too, although he doubted their Arabic was sufficient to realize that they were the unwanted houseguests, the butt of the joke, not the high heels or the hairy legs, although those were pretty funny too.

A little girl tumbled onto the stage behind a bearded maid. Her hair was cut short, and with large and vivid eyes she surveyed the crowd, hands confidently anchored to her hips. The audience laughed and applauded. She just continued glaring until Elmire broke character and wobbled over in his heels, guiding the girl to a spot behind the maid. The audience applauded again, but now in the back there was some shoving, and a man in a white djellabah cried out in Arabic: "Do you wish to make your daughter a whore? *Hchouma!* Shame! Is she for sale? You put her onstage like a prostitute!"

Some men hissed and shouted back at the man, while others applauded. The policemen drew themselves up, gripping their batons. "What is it?" Joe asked.

"He says women shouldn't be onstage. He called her a prostitute. He's a zealot, but perhaps her father was foolish to bring her out. It is a Moslem country...." He had been so proud of his Arabic that he hadn't realized his miscalculation. Joe whipped off her hood and turned on the man in the white djellabah, wrenching free of Franklin's grasp with surprising force, her slender arms batting intervening men aside.

"Say it to me!" she shouted in French. "Say I'm the whore! I am Josephine Baker! I have danced naked for kings and queens. A little girl? What is she, five, six? Have you lost your mind? Say I'm the whore!" The crowd went silent. The man in the white djellabah spat on the floor, then turned and pushed back out to the street, grumbling to himself. Up onstage the girl got down on all fours and shook her head, roaring like a lion. Joe grinned, clapping her hands in the air, and then everyone clapped and the show went on.

"You were magnificent," Felton said afterwards on the street. In the darkness palm trees clashed invisibly.

"Oh, shut up, Franklin," Joe said. "I'll take a cab from here."

3

The rain had let up for the first time since March. The men crowded around a campfire in the mud watching two scorpions fight in a tin gasoline flimsy with the top cut off. The creatures were black, with armored tails as wide as their bodies and powerful claws that looked red in the firelight. You could hardly ever tell a difference between any two scorpions until they fought, and then one would swiftly establish dominance, pinning the other's tail with a claw. Mag watched disinterestedly, holding a wad of bills. Eisenhower was now shipping out eight hundred men a day from Casablanca to the front, and scuttlebutt was that Port Battalion would be heading out soon too, to Algiers or maybe Italy. The destination changed daily, but most men didn't care. They would have preferred Antarctica to their Casablanca swamp. The worst was the Atabrine, the synthetic anti-malaria drug that Washington had shipped over as a substitute for quinine, whose supply the Japs controlled. They called it Yellow Magic, and the magic had felled hundreds of men. The Red Cross nurses did their best, but the mud between pup tents was spattered with vomit and liquid shit, and bodies moaned day and night, men lying under soaked blankets covered with their own insides.

Mag was maybe the only man out there who wasn't longing for Algiers or Italy or anywhere else. Business might be slow – here he was taking smalltime scorpion wagers and trading scuttlebutt with the unit's ten healthy men – but he still had five thousand silk stockings to unload. A fortune could be made, and he was stuck watching some genius from Oklahoma move

65

the gasoline flimsy onto the fire to make the scorpions hop. "Just watch 'em," the kid was saying. "Scorpions get scared, they sting themselves with their own tail. Only creature on God's green earth who'll commit suicide, other than humanity."

The others watched the scorpions dance until they curled up on themselves, struck their heads with their tails, and died. Mag sighed. "All you bums just did was burn 'em to death. So thanks for playing. Only winners get paid." The men grumbled, but they weren't going to cross Mag. Let the Oklahoma scientist pay for the pleasure of killing two perfectly good scorpions. There was your better example of suicide.

Some units had started moving out to the old Nazi airbase at Cazès, so maybe that was a solution. He'd driven over with Stec, and they could make something of it, all the loaded transport planes landing. He only needed to hold out long enough, keep greasing the lieutenant. The thought of Europe kept him up at night. He'd even hoped to get knocked out for a while by the Yellow Magic. Some of those poor boys wouldn't be fit to travel for weeks. But after taking his dose, he'd waited and waited and hadn't felt a goddamn thing.

Now they were out of scorpions. Numbskulls. He squished back to his tent, lifted the flap, and lit the oil lamp. In the corner of the tent were the two bottles of Atabrine he'd instructed the commissary to set aside. Grabbing the bottles, he sunk down onto his cot. His boots hadn't come off in days, and now wasn't the time to start homemaking. Better to keep the vomit out of your socks if you could help it. Personal hygiene. Uncapping the bottles, he drained them both down his throat.

Then it was midnight or later, and the Yellow Magic might as well have been Coca-Cola. He couldn't sleep. Men groaned in the night. He sat up in his cot and strained to see his watch face. He pressed fingers into his belly, but it made no sound, and he couldn't feel any nausea in any part of himself. Pulling on a long brown trench coat over his uniform, he ducked out of the tent and walked towards the guard's hut that separated the base from town.

Spanky was on duty and actually gave him some lip. Mag shoved over five bucks, but the fat guard wanted cigarettes. He'd used up his ration, but Mag wasn't selling. "Let me out, and maybe I'll bring you a pack." Spanky didn't like it: "They'll have my ass if you run off."

Mag chuckled. "Now why the hell would I do a dumb thing like that?" Finally cracking the gate, Spanky mentioned that Signal Corps had been coming round to ask about their pigeons. "I'll take care of the pigeons," Mag grumbled, and slipped off the base.

Town leave was now permitted during the day, but Mag preferred escaping at night. His new power should be exerted, he felt, or it could vanish as quickly as it had come. Sometimes when he worried, he still whiffed the scent of dead flesh on his skin, but with every new influence he obtained, the scent faded. Still, it wasn't enough. He needed to put something away, stash some gold or cash, to ever have a dealer's odds of escaping his old fate. Leaving the base like this, an hour or two snatched after midnight, maintained his faith in his future.

Along the shore you were unlikely to run into anyone. South past the fishing port, the ocean glided in over a shelf of jagged rocks, and then you came to the municipal swimming pool, separated from the Atlantic by a concrete barrier and said to be the world's largest, five hundred yards long by nearly a hundred wide. In spring the pool was still empty, but Mag liked it empty, a smooth, squared hole at the edge of an endless ocean.

Sometimes on moonlit nights you noticed a sentry down on the rocks, darkly silhouetted against silvery waves, but tonight the waves were hidden in mist and hushed by the weight of humidity. It was a shitty job, patrolling the coast, one of those military jobs that had to get done even if everybody knew it was pointless. The Germans would never attack Casablanca. Mag personally didn't give much of a damn about the war, but everybody knew the Allies had kicked the Krauts back across the Med and out of Africa, and that in Russia they were getting more than they could handle. For those poor sentries, however, boredom wasn't even the worst of it. Bucketfuls of fish drowned in black oil leaked from sunken French ships were still washing up on shore, and the stench was apocalyptic.

Stec had told him that one night two dago sentries had caught the British prime minister walking the beach out by the El Hank lighthouse at three in the morning. He'd been drinking and ordered the sentries to sing *You Are My Sunshine*. They'd called it in: some buffoon down on the beach was claiming to be the British prime minister. Eventually they'd sorted it out and had sung for him. Churchill had chimed in on the refrains, they said.

Looking inland you had the medina, the old Moroccan town, the windows in its white wall like pale blue eyes, all of them shut. Occasionally you heard someone singing or playing an Arab guitar, making a sound like somebody had died, or had their dumb heart broken. Mag had never entered the medina. He was curious about it, he guessed, but he didn't see much point. He liked the Moroccans he'd met well enough – the French had sent them a few crews of stevedores, and as long as orders were relayed through their sheik, they worked like dogs. It was just that the money was in Frenchtown.

He checked his Gallet Flying Officer in the moonlight – only just past one – and decided to walk up Boulevard du 4ème Zouaves into town, where a few bars might be open late. He'd gotten Stec his own Gallet Flying Officer now. Everyone with the watch you could eliminate – one way or another, they were a part of Mag's network. Most everyone else, however, he worried about, and he knew walking into Frenchtown was a risk. Not that he'd be immediately spotted as an American in his trench coat, as long as he kept his mouth shut. And hell, getting thrown in the stockade for a week or two might not be a bad idea. Maybe he'd miss shipping out for the front. Because that damned Yellow Magic sure as hell wasn't doing the trick.

From the port Casablanca was unimposing. It wasn't a city you could observe from a distance, but once you were inside, it became immense. Massive boulevards stretched on forever in straight lines marked by crippled palm trees whose tops had been smoked off by American planes but were now returning. Around the Place de France, a few Europeans hung around, no Moroccans. The Cinema Vox had shown the night's last movie. Mag had turned up onto Rue Oulad Ziane when a black Buick Century with red officer's plates came flying around the corner and hit the brakes. He froze. The driver cut the headlamps, then drifted back in reverse for a few dozen feet, then the wheels spun and the car leapt forward past the spot where Mag stood rooted to the sidewalk. That was strange, but even stranger was that the Buick appeared to be driving itself. No driver sat behind the wheel. And then the car was gone.

Mag half wondered if he'd seen a vision, some side effect of the Yellow Magic. He retraced his steps back to the Place de France, now anxious to return to base. Before he reached the corner, however, the Buick reappeared. It had circled the block and bore down on him before screeching to a halt not more than three feet from where he stood. The passenger door flew open. Mag gritted his teeth and bent over to look into the car. Crouched behind the wheel was a Moroccan, about twenty years old, wearing the uniform and cap of an American Army colonel and holding a liquor bottle in one hand. The two men glared at one another. Then the driver smiled and said, "Get in."

Still stunned, Mag made a quick calculation. The Moroccan had more to lose, so maybe Mag had something to win. He got into the car.

The city flew past. The Moroccan's bloodshot eyes narrowed to the mouth of the liquor bottle. Mahia, the natives called it, distilled from figs by the Jews. The officer's cap sat crookedly on his head, and with every few sips his pimpled face contorted into a yawn so wide it squeezed his eyes shut. They whipped through an intersection. Passing the bottle to Mag, he said, "We go drink?" His voice was hoarse, as if he'd been shouting.

Mag took the bottle but kept his mouth shut. The speedometer said they were travelling at precisely zero miles per hour. The odometer was dead too. Also, a wooden match was pressed into a wad of chewing gum stuck to the gas gauge. Mag took a pull from the bottle and winced. This *mahia* made Atabrine taste like the finest whiskey.

Frenchtown's splendor receded. Mag had never moved this far inland, where the streets got dirty and derelict. These were Moroccan neighborhoods, home to the tens of thousands who'd come to the city looking for work since the start of the war. Cheaply built concrete apartment buildings squeezed the streets. "I love America!" the driver cried in response to nothing, jamming his fingers at the radio, but nothing broadcast at that time of night. "My name is Ahmed Touil. You?" Mag grunted.

They came to a mechanic's garage on a broad, dusty street. Over two giant sliding metal doors, a sign read *Société des Transports Bradley*. Ahmed stopped the car. "First we have to make a drop-off." He spoke English well, with an American accent. Mag watched as he reached over the seat to fetch a dirty sweater from the back, which he pulled on over the colonel's jacket. He then removed his cap and snaked an arm up under his sweater to extract a thin-barreled Astra from the jacket pocket. The gun went into his pants waist beneath the sweater. Then he turned to Mag as if it had just occurred to him that his new American friend might still be sitting there. "Don't move," he said. "You're not supposed to be here, and these guys are assholes. Okay buddy?" He laughed, slapped Mag on the shoulder, and burst from the car, leaving the motor running.

Mag watched as Ahmed approached the garage and disappeared through a door. He knew he was a fool to sit waiting patiently for some nutcase who'd stolen a colonel's car. He should run, find his way back to base on his own, but he wouldn't have known even which general direction to take. So he lit a cigarette. Fog rolled in off the ocean. For the first time in weeks, he couldn't smell vomit or shit.

Soon Ahmed reappeared with three other men, Moroccans. Mag watched in the rearview mirror as they circled around to the back of the Buick and popped the trunk. For about a minute they were hidden, and when Ahmed slammed the trunk shut, each man was holding two carton boxes of Chesterfields. They retreated into the garage, and Ahmed hopped into the car again, squirming out of the sweater. Before he got both arms free, however, he froze and glared at Mag. "You smoke in this car? You can't smoke in this car!" Mag tossed the cigarette out the window. Ahmed shook his head and muttered, a professional among amateurs, and once he'd extracted himself from the sweater, he flapped it around attempting to vanquish the smoke. Then he slid the pistol back in the jacket pocket and wedged the cap down over a head of dark, greasy hair.

"How much you's selling them for?" Mag asked once they were moving again. Touil whistled through his teeth: "Ha! You some kind of businessman?"

"How much?"

Ahmed paused as if trying to decide on a number. "Hundred francs a carton," he finally said.

Mag raised an eyebrow: "And you's paying how much?"

"Eighty?"

Mag chuckled and lit another cigarette with the match from the gas gauge. Ahmed angrily puffed up his cheeks until they burst, and then he violently yawned. "How much would you pay?"

"A pack's ten cents at the base PX. That's two bucks a carton, say eighty francs – buying by the pack, okay? The carton's worth prolly one-sixty in town, retail, so you's making twenty while some punk takes sixty. And driving a stolen colonel's car."

Ahmed remained absolutely silent, but in seconds Mag watched whole movies play across the kid's face. "Don't pay more'n sixty – it's all profit for them – and don't sell at less than one-ten. Who's ya source?"

"A base guard up at Fedala."

"Jesus. Spending that gas money for fifty cartons of cigs?"

Touil looked at the nub of chewing gum on the dash and muttered something in Arabic. Then he pounded the steering wheel three times with the balls of both hands and stomped the accelerator to the floor.

They flew deeper into Moroccan neighborhoods, past shabby hospitals and mosques. Occasionally a shadow darted along the street, men in hooded djellabahs, the orange flare of a cigarette. Ahmed's manic face glowed in the dashboard light. He blazed through intersections with eyes narrowly focused on the road, the engine roaring in the night. Mag still figured his best play was to ride along and see if they might end up someplace interesting, or at least someplace he could disappear. He was lost. They seemed to be moving further away from the ocean. He asked Ahmed about the car.

The crazy kid couldn't have been happier or prouder to tell him. He'd been strolling through town one day, he said, when he'd noticed three American Army colonels moving into a house off Rond-Point Shell. So he started coming by regularly to wash the colonels' cars, including this very Buick. The colonels hadn't asked to have their cars washed, and Ahmed never demanded money, but sometimes they'd give him fifty francs, sometimes nothing. Once the Americans had gotten used to seeing Ahmed around, he made his proposal: for three hundred francs a month, he'd take their cars over to a proper car wash each week on a scheduled evening, and if it rained or the car got dirty, he'd wash it again. Minor repairs – punctured tires or sparkplugs – he'd also handle. Each of the colonels agreed, and on their scheduled evenings, Ahmed appeared to collect the keys. Then he would drive the car around the corner, disconnect the gauges, mark the level of gas on the indicator, and drive up the coast half an hour to Fedala. He had just returned from there in the colonel's Buick when he'd spotted the American. First he'd tried to hide, but then he'd decided an American soldier walking alone in the middle of the night was worth investigating. Because Ahmed had an instinct about people and was rarely wrong, he said. "And now we're friends!"

And now that he'd fenced the cigarettes, they could enjoy themselves till dawn, when the car would need to appear back at the colonel's, washed and gassed. Incidentally, maybe his new friend could chip in on gas.

"Pretty risky," Mag murmured, bracing himself

against the door as they slid through a turn. Ahmed was now steering with two fingers while knocking back mahia. "So why the uniform? Seems even riskier."

Ahmed said he'd had a couple of close calls and had asked a tailor friend to make him a uniform. A Moroccan driving an American officer's car was too suspicious, but in the uniform and cap nobody ever noticed. He was practically untouchable.

Mag chuckled. A dog darted out into the road, big and yellow. Stunned by the headlights, it looked Mag in the eyes before a wheel jolted over it with a thunk. Ahmed braked hard, but too late.

Mag flung open his door and jogged back towards the motionless heap on the road. You wouldn't have guessed the thing had ever been a dog. The hind legs were snapped, and the head lolled like a separate piece, the neck broken. With its forelegs it still struggled to drag itself forward, leaving a wet trail of guts and blood glistening like oil on the asphalt.

Ahmed stood beside him now, laughing. "That is one tough dog! Look how stupid he is. Where you going, doggie? Huh?"

"Shoot it," Mag muttered.

Ahmed whipped the pistol from his jacket pocket and clumsily twirled it on his index finger. "Hold it right there, partner!"

"Shoot it!"

"You crazy?" Ahmed whined, letting his arm fall. "We get caught with a gun in this neighborhood, those French bastards will torture me all night and kill me in the morning." He shook his head and walked off as if his feelings had been hurt. "It's only a dog."

Mag took a last look at the animal, turned back towards the car, and cursed himself. He should never have gotten in the damned car. He turned back to the mangled creature, sighed, and brought the heel of his boot down hard on the dog's wounded neck. The dog twitched once and died. At least he could do that much. A distant motorbike sounded like a buzzing fly. Mag then walked back to the car, where Ahmed knelt before the bumper inspecting it for damage. "Get in the car," Mag said, slumping into his seat, printing a bloodstain on the floormat as he slammed the door. "Get in."

Ahmed obeyed. "Poor doggie," he sighed while starting the engine, and they drove for a couple of blocks in silence. Ahmed kept fidgeting with the radio buttons, dialing up static, and Mag kept wanting to punch him. Finally Ahmed said: "So you can get me cigarettes?"

"I don't pilfer cigs," Mag growled. "Clothing, whiskey, perfume – fine. But G.I.s smoke cigs. That's the rule. But what would you know about fuggin principles, right? Just drive me to the ocean, and I'll walk the rest of the way."

Ahmed nodded repeatedly, then yawned and said, "I know where we should go!"

Down a narrow side street in a neighborhood called Derb Chorfa-Tolba was a bar called Les Nations Unies. Ahmed ran the Buick up onto the sidewalk and cut the engine. Then he pulled the sweater down over the uniform again and nodded for Mag to get out. The air was greasy with humidity. Against a moldy white wall an old man in a tattered three-piece suit sat on an overturned gallon tin of Dutch Boy paint, holding a flimsy stick. Ahmed tossed a coin at the man's feet and gave an order. The old man halfheartedly wagged the stick and said nothing. Ahmed tossed another coin, shouting this time, and the man bent over with his palm to the ground and slowly raised himself to his feet. Ahmed looked at Mag and smiled. "He's a thief. Come on. We have a drink."

Mag held back. "I told you, man," Ahmed groaned. "Only Moroccans around here. But don't take off the coat." When he pushed open the door, light crashed into the night, momentarily blinding them both.

Inside a dozen men sat on stools at a long wooden bar decorated with a vase of plastic flowers. They drank bottles of Cigogne beer and conspicuously avoided noticing Ahmed or Mag. The bare bulbs overhead illuminated every corner of the room – the crooked wooden tables covered with plastic mats, the cigarette butts squashed into the floor, the pink latticework stuck to otherwise bare cement walls. Behind the bar was an opening to an empty kitchen reeking of fried fish. At the end of the bar, a large woman in an embroidered kaftan balanced precariously on a stool. Her hair was down, her face heavily made up, and her body impressive, with wide hips, a round belly, and enormous breasts. She sang a romantic Arabic song as the men silently mouthed the words, heads bowed to the bar. Mag wouldn't have called her husky voice beautiful, but she sang with passion, as if the words grew in her chest and she ripped them up by the roots. Ahmed ordered two Cigognes, paying with a wad of francs he pulled from his pants pocket, and they sat at the opposite end of the bar.

As the woman finished her song, she raised a fist high and brought it down to her chest. The men applauded and shouted before returning to their beers, the bartender bringing over a fresh one for the woman. Ahmed hopped off his stool and went up to a man in a suit, clapping him on the back. The man smiled too widely, and Ahmed leaned in to kiss both cheeks, eyes roving the room for other faces, none of which acknowledged him. Then he moved through the room, greeting men Mag had assumed were strangers. They offered elaborate greetings, beaming until Ahmed moved on. The woman took him in her arms and sang something into his ear. Ahmed grinned and pulled back to admire her, his hands clasped together like a boy's begging for candy. "Please please please please," he said in English, which made Mag uneasy. He jiggled his bottle on the bar. Everybody must know he was American, and again he considered leaving. Nothing good would come of this. Ahmed was still flirting with the woman, laughing like some fuggin hyena. He had also passed her a wad of cash, which she slipped between her breasts. She wasn't as old as Mag had first thought – thirty, thirty-five. Now Ahmed was coming back down the bar, and he pulled Mag close. "Aziza wants to meet you," he whispered. "She is interesting for business."

Ignoring his instincts, Mag followed Ahmed back down to the woman and was introduced as an American working at the consulate. "We have business together." The woman held out her hand, Mag glumly shook it. She smelled of roses, which made him aware again of how truly filthy he was. His coat was stained, his boots still soaked and bloody. He made two fists to hide the dirt beneath his nails. "Please to meet you," she said.

"Aziza has a shop selling women's clothes. She can be interesting for us."

"Speak for yourself," Mag grumbled, knowing he couldn't afford to get involved with these people. The woman's smile didn't even slightly flicker. He wasn't sure how much she was understanding.

"You get us stuff," Ahmed said, "Aziza can move it."

Mag snorted. "I'm just a soldier. Or consulate officer."

"Ahmed just American colonel," Aziza said, wiggling her hips, drawing Mag's eyes down past the soft line between her breasts. She followed his eyes with her own, doubling her chin, a thumb looping through her gold necklace to hold out a little charm in the shape of a hand. "Hand of Fatima. Protect from evil eye."

"That's not what he looks at," Ahmed shouted, doubling over in glee, and Aziza laughed too – *krr krr krr* – like a car engine turning over on a cold night.

"Maybe I could locate some silk stockings," Mag said, more spooked by the minute. "How much you need?"

"How much you got?"

"At the moment? Five thousand pair, so don't tell me –"

"I take them."

Mag shook his head. These two were crazy. "How big's this shop?"

"Very small," she said, still with this permanent smile.

"But Aziza knows many people. It is good to know Aziza. Moroccans cannot have anything with the war rationing. Our rations are different from the French. They say we have different needs. But Moroccans need silk stockings if Aziza says they do."

Mag lit a cigarette and winced, calculating. If

they ever got caught, who was going to believe two Moroccans? He would deny it. There would be no proof. And for the moment he could only sell to soldiers. How was that ever going to get him more than a few favors? Even better, if this worked out, he could keep Stec out of it. He knew he was reaching, and he knew better than to reach, but he felt as if his options had been dwindling. Ahmed was a wildcard, but at least he knew the city. "I can get you a thousand in the next few days," Mag said. "And we'll see how that goes. If it works, maybe I can get you more."

Ahmed embraced him, and the two Moroccans went back and forth in Arabic until it was agreed that Mag would deliver the stockings to Ahmed somewhere off-base and split the profits fifty-fifty with them both. Aziza looked ruthless when she bargained, stripped of all charm, which encouraged Mag. She, at least, might know what she was doing. She took his hand and held it for a long moment, smiling too sweetly again. Mag shifted in his boots and felt his toes squish. Ahmed had gone off to the kitchen but immediately returned holding two greasy plastic jugs of Lesieur cooking oil. They said goodbye to Aziza.

As they came out onto the street, the old man careened off his paint can and blindly waved his stick at the air. Ahmed kicked him in the ass, then handed him the two jugs of oil, barking something before wrenching open the driver's door and hopping in. Mag watched the old man hobble over to the Buick, twist open the gas cap, and pour in the cooking oil, dribbling much of it over the body and back bumper.

"We going to make good business together, my

friend!" Ahmed cried as he mashed down the accelerator. "What is your name, by the ways?"

Mag thought for a moment before saying, "Mag."

When they reached Place Mirabeau, a place he finally recognized down by the railroad tracks, he rapped the dashboard, and Ahmed stopped the car. "Meet me here in two days after sunset," Mag said. "If I don't show, I will the next night. And if I don't show then, I won't show."

It was only after he'd thrust open the door that he remembered fuggin Spanky and reluctantly turned back to Ahmed. "You got a pack of cigarettes? I'll pay you."

"My brother Mag. I would never dream of taking your money." Ahmed reached down beneath the seat and tossed over a pack of Chesterfields. Mag caught the pack and stepped out into the night. Ahmed peeled off, honking the horn like an idiot.

Now it was cold, or maybe Mag was finally tired. He walked the last half mile along the railroad tracks to the gate, then whistled twice from the shadows. The gate slid open the width of a man, and Mag slipped through, tossing the pack towards Spanky, who stood at the door of the hut. "Took you long enough," Spanky said.

"Shop was closed," Mag said, and stumbled off through the shit and the vomit as the morning call to prayer bloomed from the tops of mosques across the city.

○

For the first time in weeks, he had slept deeply, at least for a couple of hours, only to awake with a powerful hangover, courtesy of Ahmed's fuggin mahia. "Yellow magic catching up with you?" Stec had asked when he arrived at his post. The port noise seemed especially loud that morning, the clanging and creaking, the ratcheting of bolts into the ships heaved up in dry dock. The port was always deafening, but that morning the noise was inside him, banging through his veins.

"Maybe so." The promise of new business with Aziza was now like a dream, along with the rest of the previous night. How could that strange world be only a mile or two from where he stood watching a green crew of stevedores tangle themselves in cargo nets? It would take days, weeks, to get these new punks trained. He needed Aziza.

A drizzle fell, and a few seagulls circled overhead against the gray sky, occasionally squawking. Mag watched this dumb kid named Petey, probably not more than sixteen, patrolling the fence without a helmet, rifle slung over his shoulder like a fishing pole. Suddenly Petey's hand flew up to his head as if he'd been stung. But it wasn't that. A seagull had shat on him, and he wiped the mess from his hair before glancing around to see if anyone had noticed. Mag sighed, and it took him ten flicks of the Zippo to get his moist cigarette lit.

About five minutes later, Petey got shat on again, but this time he swung the rifle around and dropped the bird from the sky with a single shot. It landed at Mag's feet, and Mag exploded, booming across the tarmac such that the whole base must have heard: "Petey you fuggin twot, get your ass over here!"

The kid came loping over, face bright red. "Sorry sir," he said, and actually fuggin saluted.

"Who you calling sir?" Mag barked, his arms rigid by his sides. He really didn't want to punch the kid. "I'm Mag, you's a fuggin numbskull, and we don't kill fuggin birds. We kill Nazis. Got it?"

"Yes sir."

"Jesus. Go fetch that Red Cross nurse, Jocelyne. Biceps and shiny leather boots."

The kid looked down at the bird. "You think she can do something?"

"Gimme your rifle," Mag growled. It was a struggle to get out the words. The kid handed over the rifle, which Mag aimed straight at his head.

"I'll go find the nurse," Petey said.

"Take the bird with you," Mag said, still aiming the rifle, "and toss it over the fence." The kid went pale, then tentatively reached down to tweezer the seagull between his wrists before scampering off.

Mag tossed the rifle on the ground and went out to the end of the pier, where Jocelyne soon met him. "Good looking boots, Jocelyne."

"I'm very pleased with them, Mag." Poor Jocelyne and her boots. It was never going to get much better. But he knew that was also what they said about him.

"Listen, I need a favor. A French girl and her mother came in on a passenger ship from Dakar the night of the landings. Fancy girl. French Red Cross found them a place to stay. I wanna know where."

GENTLEMEN CALLERS
1943

In 1908, four years before the establishment of the French protectorate in Morocco, Prosper Ferrieu, the wealthy French consul, bought a plot of land adjacent to the Old Medina at Bab Marrakesh. Ferrieu was a religious man renowned for his piety, and his frugality, and so when in 1913, after leasing the land to the government for a period of ten years, Casablanca's first official red-light district was established there, Prosper was incensed. Under the terms of his lease, however, he had no control over the land's use, and so he watched helplessly as the reserved quarter's fame spread throughout Morocco and beyond, known by the name given to it by the natives, a horrid deformation of his own: Bousbir.

In 1923, the city's head of Municipal Services, an associate of Prosper's, ordered that the reserved quarter be moved to a larger plot in the New Medina south of the palace. Prosper's plot could no longer contain the astonishing needs of the populace, and so a French municipal architect was engaged to design a harmonious neighborhood respecting local traditions, with courtyards and Islamic decorations, which could comfortably house at least six hundred prostitutes and receive the thousands of tourists who would flock from all over the world to visit exotic tableaus out of the Arabian Nights.

Construction was rushed to completion. High walls surrounded the quarter, pierced by only two entrances, one into the clinic and dispensary, the other the public gate, a soaring Moorish arch between two guard huts, one manned by the police, the other by the military.

Within the walls, the streets were named according to the provenance of their female residents: rue de la Fassia, de la Meknassia, de la Rbatia de la Doukkalia, de la Chaouia, de la Bidaouia. There were eight cafés, six restaurants, two barbershops for men, four beauty parlors for women, four fruit sellers, one charcoal seller, one bakery, a dance hall, and sixteen souvenir shops. On the day of the new reserved quarter's grand opening, hundreds of prostitutes traipsed across town from the old Bousbir to this masterpiece of public planning. They carried Berber carpets, rattan mats, silver tea seats, cracked wooden trunks, and also Prosper Ferrieu's name. Bousbir, they called it – the new Bousbir, not the old. The souvenir shops sold postcards printed with this mutilation of a name – *Bousbir: City of Love!* – given to a pious Frenchman by his pious, loving mother. His poor, debased name was printed beneath common Moroccan whores showing their tits, hanging from open windows, beckoning, trios of Negresses soaping one another's naked thighs in steamy hammams. Prosper Ferrieu's place in history was set.

o

○

Fadila sat on a hard wooden chair in an office at the police station on Boulevard Jean-Courtin – the department of Spectacles and Morality. She had been stopped twice before but had never been arrested until now, *hamdullilah*. A high, dirty window across the opposite wall provided the room's only light. A few posters were taped to the gray cement walls, and across the large metal desk in front of her sat the French policeman in his uniform. The door to the office was shut.

"Age?" the policeman asked, looking down at a sheet of paper.

"Fifteen maybe?" She knew some French, more than she'd pretended.

"*Bon.* Seventeen."

Fadila stared hard at the policeman. He had noticed

her near Parc Lyautey talking to those two farmers off the bus and had come running after her. She had been even angrier than she was scared. She had bit his wrist, which was now bandaged. She shouldn't have hurt him, but sometimes you couldn't help yourself. Some of the girls she knew said that if you let them sleep with you, the police would set you free. She puffed out her lips and put a finger in her mouth. The policeman didn't notice. He only cared about his sheet of paper. There was nothing inside of him.

"I see here, Fadila, that you have already received warnings from officers on two occasions. This has been recorded. Are you aware that now, with this third offense, you will be obliged to live in the reserved quarter, where you will be tested for disease before gaining the right to practice your trade under our close supervision?" Something was about to happen to her, she sensed. The window was too high to climb to or jump out. She slid her skirt up her thighs, which were covered with snaking lines of fading henna, and spread her knees.

Born in Taroudant, in the Sous Valley between Agadir and the Sahara, all she remembered of that city were its red ramparts, its orange trees, and the dirt-floored room where they had lived with three chickens, until she was nine, when they had come to Casablanca. A year later her father, a guard at an oil factory, had been killed in a knife fight, and her mother had run off. She had no brothers or sisters. A soldier married her and took her to Fez, and then he went off to France, leaving her alone, with no education or skills. She couldn't cook, she couldn't clean, and she couldn't sew. She had returned to Casablanca, finding part-time work as a maid in a family of Jews. Her salary hadn't given her enough to eat, so late in the afternoons she had started walking the streets between the Jewish cemetery and Place de Verdun, taking men back to a hotel near La Ferme Blanche, a neighborhood occupied mainly by fishermen. Each *pass* earned her between one hundred and one hundred fifty francs. Some men were Jewish, and many were Moslems, but there were also Christians with uncircumcised penises. She refused to touch penises with her hands or her mouth or any other part of herself. Only with her sex.

The Jewish family had money troubles. This was the reason they paid Fadila so little. At least that's what Hajar said. She was the full-time maid. Monsieur had been a lawyer, Hajar said, until the French had gone with the Germans, and then the Jewish lawyers, doctors, and teachers in Casablanca had lost their licenses. Now the family was also housing relatives who had been banished to the mellah, the Jewish quarter, by the pasha. Many fathers had been put in concentration camps at Azemour, Tendrara and Ouedzem, and in the mellah European refugees carried jewels to sell for food. The men wore black cloaks and gathered in circles at shopfronts, always haggling except when the police appeared. Then they scattered like blackbirds, cloaks flapping down narrow streets. The Sultan had refused to send Moroccan Jews to the camps, but he would not protect Jewish refugees, so like Fadila they feared the police. In her first week at the house, a family cousin had arrived from Belgium. His name was Abel, and he spoke no Arabic. Hajar told Fadila that he had escaped to Switzerland and down to Marseilles, where he had stowed away on a Portuguese ship to Oran before making his way across the mountains to Casablanca. Fadila had never heard of any of these places except Casablanca.

Abel was hoping to get a visa to Portugal, but he was too scared to leave the house. Both his mother and father had been sent to camps in Europe, and he was the last of that line. He was twenty-six, tall and thin, with close-cropped hair, bushy eyebrows, and piercing eyes. Fadila had never seen him smile. Hajar had told her to stay away from Abel.

On Saturdays, the Jews could do no work, and the mellah was quiet. Fadila would be sent to the hammam ovens to retrieve the *dafina*, the clay pot of stew, which Hajar had taught her to carry atop her head. As she walked, she would try to imagine what was in that week's *dafina*, stuffing her head with potatoes, chickpeas, eggs, saffron, honey, and sometimes even lamb, until her head was as full as the pot itself. She was never given any of the stew to eat. There were too many mouths to feed, and so she had started leaving early on her Saturday errand to find a man for a quick *pass*. This was how it had begun. When she was late, Hajar would beat her, and then Fadila would run down to the shop at the corner and buy herself oranges with the money she hid in her clothes.

When the family went to synagogue, she was meant to make the beds. She did this quickly and carelessly, and then lingered in Madame's bedroom, where she would try on her jewelry in the mirror, covering her forearms with silver bracelets, which were heavy and beaten with hammers. She never stole anything, but sometimes she would keep a bracelet or an earring, not wearing it, but just carrying it around in a pocket. She always put them back eventually. One day, however, Abel caught her at Madame's jewelry box. He said nothing. He just sat down on the bed. She placed a ring back in the box and walked over to him, meeting those piercing eyes. Should she undress? She thought of striking him and running. Then he grabbed her wrist and twisted her towards him, pushing her head down into the mattress so that she lay facedown across his lap. His legs were sharp and bony beneath her hips. He smelled like onions. She felt a flutter at her ankle, his hand, and then at her calves, then thighs bared to the cool air as he snatched up her haik over her bottom. Still he said nothing. Then he spanked her, hard. He spanked her for several minutes, just the sound of air rushing through his gritted teeth, followed by the smack. At first it hurt, and then she told herself it did not hurt, could not hurt, and then it didn't hurt. But the mattress was wet with her furious tears. And that was how she was punished.

He punished her like this other times too, always when they were alone. She learned to tell when she had done wrong by the slightest shifts in his otherwise stony face. He spanked her for forgetting sugar with coffee, for slamming a door and breaking a plate. He spanked harder with his left hand than his right and sometimes lowered her underwear to the tops of her thighs. She learned to control herself and never cried again. She thought of other things, of the orange trees of Taroudant, which appeared so vividly in her mind that she could have reached out and plucked a ripened fruit to eat, but she didn't. He spanked her until his rage was exhausted, but she didn't feel it, and the secret of why he could not touch her was that she had magical powers. She made new worlds.

When the house was quiet, she drew in the little notebook that Madame's daughter had given her at the Jewish holiday. Some of the pages had already been filled with numbers written by Madame's daughter, but Fadila drew over the numbers – waterfalls, three-headed chickens, shopkeepers with wings. One day Hajar caught her drawing at the kitchen table. She took the notebook and scolded Fadila for coming into the kitchen in her bare feet, because the djinns lived in places where water sat, in buckets and pipes, and they would possess a weak girl without discipline or morals. Hajar beat her then, but Fadila didn't feel it. That week at the hammam a woman gave her some henna, and she started drawing on herself where nobody could see, except for the men she let come inside her for one hundred francs a *pass*. The drawings were down her front – her chest, her thighs, her feet – because her back was too difficult to reach. Also, Abel spanked her there. She was two different people, or maybe more.

The truth was that Hajar was even lazier than Fadila and always arrived late, huffing and puffing, but she blamed Fadila for everything and wept at how she was treated by the savage girl, who was possessed. Hajar had been with the family for years, so the Jewish Madame believed her, and she also beat Fadila, a demon in her house deaf to all good sense. Madame gritted her teeth and kicked Fadila in the shins. Bruises often covered her body, blotting her henna drawings. With a pencil she began drawing angels on the wall beneath the kitchen table.

Then one day Hajar dropped the *dafina*, scattering chick peas and grease across the kitchen floor. Madame came running, and Fadila was blamed. They beat her together then, and she hid in the bathroom, wiping the blood from her teeth. That night while the family slept, she crept into the kitchen and covered the walls with angels and demons, layers and layers of them with the pencil gripped in her fist like a knife, until the wall was black and senseless. In the morning she was fired, and ever since she had been wandering the streets of Frenchtown looking for *passes*. She hated almost everything. At night she huddled in alleyways, smoking cigarettes and drawing on discarded newspapers.

Now the policeman was looking across the desk at her bare thighs. She would draw him with horns and sagging breasts. According to the law, she had two choices: she could whore herself either at Bousbir or in the Senegalese barracks.

Fadila stuck out her tongue. "I don't care!"

An hour later the policeman was dragging Fadila, scratching and kicking, into the clinic at the gates of Bousbir. They made her take off her clothes to test for the diseases, and another woman came to watch. They called her Jean Bart, and after she had seen Fadila's breasts and thighs, the nurse turned Fadila around so Jean Bart could see her buttocks. Jean Bart was as tall as a man, wore a man's shirt and a man's pants, smoked Casa Sports, outdrank Spanish fishermen, and had gotten her name from a great battleship after knocking out a French soldier who had proposed taking her to bed. Jean Bart wasn't for sale, but she was one of Bousbir's most powerful *patronnes*, and her girls sold everything.

She had bribed the clinic nurses to alert her to new and pretty arrivals, and now she offered Fadila a Casa Sport as they waited for the test results. Fadila took one, but the big woman frightened her, so she didn't smoke it, as much as she wanted to. This cigarette, it seemed, might steal some of her magic power.

"You will be happy here," Jean Bart said, "but you cannot cover your body like this with henna. Men will not like it. They will say it is forbidden."

"I do it against the evil eye," Fadila murmured unconvincingly. She did not fear the evil eye.

"You are safe here with me. You will have fine clothes, cigarettes, jewelry, and money to spend. Let the drawings fade."

Jean Bart then handed her five hundred francs, more than Fadila had ever held. She would be given kaftans and jewelry to rent from Jean Bart. But for now she didn't need to worry about that. "Keep the money, get yourself started. I will send you men. You will sell them tea, and then whatever else. Just remember to always be selling tea."

Fadila nodded, still holding the money in her hand. Because she was naked there was no other place to put it. The nurse came back. She was infected – they were all infected – so they gave her pills and cream and told her to come back to the clinic in a week. "Put on your clothes," said the *patronne*, her face like a cliff, like the shore beside the mellah at Sidi Belyout where the fishermen gathered. "I will take you to your room."

On the main street of Bousbir, they pushed through the crowd, past women with mouthfuls of gold teeth selling dirty postcards, girls with faces garishly painted lifting their kaftans and shaking their hips. "Naked photos! Give me ten sous! Titty photos, ten sous!" The laughter, the hands of drunken men, French soldiers, Berbers from the mountains wearing heavy packs, skinny boys darting past water sellers to pick pockets. Two heavy Marrakshias fought over a steady customer, screeching like cats, flying in circles down a long arcade with their fingers tangled in one another's hair. Fadila's eyes widened as she filled her head. Her head was not big enough.

Jean Bart led her into a building, where in a main room girls smoked kif on pillows strewn about the floor. The *patronne* told them Fadila's name, and she glared. They went upstairs, and Jean Bart invited her to open a door. The room was nicer than she had expected. There were a chest of drawers, three stools, a copper table on wooden legs, a double bed with pillows and sheets, and a carpet hung on the wall. A small window overlooked the main street.

Jean Bart left without speaking, shutting the door behind her. Fadila turned from the window and looked at the bed, wondering if she was allowed to lie down on it. But she was tired, so she did.

○

"Marlene Dietrich was meant to have been here with us today," the announcer onstage said to the two thousand rowdy G.I.s who had gathered at the Liberty Club. "But unfortunately that's not going to be possible. An American general pulled rank for her…services." The men whistled and booed, grinning widely, elbowing one another. As if Dietrich would have really turned up to entertain this bunch of turkeys. But maybe they would bring out those USO girls again to kick their pretty legs and wiggle their cans. That'd be something. The whistling trailed off, and a voice somewhere at the back of the auditorium called out, "No, no, I'm here," and then would you believe it, Marlene Dietrich, the one and only, in a general's uniform that fit her like an evening gown, came pushing through the crowd towards the stage. The men went wild, shoving up against one another to get a better look. Mag cursed, spreading his legs to brace himself against the mob, holding the two boxes tightly. He hated a crowd and was starting to wish he'd stayed on base. So he'd seen Marlene Dietrich. Why did fellas get so excited about things they'd never have?

Onstage, Marlene opened her little suitcase and unpacked a few sequins and a pair of heels. Then she started stripping off the uniform. They roared so loud that Mag glanced up at the roof, worried it might cave in. Then he grinned and shook his head. Alright, she really was something, that Marlene Dietrich. The announcer scurried back onstage to pull the nearly naked star off behind a screen. Winking at the boys, she let herself be pulled. Oh, she hadn't meant to be a bad girl. Then a few seconds later she burst back out wearing those sequins and heels, her legs looking longer than many of these filthy soldiers were tall. She carried her famous musical saw, and to crazed applause she sat on a stool, hiked up that dress even higher, placed the saw between her legs, and performed *See What the Boys in the Back Room Will Have*. What the boys wanted more than anything on earth, more than world peace or whiskey, was to keep looking forever between Marlene's legs. Except, maybe, for Mag. Yeah, she'd gotten him excited, but what was the point of that? He checked his watch and walked out of the Liberty Club.

The late afternoon sunlight angled down into the boulevards. For once he had no place to be. There was money in his pocket, and he whistled a song that one of the dark-haired USO girls had sung, *Blitzkrieg Baby*, she'd done it swell. The two boxes were cradled in one arm. They weren't heavy. Everywhere people were out enjoying the summer. With men off at the front, a disproportionate number of women strolled by, smiling French girls in their stylish French dresses, Moroccans in airy things too, although others were covered and veiled, which Mag somehow found even more exciting, like a sealed cargo hold. The anticipation with a woman like that would just about kill you. Although almost none of the girls smiled back at him, he briefly wanted to buy them ice cream, to shout up at windows, or even learn how to dance. He chuckled to himself. He didn't want to learn how to dance. What would be the point of that? What was he going on about?

These days you saw Americans everywhere: riding past on bicycles, or packed into horse cabs, playing stick ball or flirting with girls in parks. Morocco was known as the Ice Cream Front, and although Mag knew soldiers itching to march across Italy, to sail east and notch themselves a Jap, he didn't go in for all that patriotism.

America was just a pretty story to tell yourself when the bullet came and your blood ran out. The real war would be won or lost by politicians in places like Washington and Berlin, not by infantryman with hard-ons for Uncle Sam. He was more determined than ever to remain on the Ice Cream Front, and there were enough Americans around now that you could mostly go about your business without sticking out. He'd even met Ahmed for coffee a couple of times without attracting attention, and Ahmed looked shady just stirring sugar into a cup. He'd also walked right into Aziza's clothing shop, silk slips and brassieres in the window. She and Ahmed were now moving such quantities of women's undergarments that Mag had needed to set up a new supply chain. He was paying an old Philly contact to buy wholesale and transport the stuff up to New York harbor, where it shipped to Casablanca and sold for fifteen times the price. The French in Morocco, spared occupation, still had money, unlike most of their compatriots in France.

All of this meant bigger risks for Mag, especially when smuggling the stuff out of the port in the trucks supplying the air base out at Cazès. All those moving parts had unfortunately required Stec's help, and the lieutenant got his cut. Pay somebody enough, and you didn't have to think about him. Mag was careful to keep his profits with Aziza, whom he trusted the most, and once the war was over, he'd have a different life. He wouldn't have to think about people. He'd be free.

Last week Stec had even said that he might arrange a transfer out to Cazès, with a roof over their heads and proper meals, and cargo planes arriving almost every hour from America. "We could make a fine nest for eagles," the lieutenant had said. "Now remember, four eggs tomorrow. Five eggs next week." The boys in the battalion were now experts at imitating the lieutenant and could hold extended conversations where nobody understood a single word anyone else said. Mag didn't have the time or patience for that, but these imitations were one of the battalion's proudest achievements of the war.

He didn't miss home. Philly had always been tugging him in one direction or another, like a family member always expecting him for Sunday lunch. Casablanca didn't care about Mag, and he would never be like family here. That was a relief. The city was one of those fairy tales they read back in school, filled with secret passages and blind sorcerers. Hell, traffic sometimes got blocked by sheep. At cafés shoeshine boys in red fezzes with numbered metal plaques swarmed beneath the tables, negotiating whole territories down there like ant colonies tickling at your feet. Apparently there was a red-light district too, with hundreds of naked native girls, some who smoked Casa Sports with their boogies and performed other tricks. Ahmed said at least half the girls over there were now wearing Mag's silk stockings, gifts from cuntstruck officers. Ahmed had invited him to see for himself, and maybe share a dark one with big tits. He talked of kidnapping a feisty thing to have available for special occasions. Ahmed was crazy.

Mag did sometimes think of his mother. Her back mostly, cooking fish or scrubbing floors, him coming or going, never seeing much more than her back. Their tiny apartment had been graced with only a single bed, which when he'd gotten older they swapped every night. When he'd had the bed, she'd slept on the floor, sprawled out on her stomach as if she'd been stabbed in the back. She hadn't sent him a letter. Not one, and nobody else had either, but apart from his mother he didn't think much about anyone else, and he liked the people here well enough. The French could be prickly, and mostly still resented Americans, but the natives were generally friendly and didn't concern themselves with your business, other than occasionally cadging a few francs. They would steal, but they lacked the coldness for blackmail, and Mag could live with that. One of the boxes was feeling a bit soggy. That wasn't good.

More European refugees were arriving too, hundreds every day. They came across the Algerian desert on the backs of trucks, skeletons in oversized clothes, or as stowaways on cargo ships from Marseilles. Day and night, they crowded the sidewalk outside the American consulate, hoping for visas to New York, or to Lisbon at the very least. Turned away, they would return the next day, wearing everything they owned, the women jangling with gold necklaces and bracelets, which with European inflation were surer money than paper. One day, Mag had walked past and heard Polish being spoken by a sorry-looking family of eight. He had never really spoken it – his mother had, but she'd kept to herself, and then what would have been the point? – but the Polish family had looked up as if recognizing it in him. *No you don't.* He had crossed the street, and now he avoided walking past the consulate if he could help it. So life was tough. That don't make you like me.

He walked along the edge of Parc Lyautey, watching old men in suits and ties toss silver balls at the dirt. Three barefoot boys splashed into a colorfully tiled octagonal fountain to kick out a deflated soccer ball. He thought of strolling into the park, but it felt like a waste of time. What would he do there, sit and look at flowers? The thought made him uneasy, and he lit a cigarette. He felt odd in the sunlight. Philly winters had raised him. He was more like some creature who belonged in the damp beneath rocks.

Further along near the bus stop, an attractive Moroccan girl came running around the corner from Avenue Foch, heading straight for him. She had a broad nose, thick lips, and beautiful black eyes. Shells were braided into her hair, and on her bottom lip was a blue tattoo. He noticed everything about her instantly, a disorienting feeling that made him dizzy. A white dress came to her knees, and she struggled to run in a pair of oversized yellow Moroccan slippers. He held his boxes tighter. Then a French policeman raced around the corner in pursuit of the girl, and she was caught from behind. She screamed and spat, wild with rage, contorting as if she was possessed by evil spirits. She bit into the cop's wrist, and he slapped her across the face with his good hand. Then he cuffed her and took her off someplace. In Casablanca this kind of thing happened all the time.

Mag wandered. He thought about the black-eyed girl and Marlene Dietrich. He wanted to buy some ice cream. The sun had dipped below the flat roof of the Palais de Justice. He would need to be back in an hour or so. Maybe two with the excitement after the show. But the freer he'd gotten to come and go, the more careful he'd become about seeming too free. Hell, he was thinking too much, and that had never done him any good. Better to leave things simple. And he'd waited long enough. The address had been in his pocket for over a week. Plus, Signal Corps was still asking about their pigeons.

An apartment building on Rue Nolly. Jocelyne hadn't managed to get him an apartment number. From the street he watched the building for five minutes, or ten. It felt like an hour. He didn't spot any pigeons. Finally he sighed and walked through the entrance. In the lobby he knocked at the concierge's door, but nobody answered. That was a relief. He didn't feel like making conversation. At the mailboxes, only one name was a madame: Mme Morin, 4B. Well. That was his best bet. He headed for the elevator, where a sign posted on the door read: "L'ascenseur est interdit aux chiens et aux domestiques." Mag hesitated. The sign appeared to have been there for a while, so he figured it didn't say *out of service*. So he got in, shut the gate behind him, and pushed four. The motor whirred to life, jerking him upwards.

○

"*Chante, ma belle. Chante pour moi.*" The pigeon's rough orange feet found a hold on Camille's extended finger. She stroked its pale gray feathers, and its throat bobbed, making the wheezing noise that sounded to her like screaming into a pillow. This one was a female. She didn't coo so loudly as the boys, who would spin and preen and show you how tough they were. Camille sang

103

them songs in what she hoped was pigeon. She felt so alone.

Maman worried that the sun on the rooftop, where she kept the cages, would darken her skin and ruin her chances. Men might think she was Moroccan. Maman never talked about the man in Dakar, who'd already ruined her chances, but still, Camille knew Maman was right, especially now that summer had come. Maman always had to be right.

The pigeons were her only friends, apart from the bird man at the Central Market. They were extraordinary creatures, thirty-two of them, four to a cage. She fed them twice daily with the seed from the bird man. In each cage she had also placed a water bowl borrowed from Maman's porcelain collection. Maman never came up to the roof and had blamed the bowls' disappearance on the maid.

The white city shimmered. The ocean that day was as flat as a pond. They hadn't meant to stay in Casablanca this long, and Maman said the Arabs were even worse than the Negroes, but the war had made it difficult to get new papers. The consul was incompetent, Maman said, and there were no boats. Some refugees had left on trucks for Meknes, hoping to make their way eventually to Algiers and across the Mediterranean, but Maman refused to accept such indignities. They would remain until they had received news from Maman's brother in Dakar. Every day at precisely eleven, Camille was asked to go downstairs and check the mailbox. There was never a letter. Maman didn't trust the postman or the postal service. They were all thieves.

Even if she was lonely, Camille liked Casablanca.

She was careful never to mention this to Maman, but to the pigeons she sometimes did. In Spanish the word meant *white house*. Unfortunately Maman didn't often let her go out to explore, except to the mailbox downstairs and to the nearby Central Market. Yet when she went to the market, she sometimes stayed out longer, thrilled by the colors and smells, the throngs buying and selling stacked dates, scoops of saffron from spice cones, and elegant cookies like dress buttons. Then there was the bird man, who called her *zweena*, which meant beautiful. In painted wooden cages he kept pink finches with blue crests, bright yellow canaries, and two proud cockatiels. The bird man was teaching her to talk to them in their languages. Sometimes he also had a few pigeons for sale, ones that had landed with the flock he raced from his medina rooftop. You didn't want to keep a pigeon you hadn't raised yourself. They were never very loyal. These were just some of the things the bird man had taught Camille. Also, let them settle for a few weeks, then open the cages and push them out. Pushing them out the first time, she'd had tears in her eyes. They didn't want to go, but the bird man had told her she needed to push them out. And soon enough, with a few awkward flaps, one after another they had flown off, leaving Camille squealing with joy. Every day then she let them out, until they knew the neighborhood better than she did. Some returned after a few minutes, which Camille could understand, but others were more adventurous and vanished for hours before signaling their arrival with a flutter of wings and a jingling of the bell that the bird man had told her to hang from the top of each cage. Nothing in her life was more exciting than the sound of that bell. Everywhere in her life, always, she listened for the bells.

The bird man had warned her, too. Sometimes whole flocks of pigeons could mysteriously disappear out of the sky as if they had never existed. Nobody knew why. Some said the earth contained magnets that pulled the birds off into invisible places. Others said Allied radios confused them, and they flew until they were lost out at sea. Then poachers would sometimes shoot them for food. These days everybody had a gun. The bird man had also warned her about another medina racer notorious for pigeon theft, and thoughts of the Notorious Racer sometimes kept Camille up at night. She dreaded the day when her pigeons would be ready to fly even further. She also wanted this more than anything. To wait and wait for hours and hours until she heard the bell.

The sky was where she wanted to live. The city was only stacked surfaces of underlight. Today for the first time she had written a message on a strip of paper rolled into a tight cylinder and tied to the foot of the pigeon named Henri. Now her message was out there in the sky. She wasn't supposed to know, it was supposed to be a surprise, but the note read, "*Bonjour Camille.*" She couldn't wait for the bell.

○

"*Quelle surprise!* Here is this generous man. Camille! Come see. You have a visitor. *Camille!* Please, please enter, *monsieur*."

Mag stood at the door holding his two boxes. A plump woman with red cheeks and dark hair twisted into a tight bun was smiling at him with unnaturally bright eyes. She looked forty-five, maybe fifty, wore a long gray skirt and a pink sweater filled by the great unified hump of her breasts. He'd mentioned the birds, and she'd started talking, so he guessed this was the right place. Madame Morin was calling again for Camille, which must be the girl's name. The girl didn't appear, and her mother's smile stretched tighter every second. "Please do come in. Perhaps she went down to buy some eggs. Camille is famous for her lemon tart. Unfortunately a daughter who is a marvelous cook is not so marvelous for the *physique* of the mother!"

"You look fine," Mag said, in a way he hoped was polite. Then he followed the woman into a sitting room sparsely furnished with a couple of upholstered chairs, an ornate wooden coffee table, and a couch over which a square of embroidered cotton had been draped.

"Oh, aren't you a gentleman. *Merci, Monsieur*…I am sorry, but Camille did not remember your name."

"Just Mag's fine."

"Please, Monsieur Mag, sit yourself and I will make some tea. Or do you prefer coffee? Unfortunately we do not have any *patisserie*. I am sure you are aware that the shops have been closed for rationing by the Resident General. We do not even have *croissants*, Monsieur Mag. For we French this is very difficult."

"I can't stay too long," Mag said, already regretting the visit.

"Please," said Madame Morin, the smile tightening again. "Camille will be furious with me if she does not have a chance to say hello. So tea? Coffee?"

"Coffee's fine," Mag said, and watched the woman go off towards the kitchen, swaying her hips. Back in the day she had probably gotten up to tricks. Hell, what did he know. With the boxes still cradled in his arm, he wondered about French girls. Then he sat on the couch, sinking deep into the cushions, which gave him a good view of his knees. His uniform was filthy. He guessed there hadn't been much time to notice things like that. He imagined a long, hot shower. Most of the time it was whore's baths, cold water poured from his helmet. His boots were caked with mud, so he was glad there was no carpet. The room was simple, but colored lampshades softened its edges, and vases of white lilies, so you could tell it was inhabited by women, even if they hadn't completely settled in. The air smelled of perfume and warm food. France must feel like this. Home must feel like this. It felt like something he'd never known.

The door clicked shut behind him, and he turned. It was the girl, Camille. Her dark curls stood out from her head, and she grinned into her shoulder, whispering something to herself. She wore a sleeveless lavender dress with white flowers stitched over the shoulders, and her skin looked as smooth as soap. He'd never known a proper girl like that. She was shy, but that was alright. She had class. He noticed she wasn't carrying any eggs, or anything else. Also, she'd gotten some sun since they'd first met. She was beautiful, so beautiful she made him feel ugly, even dirtier than before. "You came!" she said softly. "I knew you would."

"Yeah, Signal Corps's been riding me pretty hard."

Her head shook as if she'd lost a screw at the neck,

and then she hurried across the room, rising high up onto the balls of her feet with each step. Finally she perched on one of the chairs opposite Mag. "You saw Maman?"

"Yeah. Very nice lady. I brought you some presents." Camille jolted upright, tucking her chin into her neck again, beaming. Mag grunted up off the couch and held out the two boxes. Liquid seeped out of one box onto his fingers, so he told her to open that one first, then sunk back onto the couch. Camille set the second box aside and partially lifted the lid of the moist one, taking care to hold it away from her dress. She lowered her head to look through the gap, biting her lip.

"It's just a couple of American steaks," Mag said. "Reefer came in yesterday, and I thought you and your ma might want 'em. Tough to get steak these days. I mean, a reefer's a refrigerator ship. They was frozen when I got 'em." Camille nodded and shut the lid, whispering, "*Merci.*"

"Your ma said you's a pretty good cook."

"Not very much," the girl said. Really shy, but at least they could have a conversation, unlike with her ma. "Go ahead," he said. "Open the other one."

But Madame Morin came in then with a clatter, carrying a tray with a teapot, three cups, and a plate of broken cookies. "Ah Camille!" she said. "We feared you had abandoned your mother. And Monsieur Mag came specially to see you. Imagine his disappointment." She set down the tray with a sharp burst of air from her lips, then smoothed her skirt over her hips. "I am afraid we are not very elegant today, but our charming guest will understand. *C'est la guerre, n'est-ce pas? Alors* Camille, why don't you pour tea for Monsieur Mag, and possibly he would like to taste a little cookie. Oh! You did ask for tea, Monsieur Mag?"

"Coffee."

"*Ah mon dieu.* I remembered tea. I am hopeless, you see? Camille is so much more sensible. Camille, make some coffee for Monsieur Mag. Coffee! In the afternoons, you see, we are more accustomed to tea. Please forgive me, Monsieur Mag."

"Is that your name?" Camille interrupted, looking directly at him.

"It's Michael, I guess," he said, feeling he should do something with his hands other than letting them rest there on his knees. Why had he said Michael? "Or Mike. But nobody ever called me that. Just Mag." She nodded and mouthed it a few times: *Mag Mag Mag.* "Pleased to meet you," he muttered, "or meet you again, I guess. Just gimme the tea, that's alright."

The girl whispered something, but it wasn't his name anymore, or at least it didn't sound like it. When she was shy, she made her mouth very small, but when she smiled her mouth was full and showed a pretty set of teeth. There was a tiny black speck on her cheek that he hadn't noticed before. A silver chain hung from her neck, and bounced against her breasts as she bent over the tray, first burning her fingers on the handle of the teapot – *ooo!* – then folding a napkin around the handle to pour with a trembling hand. The table was coated in a thick layer of dust.

"You should open the other box if you want," he said.

"I forgot, Maman," she said while pouring tea. "Mag brought us two American steaks to eat." She pointed at the bloodstained box on the table.

"Oh!" Madame Morin cried. "*Merci! Notre ami,* how generous you have been to us. You are concerned for our health, no? We are so grateful."

"They were frozen, so they should be fine," Mag said. "Apologize for the mess. The other one's not so messy." Camille passed a cup to her mother and sat down with the second box on her lap. Then she slowly opened it, and gasped.

"Well what is it, *ma fille?*"

"Beautiful," Camille said, mouth agape. "Is it silk?"

"Rayon, they call it," Mag said as Camille pulled from the box a sheer yellow slip with lace up the shoulder straps and across the hem. On each hip was a deep, lacy slit. "It's the new silk."

"Well…," Madame Morin muttered. "*Très belle.* We will save this for some special occasion, won't we Camille?" The girl ran her tiny fingers over the fabric and sighed. Then she stood and held the slip to her body. Through the yellow Mag could see the darker purple of her dress and the silver necklace on her chest. "It is perfect," she said. It looked perfect to him too.

"But *ma fille,*" Madame Morin said, pretending to laugh. "You cannot try it on now, of course!"

Camille blushed and shoved the slip back into the box. "*Merci,*" she murmured as she sat back down. He'd been imagining her in the slip. He hadn't meant to embarrass her. But in any case the girl seemed pleased. Aziza had a couple hundred of them in all colors now, and they weren't selling cheap.

Madame Morin cleared her throat. "Sadly we have become unaccustomed to such exquisite luxuries, Monsieur Mag," she said. "You have made Camille very happy. Now you must tell us absolutely everything about yourself, you fascinating man." She was perched on the edge of her chair with her back as flat as a board, her breasts a solid fortress. "You must be very brave, a fine American soldier here in this barbaric country. You are an officer? A pilot?"

"Nah, I just unload ships. A staff sergeant, I guess. Before I was a longshoreman – not sure what it's called in French. Stevedore, you know. Basically keep supplies coming through. Like those birds. Told your daughter Signal Corps's been busting my chops about that."

"Ah yes," Madame Morin said brightly, "the filthy birds. I had almost forgotten about the filthy birds. But tell us: these must be such interesting times for a capable man like you. I understand so little about war. What do you think of De Gaulle? And your family back in the United States? They must be very proud of their *sergeant.*"

"My family? Dunno, really. I guess there isn't too many of us left. Just my ma back in Philly – Philadelphia – but she pretty much keeps to herself. She don't know nothing about the war. Hell, I don't know much. I'm just a sergeant in the port battalion. Don't guess I'd be much use at the front." He stared at his knees, speaking self-consciously, aware of the woman's eager eyes. Camille made little clinking noises as she stirred her tea, and he was annoyed with himself for babbling, so he raised his cup to his lips and sipped. At least the tea tasted better than the powdered coffee they served back at the barracks. Hot as hell, too. Practically burned off his tongue, but maybe they hadn't noticed.

"Does it please you? Madame Morin purred.

"Good tea," Mag nodded. "Appreciate it, but now I really gotta be getting back to base."

"Don't you want to check the pigeons first?" Camille asked anxiously. "I have been taking good care of them. I feed them twice a day…and I give them water. I have trained them. I will show you."

"Camille!" her mother cried. "Monsieur Mag is surely not interested in some filthy birds on a filthy roof. Sing monsieur a song, *ma fille*. She possesses the most beautiful voice, you will see. A very talented girl. You must not go just yet."

"I also like to dance," Camille said brightly. Mag nodded into his cup.

"Silly girl! She thinks someday she will be a star. What do I know? Maybe this is true. She is very beautiful, *n'est-ce pas?*"

"Uncle once took me dancing at the bal musette," Camille interrupted, "but Maman doesn't like the quality of the people at the bals musettes in Casablanca. I am a rather good dancer."

"*Ah Camille!* Sing a song for Monsieur Mag. For his exceptional gift, your marvelous voice."

"I gotta get going," he murmured. But Camille was already standing before them with her chin raised, her eyes closed, and her hands clasped behind her back. Light filtered through the curtains, softly lighting her face. She sang in a high, airy voice that reminded him of train whistles along the coast in the night. He couldn't tell if she was any good or not, but he liked watching her. She didn't open her eyes once, her forehead creased as if she were struggling not to forget the words. It was some French song that Mag didn't know. Really all he knew were American songs, and in France they probably had a different style. Like those Moroccans you heard weeping and wailing over the medina walls. Those songs sounded like knifings to Mag, or plucking a chicken, but to them it was just music. So he couldn't tell if Camille was any good. It wasn't *Blitzkrieg Baby*, and it definitely wasn't *See What the Boys in the Back Room Will Have*, but she was real emotional about it, and when she'd finished singing, he clapped a few times. The girl's ma applauded too, watching Mag instead of her daughter. Then Camille curtsied with her hands still clasped behind her back.

"Now I really gotta go," Mag said, heaving himself up from the couch. "Thanks for the tea. Real tasty."

"But first I have to show you the pigeons," Camille insisted. "Please come with me."

"*Mais Camille!*" her mother gasped. "A young lady does not take a man like Monsieur Mag up to a filthy rooftop! He does not have time for such silliness."

"That's alright," Mag said. "Guess I better check on the birds." His palms were sweaty. He'd been a fool to give those birds away. Probably could have fetched a pretty penny for them, but it was too late now.

"Oh!" Madame Morin sighed. "*Alors* wear your sunhat and gloves, Camille. We do not want to ruin your beautiful skin." Camille nodded and walked past Mag to the entrance, where she took long gloves and a floppy hat from a wooden stand. She looked up at him and blushed. "I get freckles," she said.

Mag thanked Madame Morin again and followed Camille out to the staircase, then up two floors to a heavy metal door which she pushed open with her shoulder. Her hips swayed just like her mother's.

The sun had set, and pink streaked the sky's western edge, which was dotted with isolated gulls. The heavy light had dissolved the contours of the city, such that the rooftop was like an island in a pink sea. Laundry hung on twine between crooked iron rods, and in the center of the roof beneath a folded tarpaulin were eight stacked cages populated by shuffling pigeons. Camille led him over, carefully opened a cage door, and stuck in a hand. The pigeons fluttered and cooed. Mag kept his distance. A bird in the air was a fine enough thing, but up close they gave him the heebie-jeebies.

Camille held one out to him, surprisingly big in her little hands, its throat working up and down like a heart. "Do you want to pet it?"

"I'm alright," he said. "They look in good shape, so I'll report back and whatnot." Signal Corps didn't care. Not really. Nobody did. Camille grinned and flung her hands in the air. Her lavender dress flapped in the wind as the pigeon wobbled up to settle on top of the cage. Camille stuck out her bottom lip, making a sad face, and scolded the bird, whose name was apparently Henry – not a bad name for a bird if you were gonna name him. The girl seemed more relaxed on the roof. He felt less relaxed by the second.

"My next test is to take one somewhere and see if it will fly back, but I am still too nervous for that. What if it gets lost?"

"He'll prolly fly back," Mag said, shifting his weight from one leg to another. He thought of that warm shower again. "I'm sure you trained 'em good. I mean that's what they's for, right? Just gotta take your chances."

Camille pinched her chin between her thumb and

index finger, giving this some thought. "I think they're ready," she eventually said with a nod.

Mag nodded too. Then he sneezed hard, then twice again in rapid succession. "I may be allergic to ol' Henry," he said through his hands.

"Then let's go over here." She led him to the edge of the roof, her gloved fingers flared out by her sides. "The bird man says pigeons will give some people a sort of pneumonia. Only lucky ones can get close to birds." Mag nodded, wiping his hands on his pants. They looked out at the last of the sunset. Camille's hat flapped in the breeze that came off the ocean. "*Merci* for the birds, Mag. And for the beautiful slip and the steaks. I am happy you came. Maman says I need to work on my social confidence. I think she is right. Maman has always been very confident."

"Yeah, she's a real sociable woman."

Camille turned to him then and studied his face for what seemed like ages. "Sometimes I also think I hate her," she said, and before he could respond, her lips were rushing towards his, knocking the brim of her hat against his forehead. The hat slid up off her head as he felt her lips, and then her tongue darting into his mouth.

"Okay," he said after a long kiss, his heart pounding wildly. "I gotta go."

53. - CASABLANCA
Déshabillé Marocain
Madeleine, édit., Casablanca - M. Trompette, phot.

Victor ordered a pastis in a shabby café on Route de Medouina, because that's what the other men were drinking. He rarely came to this neighborhood, which was mainly Moroccan. He spent his days at the Tit Mellil airfield, where he had begun training for his pilot's license. But his body had led him again to these dirty, treeless streets, a stranger here with complicated desires. That night over a year ago with the girl in the shadowy passage had rewired him. He now moved differently through the world, wanting different things. Often he wondered if he was wrong.

The pastis was undrinkable. A defeated donkey clopped past pulling a cart stacked high with mint. The fresh scent briefly lingered. Basketfuls of laundry hung from windows. The mess of life was never contained in these native streets, and any privacy there was an illusion, which always unsettled Victor, who increasingly strove to maintain perfect separation between inside and out. Leaks in the self were weakness. He looked down at the photographic postcard on the café table. A tall Moroccan woman leaned against a white column, smiling out of the frame as if spying someone familiar. She wore baboushes, her ankles exceptionally slender. He followed the line of her long leg up to the white fabric wrapped carelessly around her waist, and then to her breasts, which were bare, large nipples pointing at the ground. *Casablanca: Moroccan Undressed.* As a boy he'd spent hours looking at that postcard – the others too. He had forgotten that they were in the leather pea coat he'd lent Tommy, the American pilot. Then when Tommy had disappeared with the coat, his embarrassment had been infuriating.

Now Tommy was sending them back to him with

news from the war, each one a fresh little wound. One from Virginia (*Young Moor*, pretty, with a headband of silver spangles, heavy earrings, and a sheer white kaftan lit from the side, outlining a pair of enormous breasts), and then one from out at sea (*Young Arab Women Amusing Themselves in the Kasbah*, a former favorite, three dark-skinned beauties with flat bellies and full breasts looking brazenly at the camera, draped around a central fourth fully covered by a kaftan), and now the one from Manila. Tommy wrote directly on the postcards, but he always posted them in envelopes.

In Norfolk, Tommy had married his girlfriend, whom he'd found pregnant. He was excited to become a father, he'd written, and he hoped Victor would someday find someone as fine as Lucy with whom to share his life. Then from sea he'd written that there was no time to think about music, or even listen to it, and he was finding this frustrating, but the Japs weren't going to wait for Tommy August to compose his masterpiece. He wondered if Victor was still listening to Stravinsky, which reminded him – in Norfolk he'd heard a recording of Stravinsky and his son playing the *Concerto for Two Pianos*, which he had admired, and which Victor should try to find. Now in Manila he wrote about the girls, brown, slim and unusually tempting. He was having a tough time keeping his eyes from wandering, as Victor could imagine. Now he and the boys were at a bar called the Lonely Mango on their last night before sailing for Japan. If only Lucy could see him now…or maybe not!

Victor sighed. He'd written back once, and then he'd grown impatient with the game. He did look forward to receiving the postcards, however, and not only because they reunited him with his photographic harem. Tommy's adventures drove him to want to earn his wings all the more urgently. Now almost nineteen, he desperately wanted the world. Wincing back the last of the pastis, which apparently he'd drunk anyway, he whistled a few bars of the beginning oboe solo of *Rite of Spring*, that single warbling line before the thunder and the lightning. Out on the sidewalk, two Moroccans lunged at one another, gesticulating so violently that it appeared each would be dead before nightfall. Victor knew better. Frenchmen might fight to the death for honor or some other ideal in which they chose to believe, but Moroccans could simply perform their bouts of rage, judged by a guaranteed audience like actors on a stage. Nobody would get hit, or stabbed, unless somebody was drunk. Victor smiled and put a coin on the table. Sometimes just whistling a line played by an oboe could change his atmosphere.

He pushed through the crowd towards the gate of Bousbir, where he handed another coin to a blind staggering marabout and watched him slip it into a wet smile. The holy fool always stood there at that spot in a moth-eaten djellabah, palming coins from passersby and popping them into his mouth to chew until he felt their weight and size and knew their value.

Within the walls Victor's eyes roved over passing bodies. Some turned up their noses and crossed the street, contemptuous of Nazarenes, but others were eager to secure what might be a profitable *pass*. They pulled at his jacket, even shoving hands between his legs. Their boldness did not excite him, however, at least not today. Being chosen was no thrill compared to choosing. Yet he was anxious of lingering in the public street, so he ducked into a house he'd visited once or twice before in search of the unusual.

The *patronne* didn't seem to remember him, which was just as well. He never wanted pleasure to become a mere habit. He had vowed to smash habits like champagne glasses into the fire. She said that only one girl was available, new and young. Victor nodded, and the *patronne* led him up the staircase, indicating the door. He took a deep breath and walked through it.

The new girl sat on a stool smoking kif from a clay sebsi. Smoke floated over her head in the light from a cracked shutter. She was savagely beautiful, eyes dark and wide over high cheekbones. Her nose was broad and straight, and her mouth was large, with thick lips turned down at the corners, hinting at sadness or imagination. On her chin was an indigo tattoo, a single vertical line, and around her neck hung several necklaces of copper medallions and heavy stone beads. These fell deep into the neckline of her loose white cotton dress, which she wore with the sleeves rolled up. A leather belt loosely encircled her waist, copper bracelets ringed her arms, and white woolen strings wove through her dark hair like the tentacles of a jellyfish.

"Some tea, *s'il vous plaît?*" she said, hardly parting her lips.

Victor shook his head and sat on the stool beside her. He was not certain he wanted the bed. A bed was already an ending. He asked her name.

"Fadila," she said with frightening composure, picking a fleck of tobacco from the tip of her tongue. She had not offered him the pipe.

"Undress, Fadila," Victor said hoarsely. "*Déshabille-toi*."

The girl set the sebsi on a low table and rose to her feet. She did not undress, and he assumed she hadn't understood. What she did was bend herself over his knees, and then with one practiced motion she lifted her dress to her waist and lowered her underwear. Victor was astonished. He looked blankly at the girl's unblemished bottom, his flesh quivering. Dizzy with excitement, he lifted his palm, feeling every molecule of air slipstreaming around its edges in little spirals. He was moving through water and breathing from gills. Then once his arm was extended, he felt himself surface like a dolphin, and when he brought his palm down with more force than he could have imagined, he was no longer swimming, but bouncing off planets with no weight or heat.

ANIMAL KINGDOM
1944–46

Day and night massive transport planes rumbled down the narrow runway of the American base at Cazès. Sometimes at night armies of melon-sized Moroccan toads would hop out onto the runway to starbathe, and exhausted privates were sent out to chase them off, but just last week after taxiing over a stray toad, a C-54 Skymaster had run smack into a C-46 Commando, destroying both planes. Miraculously the only casualty, apart from the toad, was some no-name Navy mechanic who had tripped and broken his foot hopping clear of the Skymaster. This yokel from Idaho had never said a word but was now the life of the infirmary, telling anyone who would listen about his run-in with a transport plane. Some guys had all the luck, Mag thought, smoking a post-breakfast cigarette in the hangar, while watching a circle of insufferable cargo pilots jabbering, while trying to catch the eye of Bones.

This is the Armed Forces Radio Service. It's eight o'clock. If you're not working, you're in trouble, but! Mag grunted. Mechanics and their fuggin radios. He was beginning to regret the transfer to Cazès. Yeah, he slept in a proper bunk with a roof over his head, and there was actually a mess hall that served fairly respectable mess, but his opportunities for pilfering had dwindled. A few guys back at the port still looked out for him, but work at the airbase was concentrated on assembling the P-40s that arrived packed in crates and were trucked over from ships or brought right in on cargo planes. The center section was lashed to a skid, and the wings were fastened to the crate's sides. You broke open one end of the crate to get at the fuselage, slid it out, attached the wings, and then installed the engine. The assembly line could pop out twelve to fifteen planes per day. Then the P-40s dodged some toads and took off for Europe, and the crates got stacked behind the hangar. Sometimes those crates were about all Mag could sell, and it didn't take a genius to know there wasn't a hell of a lot of money in busted wooden crates. Not only that, but Stec was growing impatient. He'd gone so far as to say that if the swimming pool didn't get filled quick, he'd fill it with spaghetti. Which Mag didn't get, apart from spaghetti meant Italy, and he didn't want to go there.

Which was why he needed to talk to Bones, the bastard. Cargo pilots were now his best option for importing valuable merchandise, and through a New York contact at American Export Lines, Mag had been buying quality wool in Natal, Brazil and flying it in to sell through Aziza or one of the other local contacts he'd developed with Ahmed's help. Thirty meters of Brazilian wool cost him two hundred dollars, he sold it to the Moroccans for six hundred, and they resold it for eight. There were also watches sometimes, bought from pawn shops along the East Coast, but the Brits were smuggling them in from Gibraltar and beating him on price. None of this was going to make him rich, which was why he needed a new plan, and Bones.

The P-40 assembly line hated pilots unanimously. Hell, they probably hated Mag too, but at least he was one of them. He didn't stand around jabbering in heroic little circles. Bones was ignoring him, a grin on his face. The pilots were gossiping about their Moroccan whores at the Bousbir brothels. Everyone knew they flew in Berettas from Italy to offer as gifts, which then got passed on to the girls' Moroccan boyfriends. At least that's what Ahmed had told him. Ahmed wanted guns, but Mag knew better than to take dumb risks. Still, he was fuggin sick of this penny ante stuff. And, finally, the great Bones edged away from his buddies to stroll in Mag's general direction.

Light streamed through the hangar opening. September was Casablanca's finest month, everybody said, not that he was seeing too much of it. Deep in that hangar he was like a bear in hibernation. Bones reached out a hand and took the letter Mag held. "This time my guy in Philly will be waiting," Mag said. Bones nodded, said he'd do what he could do. "Thousand dollars in it for you, Bones. I'm not fuggin around. Just one trunk." Bones nodded again and walked off. So that was that. Or not. You never knew with Bones.

Some days Mag felt as if he was officially losing his mind. That day before lunch he was washing his face in the latrine of his Dallas hut when he caught a glimpse of someone in the mirror and nearly jumped out of his skin. Then he realized the face in the mirror was his own, and he forced himself to look. Yeah, I guess that's it. What the hell.

Back out in the bunkroom, Stec was sprawled on Mag's bed. His boots had streaked mud across the blanket. Mag felt sick to his stomach. Soldiers were moving more bunks into the room. Something was up. Stec rubbed his head into Mag's pillow and luxuriously stretched out his legs like some Arabian sheik. A new battalion had just arrived from Norfolk, he said. "I want you to get to know these guys. I mean really get to know them. They're infantry, but they're going to lend us a hand. Unfortunately they're not staying for long. Their orders are to head for Sicily in three weeks. You like spaghetti, Mag? I hope so, because you're going with them. Gonna take out Il Duce once and for all, Magursky. You got what it takes."

"Just a few more weeks, Stec. I'm onto something."

"Lieutenant Stec," Stec said. "And you got three weeks. In which time I expect you to prove your worth to this battalion." And then he just kept lounging on Mag's bed like he was Rudolph Valentino, so Mag walked back out to the hangar, hoping to find Bones again, figuring he'd offer twelve hundred.

Later that afternoon he met Ahmed at the base entrance in another of his cars. The American colonels had left town, but Ahmed never lacked for something new to drive, and Mag no longer bothered asking. He didn't ask about the new suits either, each fitting Ahmed a little better, as if he was slowly coming into focus.

Mag glanced up at the sky as he slid into the passenger seat. Since breakfast it had grown hazy. Maybe a storm was rolling in. Ahmed nodded hello and took off, but didn't turn down the radio. He was always listening to namby-pamby French love songs, which never failed to drive Mag nuts. "Turn off that shit," he shouted over the music, but Ahmed just kept singing along to French nonsense, grinning idiotically. "Fuggin Edith Piaf," Mag growled. He knew how to get Ahmed's attention, although once you got Ahmed's attention, you almost always regretted having it. Ahmed slammed on the brakes and turned up the volume so loud that Mag had to cover his ears. *Y'A PAS DE PRINTEMPS!* One time Ahmed had even pulled a gun on Mag for insulting Edith Piaf, whom he called his Little Sparrow, and who, Ahmed said, spoke straight to his heart.

"Ah, knock it off!" Mag shouted, flicking off the radio. Behind them cars honked. Drivers pulled past waving fists. "We got bigger problems than your little sparrow."

"Yes," Ahmed hissed, nodding like some revved-up machinery. "You are the problem. We do no business. I bring you a good contact, my friend Jimmie in NATS at Port Lyautey, but you do not want to work with Jimmie."

"I don't trust your Jimmie," Mag growled. "I know it's been slow, but I'm onto something. Now drive." The car rolled forward again. Overhead the sky grew darker. "You want some crates? Get four trucks over here tomorrow night around ten. I'll get you in."

Even that wasn't so easy anymore. The Captain had stepped up armed patrols around the base perimeter after American intelligence had warned that the French army in Morocco might actually revolt against De Gaulle and attempt to seize Allied positions. So it wasn't enough anymore to worry about the Krauts. Now you had to worry about the fuggin Frogs. Not to mention fresh patrols of guards from Norfolk with hard-ons as big as the Atlantic. Not to mention the prospect of getting transferred to Italy.

"More crates?" Ahmed howled. "I need another thousand francs for that, or my drivers will quit."

"Come on, Ahmed. I can't do it right now. Be fuggin patient. Something big's coming." Ahmed banged the steering wheel and barked at the windshield. The car swerved, and he kicked the accelerator to the floor. Ahmed was a fuggin lunatic. He was entirely capable of driving them both into a ditch for some kind of crazy revenge. It occurred to Mag that Ahmed was also his best friend. Fuggin hell. They were speeding into Casablanca now, large insects splatting against the windshield. If Mag could pull off this job with Bones, he'd be free. He wouldn't need Ahmed or anyone else.

Ahmed seemed to get an idea then and eased back on the accelerator as they moved through the mostly Spanish neighborhood of Maarif, home to thousands of refugees from Franco's civil war, a whole lotta drunken communists. They passed Les Arènes, the cylindrical bullfighting arena, as big as the Roman Coliseum, they said, and then, off Boulevard Camille des Moulins, the Italian prison camp, Camp 24, coils of barbed wire, home to thousands of suspected fascists. Mostly it was neighbors who had turned them in after the Americans had landed. Tough luck, but served them right for throwing in with Il Duce. Shoulda killed Mussolini when they had the chance. Now Stec was pretending that was Mag's job.

Mag's immediate problem, however, was fuggin Ahmed, who was grinning slyly, a look that unfailingly introduced more problems. "I know why Mag is in a bad mood," he purred. "Mag is in love. The Freeench girl. Did she betray you? I told you not to trust the French."

Mag clenched his fists. "I swear, Ahmed, don't ever mention her again, or I'll –"

"Mag is in looove," Ahmed sang. "Mag got some French pussy."

Mag lunged and grabbed Ahmed by the neck.

Ahmed cackled and wove up the road, speeding faster. A massive cloud hurtled in from the desert. "Let me out!" Mag roared.

"How is she, Mag?" Ahmed whispered, his face reddening. "I thought I might try her sometime. I found out where she lives." Mag tightened his grip. He'd kill him. He'd be happy to kill him. One problem solved. "Stop the car! Let me out!"

"First tell me what's coming that's so big," Ahmed gasped. The sky was black, and it wasn't a storm, Mag saw out the corner of his eye, but a cloud of insects. They smacked the windshield like hail. Traffic ahead had slowed to a halt. Vehicles pulled over to the side of the road, which was already coated with insect carcasses. In the opposite lane a truck went into a skid and spun into the car in front of them. Ahmed eased to a stop, and Mag cursed. Sheets of insects rained down, making a noise like hard rain on the metal roofs of the Dallas huts. Grasshoppers. Mag shoved a hand into his pocket and pulled out a twenty-franc note, which he thrust in Ahmed's face. "Read it."

"Twenty francs?!" Ahmed snorted. "Now I'm your shoeshine boy?"

"I said read it, you bum." But Ahmed just laughed and shook his head, so Mag shoved the bill back into his pocket, wrenched his door open, and ducked out into the grasshopper storm, shielding his face with his arms. Blindly he ran for shelter, pushing through the whirring of thousands of wings, hard insects pelting his body like gravel. A field of grass alongside the road had turned black, and you could actually hear the creatures chomping. Some were as big as cigars. Mag ran.

Across the street he flung himself beneath a café awning, wedging himself into a crowd. Grasshopper bodies bounced off the overhead canvas like drumbeats. Mag looked out in astonishment across the blackened landscape. Here he was in a uniform surrounded by men in woolen djellabahs watching grasshoppers rain from the African sky. What the hell.

Eventually the pounding subsided. Maybe the creatures had moved on to another section of town. Maybe they'd all flung themselves to the earth and died. A few onlookers tentatively stepped out into the open, glancing around as if expecting to be whisked off somewhere and chomped. Other onlookers now studied Mag. Probably it was the uniform. He was meant to take control. He'd give it another few minutes. Pulling out the twenty-franc note, he read it again, because he needed to remind himself. Right there across the bottom in tiny letters: *E.A. Wright Bank Note Co. Phila.* The old Moroccan bills were still in effect, but the new ones were coming in – 5, 10, 50 and 100 Moroccan francs. The contract for the design and printing of the bills had gone to a company in Philly, where Mag had a guy. Just give him some more time, and back home printing presses would run throughout the night, making him a very rich man.

○

AT WO GIRAUD AIDES FLEE TO MOROCCO

LEMAIGRE-DUBREUIL AND RIGAUD BELIEVED ON WAY TO SPAIN TO AID VICHY BACKERS

By Harold Callender, by Wireless to The New York Times

ALGIERS – Jacques Lemaigre-Dubreuil, formerly chief economic adviser to Gen. Henri-Honoré Giraud, who was about to be arrested by order of the French Committee of National Liberation, has escaped from French North Africa to Spanish Morocco, it was revealed today....

The police searched his house when it was found that he had escaped....

M. Lemaigre-Dubreuil, who was a rich manufacturer, worked with American consular officers here before the Allies' landings....

The escapes have caused much concern that has diplomatic aspects. It is believed that M. Lemaigre-Dubreuil is on his way to Madrid or already there. In Madrid are Vichy's Ambassador and, it is said, Gen. Charles Noguès, former Resident General of French Morocco.... These and other persons there are supposed to be active agents for Vichy and to be trying to get into touch with the Allies in the interests of Vichy, or of those who backed Vichy and now may seek another horse to back against Gen. Charles de Gaulle....

M. Lemaigre-Dubreuil has been accused of

working with German industrial and financial cartels even after the Allies' liberation of North Africa....[8]

○

Crusoe was travelling undercover. Ever since the Americans had shortsightedly cut him out of their invasion plans, much had gone wrong for him, as well as for the Americans, as far as Jacques was concerned, not to mention for France, whose campaign had been disastrous since the beginning. Captain in the Army of the Levant in Syria during the Great War, Legion of Honor, medaled after escaping German capture in 1940 at Nogent-sur-Seine…and nobody would listen to his counsel. He had met with Bob Murphy at Algiers to plan the North African invasion – Operation Torch – but Murphy and his vice-consuls' impatience had denied him time to prepare his chosen commander of the Free French, General Giraud. Subsequently Giraud had been steamrolled by De Gaulle at the Casablanca Conference, with Roosevelt's blessing. If Jacques now hated anyone more than the Americans, it was De Gaulle and his cronies. They had slandered his reputation before illegally handing over the Casablanca cooking oil refinery of his company, Lesieur Oils, to a competitor, the Société des Huileries Marocaines. And now he was a hunted man.

Even employing a driver had become too risky, so he had been driving himself through the Maarif when the locusts had swarmed. The symbolism of this was not

---

8   *The New York Times* – 6/1/1944

lost on Jacques Lemaigre-Dubreuil, although he was not a superstitious man. He knew that plagues were part of the natural cycle of things. The locusts bred in the desert, typically solitary creatures, but every decade or so they would malevolently transform, uniting in a mindless swarm that destroyed everything in its path. But Jacques was too intelligent to let himself be destroyed by the mindless swarm.

As soon as the sky had cleared, Moroccans rushed to light fires on street corners to cook the insects in oil they poured into large frying pans – his own Lesieur Oil, Jacques noticed with glum satisfaction. They scooped handfuls of the brittle carcasses into the oil, and when the locusts turned dark brown, they used sticks to flip them back out onto wooden planks.

Jacques parked the car and got out. Now fifty years old, he had a prominent forehead, bushy eyebrows, and a bulldog's low-slung jaw. He strode over to a fire, his short, compact wrestler's body neatly contained in a pin-striped suit. This drew some attention, but he felt at ease among North Africans, and had first encountered locusts in Algiers, knowing them to be a delicacy. He nodded at the man tending the fire and plucked the largest grasshopper from the plank – a female, by its size, more suitable for eating. Then he stripped off the creature's wings and legs, held it aloft, turned up his head, and dropped the locust into his open mouth. "Delicious!" he eventually said in Moroccan Arabic, then handed over a coin and walked into a bar to see if he could find a glass of champagne to wash the critter down.

Now he sat at the bar with a glass of *fino* – naturally they hadn't served champagne – next to a heavyset young American soldier slouching on his stool. Jacques couldn't imagine the boy being in any kind of fighting shape, but then lack of discipline was what he had come to expect from Americans. A lick of sloppy hair stuck to the soldier's forehead – such disregard for military standards was forbidden when Jacques had commanded men. But the boy was not entirely unattractive. His features seemed to have been modeled after a Greek statue, although from the softest clay. Still, the nose was commanding, and his hooded eyes, while evasive, burned with an unmistakable fire. Perhaps he felt Jacques's eyes on him, because he finally grunted and said, "You like those grasshoppers?"

Jacques chuckled. "They're locusts, actually. Quite a delicacy."

"Too fuggin delicate for me," the soldier growled, and Jacques laughed again. The soldier's sloppiness now intrigued him. Perhaps it indicated a welcome independence of character. The boy might lack focus, but he had aspirations. Jacques looked him over again, liking him more by the minute.

"Awfully nosey," the American growled. Jacques struggled not to laugh. It was time for some reassurance: "My apologies. I'm afraid I'm too curious about Americans. My experiences with them have not been exceptionally positive. Although of course I'm always happy to meet an…exception."

The soldier only grunted, so Jacques went on, feeling an instinctive need to gain his trust: "They have made it quite difficult for me to do business here. Now I fear circumstances will prevent me from seeing my wife and children in Paris for quite some time. My enemies, alas, are not on the battlefield."

The soldier muttered something into his beer. What was he doing in a bar off base in the middle of the day? Perhaps he had deserted. "Perhaps we're not so different," Jacques said.

"Yeah buddy," the soldier said, eyeing Jacques's suit. "We're different."

Jacques chuckled again. "Forgive my curiosity. But you look as if you might have enemies too. If there is a problem, perhaps I can help. I happen to know many high-ranking officials. I hope that is not indiscreet."

The soldier slumped further onto his stool and gave Jacques a crooked grin. "Oh yeah? How those high-ranking contacts working out for ya?"

"Everybody needs a friend," Jacques said, running a finger around the rim of his glass. "I also have contacts at the American consulate. Perhaps useful. Perhaps not. Take my card." He slipped a card and a pen from his jacket pocket, wrote his secret name across the back of the card, and slid it across the bar. "If you find yourself in Morocco for a while, let me know. I may not be… available…for several months, but if you need a friend, show this at the factory. We're in the industrial district at Roches Noires. They'll know how to reach me."

The soldier took the card and read it. "The cooking oil," he said, without commenting on Jacques's title: *Président Directeur Général.*

"My name is Jacques, but you can call me Crusoe."

"Like the guy on the island," the soldier said, flipping over the card.

"Yes, civilizing the savages. Converting lost souls." He looked at the young man intently, running the tip of his tongue over his upper lip.

But the soldier didn't appear to be listening. He had turned away to stare at the beaded curtain hung over the open doorway.

"So since you's so smart," the soldier finally said, "you think a swarm of those grasshoppers of yours could take down a bird?"

Strange boy.

○

○

She wasn't on the roof, but the grasshoppers didn't seem to have made it this far. He guessed that deep enough into a city, they ran out of green to eat. The pigeons were all present, doing their creepy warbling. Downstairs he knocked and was relieved when she answered. "You okay? Your ma not around?" He glanced past her into the apartment.

"No," she murmured with a little shake of her head. He grabbed her by the shoulders and pulled her close for a kiss. He'd been afraid for those birds, had imagined her up on the roof inside a cloud of whirring insects. She gasped into his mouth and pushed him away. "Aren't you gonna invite me in?"

She hid a smile behind both hands, turned, and led him into the apartment. He shut the door and she came to him again, flinging her arms around his neck and peppering his face with kisses that popped too early or too late. His palms were wet, his guts churned. "She gonna be back soon?"

"Not until after dinner."

Her room was a mess. Mag had never been too tidy himself, but Camille had dirty coffee cups on the table beside the single bed, clothes strewn everywhere, bubblegum stuck to the headboard, wet towels on the floor, their rancid smell mixed with musty sheets and perfume. "Wait here," she whispered, stooping to kiss his elbow before scampering off. He sat down on the bed, then stood up again. He thought about taking off his boots. He didn't understand anything. She was one of the most beautiful girls he'd ever seen. That was all. He sat back down on the bed.

She knocked before entering. Mag grunted. The door crept open, and she darted through the crack, wearing the yellow lingerie he'd brought her, her arms clasped tightly across her breasts like she was about to dive feet-first from a cliff into a lake.

"Let me see," he said softly. Tentatively she dropped her hands to her sides and looked at the floor, humming one of her songs. His eyes devoured her. Her breasts were fuller than he'd imagined, and pushed out of the top of the slip, which was too small. Her nipples showed through the sheer fabric, and the curve of her hips, the dark triangle of hair. He breathed heavily, heart pounding.

"Do I look like a lady?" she asked, glancing shyly up at him, her fingers teasing the slip's lacy hem. "Turn around," he said, and she did, rising up on her toes as if she were wearing heels.

Then he said, "Come to bed."

Mag had been with a few girls before, professional ones who hung around the bars near the docks in Philly, but Camille didn't know any better than to give him everything. She was unspoiled, and he'd never had anything good like that before. Her body was soft, and she hugged his head tight to her shoulder as he pushed into her, chirping into his ear, sighing, nibbling his cheek. Traffic honked below in the streets. When slowly, after much coaxing, her legs spread wide, he felt as if he might burst open with happiness.

Afterwards she clasped his body to hers with suffocating force, occasionally shifting around on the narrow bed as if to get more comfortable, but really just drawing back to look at him, then muttering something and smothering him again with kisses. In the light from the open window, he looked down over her curves, the tiny hairs on her arms. He wanted to see this forever. Later he kissed into the mess of her thick hair, smelling her neck. He touched the tip of his tongue to the black speck on her cheek. "Hee hee. What are you doing?"

"I don't know."

She sighed. "I heard the bell."

"Huh?"

"*Rien.*"

Most of the time she made no sense at all. Her mind was a total mystery to him, and that made him nervous, but maybe it didn't matter. Most of the time she didn't understand a goddamn word he said either. He was just grateful for the tenderness she'd shown him. "Cam," he said, "I'm never going home."

She murmured something into the pillow. Outside the light was fading, and there on the ledge, rubbing its legs as it watched him, was a lone green grasshopper.

2

JOSEPHINE BAKER A LIEUTENANT

PARIS – Josephine Baker is the latest theatrical star to show up in Paris, but admirers might not recognize her in her air auxiliary lieutenant's uniform. Miss Baker said that if she were not in the service her greatest wish would be to appear again at the Casino de Paris. She has been working as a liaison officer after a serious illness in Casablanca.[9]

○

Franklin Felton walked into the bar of the Transcontinental in a short-sleeved shirt, having smoked a reefer while driving over in the Pontiac, which after a minor collision and a local repair job now sported a swath of red paint across its side that wasn't quite Parma red. After parking he'd smoked another with the windows rolled up until he wondered if the heat might explode him, and then he'd crashed out into the sunlight. Now he was vibrating like a sound wave aimed at Arkady Zubov, who sat at his usual table in the corner. As predicted.

Arkady was one of the last of the '42 crowd still in town. Joe had gone back to France, or America, or wherever she was now. He was trying not to keep up, because she hadn't written. And King and Reid, then poor Canfield, for what Bob Murphy had tactfully

---

9   Associated Press – 10/11/1944

called "indiscretions and undue exuberance", escorted to a cargo ship for an ignominious ride home atop several thousand oranges. Franklin was different. The others, even Joe, had been only tourists, and fundamentally tourists were counterfeiters. They did not see what they thought they saw. They only registered surfaces, further obscuring the truth, while Felton had learned to pierce deeper into the world's essential secrets. Also, if he had gone *home*, the story people told about him would have simply been that he had returned. Not that he had left in the first place. That he was a man of the world. Of course that was all beside the point. He didn't give a damn anymore about what people thought.

"Salaam alaikum," Felton said, pulling out a chair at Arkady's table and flopping down into it.

"Alaikum salaam." Arkady smiled warmly and slipped his notebook into his jacket pocket. In *Darija*, they exchanged the customary formalities, how are you, your family, then again and again. Arkady's Arabic had improved, Felton noticed, but then so had his own. They hadn't crossed paths in many months.

"Would you like something to drink, Franklin?"

"No thanks. Not sticking around, just wanted to say hello."

"I'm so pleased to see you." Arkady looked lost behind his spectacles, innocent, his cheeks flushed in that look of permanent embarrassment. How could he sit so placidly in that stifling uniform? "I've missed our idyllic Sunday afternoons."

Liar, Felton thought. What else could you say about a birder who invented sightings? What was the point of that? Might as well just say you'd seen every bird on the planet and stop looking. Might as well put on a cape and call yourself Superman. What was the point?

Felton had mostly lost interest in the sport. For a while he'd gone walking through the countryside alone, until the day he'd encountered Patton and his officers hunting boar, and had been accused of spying. Russell had needed to bail him out, which had been an additional pain in the ass, but Russell was gone now too. "Any more sightings of the famous slender-billed curlew?" he asked, a grin sketched across his face. "Remember? *Coor-lee! Coor-lee!*"

"Unfortunately not," the Soviet replied, pouring a few drops of hot water into his coffee from his customary miniature pitcher. Jesus. "I'm afraid I was extraordinarily privileged that day, but it would be wonderful if we could both go up to Merja Zerga sometime and try our luck."

"That would be some luck, wouldn't it, Arkady?"

"It certainly would," Zubov said, smiling contentedly. "You can't imagine how happy I was that day."

"No, I guess I can't. Can't imagine a slender-billed curlew up there either," Franklin murmured, feeling his face go as numb as a punching bag. The blood from his fingers and toes all flowed into his belly and boiled like a red sun. "But you know what's even harder to imagine, Arkady? How you ever thought I'd believe that cock-eyed story. Ha! *Coor-lee! Coor-lee!* My ass."

"Franklin –"

"You're full of shit, Arkady. Even if nobody else realizes it, I do, and that's what I wanted to say. You may still think we're allies in this war, but I don't countenance liars or cowards."

"I'll take you to Merja Zerga," Arkady insisted,

mistakenly lifting the pitcher of hot water to his lips. The water burned his tongue, and he spilled the pitcher across the table. Felton laughed hysterically.

"Please, Franklin," the Russian said, but Franklin was laughing too hard to hear anything else. It was just too funny.

○

Across the bar a waiter set down a cup of coffee in front of Victor Tessier. "Warm out there today, isn't it, monsieur? Ah, *pardon*, did you want milk or sugar?"

"Just leave the coffee," Victor said without looking up. On the table in front of him was the last postcard. His harem was reunited, although he had no use for them anymore. This one was an overhead view of the city with four bare-breasted portraits inset at the corners. Tommy wrote that he had been on the USS *Essex* when it had been hit by a kamikaze. Several men had been killed, and Tommy's plane, which had been on the flight deck, had been destroyed. He was still in one piece, though, and morale was as high as ever. They were hard-bent on licking those Japs once and for all.

Victor put down the postcard. He'd barely read the past few. They seemed to be asking for something, Victor wasn't sure what. Tommy's wife had given birth to a boy, which had made him happier than he'd ever imagined possible. He also wrote of the indescribable sense of loss he felt as each postcard was sent out. Why was Tommy telling him all of this? Victor was bored with it.

At a table near the entrance, two young Frenchwomen in pillbox hats sat drinking tea. Victor wondered if the brunette recognized him. Maybe not in his uniform. He stared until she caught his eye, and blushed. *Oui.* She recognized him. He kept staring, wanting to see if she would mention anything to her friend, but of course she wouldn't, and didn't.

Crazed laughter burst from the corner of the room, and he looked over to see the American vice-consul – what was his name? – standing over a table where Arkady Zubov sat. Sweat poured down the American's face. His laughter sounded like radio static coming and going. Zubov had knocked over a pitcher and was righting it with his eyes downcast. Poor Arkady. He'd tried to recruit Victor, in a vague fashion, a month or two earlier. "Boring, Arkady," Victor had said. Perhaps he'd tried to recruit the American too, although Arkady was almost certainly too cautious for that. Victor should mention the incident to his intelligence officer, but he knew he wouldn't. Boring again.

When the American left, Zubov came over with trembling hands to congratulate him on his new mission. "My country will be honored by your service," he said. Victor nodded. In two days he was off to join the GC3, the Third Fighter Group in the Free French Air Force under the First Air Army of their allies, the Soviet Union.

3

On a Sunday in the winter of 1944, hundreds of servicemen crowded the boxing ring at the center of the Stade Philippe. They had been drinking all morning, as had the Frenchmen who lingered at the back of the crowd, wary of the rowdy Americans. Beyond the fences of the stadium, on a dusty plot by the port, Moroccan boys were kicking a rag ball in fits and starts, eyeing the fence and the crowd within. Armed sentinels had been posted along the fence, and whenever the boys approached, they swatted them back. Mag watched a boy waving his hands and dancing, daring a guard to come after him. He led Camille across the field to the bleachers.

This had been a fuggin mistake. Men whistled and gaped, and Camille cowered on his arm. He had wanted to show her off, to impress her with his freshly pressed uniform, with their seats up in the bleachers among the brass, but this was a pack of wolves, and for weeks the men would be whispering. He glared at the smirks on their fuggin faces. He shouldn't have brought the girl.

They climbed up into the bleachers, passing Stec and some other lieutenants, most of whom also ogled Camille. Quickly they found their seats and sat. Camille didn't seem to have noticed the bastards too much. She was mostly just pleased to get out of the house. Mag grunted, catching sight of Bones in the next section with the other transport pilots. Again the bastard had returned empty-handed from Philly, again wanting more money, which Mag had promised, although not much was left. Stec had required a big payoff to delay the transfer to

147

Italy, and time was running out again. Time was always running out. Mag had a week, enough for Bones to make a roundtrip and return with the half million Moroccan francs that Mag's man inside the Philly printers had produced during the nights. But how likely was that? Worries kept him up at night, when all he really wanted to think about was what he and Camille could do with the money. He could retire, disappear, desert, anything, everything.

Stec turned to wave, nodding approvingly at Camille, as if Mag hadn't already gotten the message. Anybody else would have thought he was waving hello, but Mag knew he was waving goodbye. He glanced away, fiddling with the Frenchman's card in his pants pocket. Crusoe. Mag doubted the Frenchman could do anything to hold off Stec, but he was desperate. He'd also done some research on Lesieur Oils, which sent out more ships from Morocco than anyone except the American military and the phosphate conglomerates. How hard could it be to pack cargo in oil drums and expand into the European market?

A French family of three pushed up into the bleachers. The scrawny boy was probably fourteen. His father was equally scrawny, balding with spectacles, but the mother was a head taller, with a full body and a jolly face. Soldiers parted to let them pass, stripping her with their eyes. With her arms outstretched, the woman steadied herself on a step, clucking like a chicken, flushed by the attention. The boy clutched his fists to his chest and ducked his head, frightened by the pressing crowd. This was no place for a woman, Mag thought again.

Beyond the fence one of the older Moroccan soccer

players, sixteen or seventeen, was now running the game, pointing players left and right, setting up a slump-shouldered American sentinel as a reluctant goalie, goading him until the soldier leaned his rifle against the fence to bat away shots. Mag watched as the boy orchestrated a low, hard shot, and when the soldier dove for it, both teams made a dash for the fence, clambering up over it and onto the stadium field. By the time the soldier had struggled to his feet and snatched up his rifle, it was too late. The boys were going to see the fight, and Mag grinned for the first time that day. Probably nobody else in the whole stadium had noticed, but he'd been rooting for the kids. All but a few made it over. The stragglers were chased down by French police, who beat the shit out of them.

Army vs. Navy was the undercard, heavyweights, and as the fighters were announced, G.I.s packed closer to the ring and the crowd in the bleachers rose to its feet. The Army was outnumbered that day, but their fighter was quicker and put the Navy man on the canvas twice before knocking him out in the third. The Army contingent cheered, including Stec and his cronies, but Mag didn't care one way or another, and it hadn't been much of a fight anyway. He'd been watching the French family a few rows below, the father stooping to explain ring mechanics to the boy – Albert was his name – who asked questions in an excited stutter. The mother paid them little attention. Between rounds she had been getting ample attention. "Shocking," Mag heard her say in English as two sailors pushed up close to her, but her eyes shone, and when one passed her a bottle of beer, she laughed and took a sip. One sailor put a hand on her arm, the other brushed his knuckles against the sweep of her hip. The husband had been too intent on the boy to notice any of this, not that he was the sort of specimen who could have done anything about it.

Mag had watched Camille watching the mother and had attempted to read her thoughts. Was she thinking of how horrible it would be to be manhandled like that, or did she want to be manhandled? He couldn't figure her out. Stuttering some more, the kid Albert had pulled at his mother's skirt, but she was too distracted to notice. "Why isn't he off at war?" one of the sailors had asked of the husband. "Yeah, why aren't you in uniform?" the other shouted, but the husband either didn't speak English, or didn't hear. Mag had gritted his teeth. He'd wanted to plug the two assholes, but the last thing he needed was more enemies. When another round had begun, the boy had watched closely, wincing with each punch, bobbing his head with a tiny fist extended.

After the fight the crowd surged down from the bleachers towards the concession stands, some pulling flasks from their pockets to pour into Coca-Colas. Mag pulled out his flask, took a long swig, and held it out to Camille, who shook her head and frowned. Then Stec appeared beside them, pretending he was some bigshot, saluting crisply so that Mag was forced to slide the flask back into his jacket pocket and respond with his own half-assed salute.

"And does this lovely breath of fresh air have a name?" fuggin Stec actually said. Of course poor Camille couldn't get enough of gallantry, or whatever, and rose up on her toes, positively beaming. "I'm Camille."

"Well the pleasure," Stec purred, taking her hand

in his, "is most certainly all mine." Then he lowered his lips to kiss her fingers. Mag stared hard, searing into his mind the image of Camille's five pink-painted nails, whose color he'd just noticed. He reached into his pants pocket and dug the corner of Crusoe's card up under his thumbnail. Then they heard the French mother scream.

"Guess somebody finally put a hand up her skirt," Mag snarled. Camille shot him a look of hatred, and Stec laughed, then pushed his way back down towards the other officers. The woman kept screaming, rooted to the spot, arms whirling. Her husband timidly raised a hand, trying to calm her, perhaps, but looking more like he was preparing to get hit. Apparently the boy had vanished. "Albert! Albert!" she screamed. Camille looked on in horror. "Do something!" she cried, pulling at Mag's arm.

"Ah, he just went off to get a Coca-Cola," Mag growled. "She likes to be the center of attention, that's all."

They watched as the husband gingerly escorted his overwrought wife down the bleachers, swiveling his head about in search of the missing Albert. Mag took out his flask again and poured the rest of it down his throat.

In the main event that day, Marcel Cerdan, "The Casablanca Clouter", was facing Willie Sampson, an American sailor making his debut. Cerdan was a Frenchman who'd been raised a dozen blocks away in Mers Sultan. He was European Welterweight Champion and had knocked out the American Bulldog Milano in this same stadium the previous Halloween. Only twenty-seven, he had already fought seventy-seven bouts, with just two losses after disputed disqualifications.

The announcer began his introductions, and as the spectators quieted, you could hear the Frenchwoman again, off somewhere crying out, "Albert! Albert!" The crowd in the bleachers murmured in annoyance. The voice came from below, and Mag looked down between his legs, through the gaps in the slats of the risers. The woman and her husband were down there in the dead space wandering in blind circles through a wasteland of discarded bottles and trash. "Albert! Albert!"

"Shut up!" somebody yelled, and people laughed. Then the announcer spoke Sampson's name, and the Americans roared as he made a path towards the ring, his strong, stubby arms raised optimistically into the air. Mag kept his eyes on the couple down below, appearing through adjacent slats as they wandered. They seemed to have slid into a parallel world, and for a moment Mag had the sensation that he and Camille were the ones wandering down there alone. For a moment he felt dizzy. He brushed his hand against hers, and still she was next to him, still his girl. "Sampson looks tough," he said. "I think he might have a shot." She nodded, unable to tear her eyes from the scene beneath their feet.

Cerdan was announced, and he popped up from the crowd in a striped bathrobe to dance in his corner. Mugging for the hometown contingent, he got a lot of cheers, both French and Moroccan. Mag couldn't spot the soccer boys, but they had surely pushed up close into the mass of bodies. When Cerdan's corner man stripped the robe from the fighter's shoulders, he looked thin, underfed, and half the size of Sampson. The referee drew them into the center of the ring. Then they rang the bell, and Camille jumped.

At first it was difficult to observe the extent to which Cerdan outclassed Sampson. He was so quick that his punches blurred like a hummingbird's wings. Occasionally the big American would crumple forward in pain, as if these separate actions were unrelated. Mag glanced at Camille, but she wasn't paying any attention. She was still looking around for the missing boy, clutching the sides of her pretty dress in her fists. He wished there was more booze in the flask.

Sampson hit the mat twice in the first round, and not long into the second he was knocked out by a quick stab between the eyes. The fight left everyone unsatisfied except Cerdan's biggest fans, but that was what you got when you fought Marcel Cerdan, and the crowd began dispersing into the city. The soldiers had been given the rest of the day off, and they would fill the city's brothels. Mag waited until Stec and the others had cleared out and the bleachers were almost empty before taking Camille's arm. But she wasn't ready. She was still scanning the space below the bleachers, where there was no longer any sign of the French couple. "What about the boy?" She gently pushed away his hand. "We should help find him."

She was funny like that. She'd watch the sky for hours waiting for one dumb pigeon to come home. "Ah, they'll find him if they haven't already. Kid just wanted a closer look at the fight."

"He didn't look like it. He looked scared."

"Come on, Cam. I'll take you home."

She took some coaxing, but finally he got her back to the base jeep he'd requisitioned for the day. Fortunately he'd stashed a bottle beneath the driver's seat, which he immediately uncapped to pour whiskey into his mouth. Then they drove in silence through traffic to Rue Nolly, where he parked beneath Camille's apartment. He knew her mother had invited several church ladies for lunch, so he wasn't going to get what he wanted, but Camille begged him to wait anyway. "You smell of alcohol," she said, pecking him on the cheek before scampering off into the building.

Now he was even more annoyed. Sitting there following orders like some kind of fuggin pigeon in training. Another swig. At least fifteen minutes passed. His mind was a crowd of screaming worries. Hard as he tried, he couldn't shut them up. Another swig. Was this how people went cuckoo? What a pitiful sight he was, a shell-shocked supply sergeant on the Ice Cream Front. Ha.

A thump at the passenger-side window startled him from his thoughts. There she was, finally, holding a pigeon in two hands, her pink nails against its white breast. Her head dipped to murmur into the bird's neck. Mag leaned over and thrust open the door. "What the hell, Cam?"

Solemnly she spoke a few last words to the pigeon before glancing up at him. "Henri is ready. I know he is." Mag smirked. Fuggin Henry looked exactly like all the other pigeons. Girls with their pets. "Please, Mag. Take him to the base with you. You see this little cylinder tied to his leg? I have put a white roll of paper inside. Write something on the paper for me when you are home, and then let him go into the air. I will be waiting on the roof for your message. I will listen for the bell. Please, Mag."

Crazy girl. Cuckoo. "Write something like what?"

"Anything you want to say."

He grunted, taking the bird from her outstretched hands. Its feathers were warm, and he could feel the beat of its lungs or heart inside, the kicking of its legs. He sneezed as he set it down on the back seat, and the bird fluttered about, banging into windows and the roof before settling onto the seat and cooing. Camille leaned into the jeep and cooed back at it. She probably thought she was saying something, but one natural law Mag felt pretty certain about was that a girl would never learn to talk pigeon. Then she kissed him on the cheek and fluttered back into the building. So that was that. Lotta good the day had brought, and now it was just him and Henry.

Maybe Ahmed was around. Another swig, and he decided to drive over to Les Nations Unies, the bar where he'd first met Aziza, and where they'd met many times since. Henry flapped around in the back. Mag drove hunched over the steering wheel, worried the thing would start pecking at the back of his head. Occasionally he sneezed, and the jeep swerved.

In front of the bar, he parked up on the sidewalk and slammed the door before Henry could follow, although the pigeon now seemed to have settled into an invisible little back seat nest. The old guardian creaked up from his stoop and shook his stick at Mag, who dug into his pockets looking for a small coin. His shirt had come untucked, and there was a stain down the front of his jacket. When had that happened? Before the fight he had been looking pretty sharp. He didn't have a coin, just that business card, so he waved off the guardian and poked his head through the bar door. Sure enough,

Ahmed was on a stool telling some dumb story to anybody who would listen. Mag caught his attention, and the lunatic hustled out to the sidewalk with this big grin on his face. "Something wrong?"

"Nah. Just thought we could have a drink."

"Come inside. I saw Aziza this morning. She might come by later."

"Not today. Let's drive."

So they cruised around town passing the bottle. When Mag wasn't drinking, he was cursing that scumbucket Stec, who had him trapped and needed to be handled. Ahmed grumbled about business and took the cursing up a notch, until he banged the dashboard and shouted, "I'll kill the bastard!"

In that instant a winged demon sprang up from the backseat into the space between their heads. They screamed for their lives. Mag slammed on the brakes. "What in hell!" Ahmed shouted, slapping his head with his palms as if he were being stung by a hive of bees. The pigeon flapped its wings several times before settling again onto the back seat.

"That's Henry," Mag snarled. "Cam's fuggin bird. Never mind. How do we get to Roches Noires from here?"

Ahmed shook his head, cagily eyeing Henry out the corner of his eye, as if that bird, not Stec, was their new biggest enemy. The sun dipped low over the ocean, and any warmth in the air raced after it towards America. Near the rail station Ahmed indicated a turn east on Boulevard Colonna-d'Ornano, and Mag drunkenly swerved. They drove past the vast slums known as Carrières Centrales, where a hundred thousand people, new arrivals to the booming metropolis, lived in shacks built of tar paper and wood, roofed with flattened tin cans, American detritus labeled Texaco, Esso, Budweiser, and Spam. Trash fires belched up black smoke, and packs of wild dogs spattered with mud foraged through narrow alleyways between slumping constructions. Mag saw where the wooden crates he'd hocked to Ahmed had gone. They were walls in which people were attempting to live. Fuggin Ahmed. He felt like he was moving slowly through some endless human graveyard, and he wanted to disappear. His slums in Philly had never been so rough, but he knew the story.

They turned left, then right onto Boulevard du Commandant Fages. Another group of tattered Moroccan boys kicked another ball around a field of dirt, this ball looking like plastic bags tied around a rock. Soon a huge factory appeared off to the right. *Huiles Lesieur rend la bonne cuisine encore meilleure.* Another pull of whiskey. "What's the rest of it mean?"

"It makes good cooking even better."

Mag nodded as the jeep rattled into the parking lot. Two cars sat in the lot, so there was a possibility. Or he was going cuckoo. Sunday, doneday. Nobody could do a goddam thing for him here or anywhere else anymore.

"What are we doing?" Ahmed asked.

"Gotta friend who can help us."

Touil raised an eyebrow.

"Keep your mouth shut. And roll up that fuggin window."

Along a concrete loading platform a row of truck bays punctured the factory, all of them shut. A narrow glass door looked as if it might lead to an office. The gravel parking lot was potted with mud puddles, and even here Mag could smell the putrid fires of Carrières Centrales. The sun bled orange as they tromped across the lot and up three steps to the concrete platform. The glass door was locked. Mag banged at it until his fists ached, then went around to the nearest truck bay and banged at that too, but the place was deserted. Lifting his face to the fading sky, he shouted. Put my guts up in the clouds. Bones wouldn't bring back that trunk. This was all a big joke. He slumped down to the concrete, and for once in human history, Ahmed didn't have anything to say.

They sat in silence against the locked door of the bay until the edge of the sun swelled out across the sea and prepared to vanish. This was a beautiful place, Casablanca, but it didn't matter. They watched the sky until they heard a sound out at the edge of the parking lot. Mag turned his head. In the dusk the source of the sound was hidden, but it was approaching. Eventually their eyes discerned a new shape.

Across the lot walked an enormous pig, as big as a baby hippopotamus. Its fur was white and patchy, caked with filth, and its giant, pointy ears flapped down over its eyes. Scraggly whiskers grew from its broad, wrinkled snout, which sniffed at the ground along a wandering path. She was a sow, and waggled a dozen swollen teats along her belly, muttering to herself as she lumbered along. They watched her move across the sunset.

"Probably been living in Carrières Centrales," Ahmed whispered. "Maybe escaped from the *abattoirs*. She is old. Probably been wild for a couple of years."

Mag felt deeply uneasy. "I once saw a pig eat Paddy

Spillane," he murmured. He had a nauseating feeling of being on deck of the *Buenos Aires* again, and a pig, half the size of the one in the twilight, was chomping off a piece of Paddy's mangled face. Poor Paddy, who hadn't wanted to fight, cutting off his trigger finger in the latrine the night before the landings. Did pigs scent blood like sharks? Why had he never asked himself the question? Ah, he couldn't have saved Paddy. Paddy had been born for that pig.

In his pocket he ran a finger along the edge of Crusoe's card, but there was no longer any use for it. He was embarrassed now for having put some faith in the pompous Frenchman. That was when you got into trouble. People didn't care, or they didn't for long. The world kept turning. All you had was you. Somehow he'd forgotten that for a moment, and into the dark clouds filling his mind, he sent one urgent message, a vow never to forget it again. Wait for no one. The card he left in his pocket. Instead he took out a handkerchief.

"Give me your knife," he said, wishing they'd brought the whiskey from the jeep. If he went back for it now, he might attract the pig's attention, which was an especially unappealing thought.

Ahmed pulled out his knife, flipped open the blade, and handed it to Mag. "Filthy animal."

"Then you and the fuggin prophet Mohamed don't have to eat it." But Mag wasn't planning on eating it either. He placed his palm on the concrete platform and spread his fingers wide. He held the blade of the knife to his index finger. Two weeks in the infirmary at least, and exemption from the artillery. He shook his head. He couldn't do it.

"Take it," he said, thrusting the knife at Touil. "Cut off my finger."

"What?"

"Do it," Mag said, pressing his outstretched fingers to the platform again. "Stec can't send me to the front without a trigger finger."

The logic of this immediately appealed to the Moroccan, especially his business sense, and he excitedly shifted onto his knees, gripping the knife. "The whole thing?"

"Fug no! Just below the little knuckle." Mag spread his fingers even wider, indicating the place to cut while shifting his body away from where the blade would come. His arm trembled. His face was greased with sweat. Ahmed seemed paralyzed. "Don't tell me you haven't done this before, Ahmed! Chop it off!"

"You sure?" Ahmed asked nervously while making a slow practice chop with the blade.

"Do it!" Mag groaned through gritted teeth. "We're out of business if you don't."

So Touil firmly held the point of the blade to the ground between Mag's index and middle fingers, and with his free palm pressing down on the back of the blade, he gently lowered its sharp length until it touched the skin below the knuckle. Mag felt as if all of him had been compressed into that one little spot, and he shut his eyes tight.

"*Allah u akbar*," Ahmed hissed, and with all his force he levered the blade down through the finger until it crunched into the concrete. There was a snapping sound, and the fingertip twitched slightly away from the hand. The spot went immediately red.

Tears ran down Mag's face, but he hadn't made a sound. His eyes were still clamped shut, and his whole body trembled, all his force still pressing down on the hand as if he was determined to drive it through the earth. Blood was everywhere, flooding around his palm and streaming towards the edge of the platform. He opened his eyes, grabbed the handkerchief, and gingerly lifted his palm. Blood raced in to fill the negative print of his severed hand in the concrete. He wrapped the handkerchief around the bloody nub, and with tears still pouring from his eyes, he laughed like some shell-shocked looney. He laughed and laughed as he struggled to his feet, using the bay door for support while still gripping the finger with his good hand. "You drive." His voice was slurred, unrecognizable. "We have to get to the base infirmary. If anyone asks, this happened there."

Ahmed nodded, watching his friend with a mixture of admiration and horror. Then he picked up the severed fingertip and slipped it into his pocket along with the bloody knife.

"What are you doing?"

"You don't want me to leave it here, do you?"

"Fuggin Ahmed," Mag muttered, and staggered down the three steps into the parking lot. The pig was gone. He checked. It wasn't there. They made their way across the gravel, through the mud to the jeep, where Ahmed ripped open the door, and a panicked pigeon named Henry flew out and vanished into the dark sky.

4

Abdelwahed Chaoui walked into Aziza's women's clothing shop in a gray three-piece suit, smelling of Richefleur cologne, a sack wedged beneath his arm. Slender and handsome, he had a sharp nose and a thin mustache. His gait was breezy and confident. The only hint of today's unusual worry was a slight crease between his eyebrows and an almost imperceptible slump in his shoulders. Aziza could be tough, and he was returning his dresses several weeks late.

Bells jingled against the glass door. She stood behind the wooden counter in a V-necked kaftan prominently featuring her breasts. That was no surprise. Behind her were dense racks of hanging dresses, djellabahs, blouses. On the walls were more colorful kaftans pinned like butterflies. Around him, bins of hosiery, underwear, garter belts, lingerie.

"*Voilà le Français*," Aziza said with a broad smile. This was her nickname for him. Several of his friends had arrived at the nickname separately. After all, he was one of the few Moroccan journalists to write his columns in French, for the *Courrier du Maroc*, and then there were his popular theater performances of French classics, which he translated into Moroccan himself. Also, Abdelwahed was a bit of a dandy.

"I was just about to close up," she said. He strode over to the counter and placed a hand over hers. "I've missed you, Aziza. How have you been? How's your daughter?"

"You'll see her. She's in the back. And you? Touria and baby Salah? Zina?"

"They're all well. Tonight I return home to Fez. So I've brought you the clothes I borrowed, and thought maybe I would pick up something for Zina. She's always so happy when I say I've been to Aziza's."

Aziza's breasts shook as she laughed – krr krr krr – bouncing the hand of Fatima that hung from the chain around her neck. "If I had such a handsome husband, I would never be happy if he'd been to Aziza's."

Abdelwahed chuckled and set his sack on the counter. The crease between his eyebrows had vanished. He pulled out two dresses, one bright red, the other floral, and three pairs of sheer silk stockings.

"Oh, you must have been *zweena!*" *Krr krr krr.* "I wanted to come to the performance, but I work like a donkey."

"I *was* zweena. Even with the mustache." His fingers danced into the air, and he gyrated his hips.

"*Willi willi!* Come to the back, *zweena*, and we can drink something."

Leaving the clothes on the counter, he followed her, saying, "I, ah, could pay for the stockings if you like."

"Nonsense," Aziza said, wiggling down a narrow gap between racks of clothes. "They'll go right back into the package." Abdelwahed nodded to himself, relieved, and followed her broad, swiveling buttocks into the back of the shop. His eye caught a pink jacket and skirt combination that was absolutely made for Zina, but surely it was too expensive.

Beyond the racks Aziza's ten-year-old daughter Suzanne – two years older than Touria – sat in a chair moving scraps of cloth around on a wooden table. Abdelwahed said hello, but the girl didn't look up. Aziza had stepped into her office and brought out two warm beers, which she set on the table. "Now what would please Zina? Last week I got in some beautiful silk *takshitas.*"

Abdelwahed said nothing. He preferred Zina in Western clothes, skirts and heels, like a French movie star. He dressed her to be the most beautiful woman in any room. And if the *takshita* was silk, it would be even more expensive than the pink combination. But Aziza reached up and brought it down from a rack. "Do you want to try it on?" she asked. *Krr krr krr.* She held it up to her body so that he could see. "Zina's skinnier than me, but let me show you." She went off to the office again, leaving Abdelwahed alone with Suzanne, who finally glanced up, humming a song of Umm Kulthum's – *Remember Me.* Her skin was unusually dark, her black hair tightly curled, and her wide brown eyes held his.

Abdelwahed glanced towards the office. Aziza had not shut the door. The kaftan flashed through the air. He looked back at the girl, whose cheek now rested coquettishly on her palm. Sipping from the beer bottle, he looked back towards the office as Aziza emerged in the *takshita*, much too tight on her, overemphasizing her innumerable curves. As she moved towards him, the hanging dresses danced on their racks. "Very nice," he said, pulling out a chair for her and sitting in another opposite Suzanne. "I'll make you a price," Aziza smirked.

"You're generous to me, Aziza, and I'm glad I've seen the *takshita*. I will remember it for when Zina has a special occasion." Aziza nodded sharply and looked down at her daughter. "She won't go to school anymore," she said bitterly. "She's dreamy. Where will that get her?

Where will that get you, Suzanne?" Suzanne glanced back at Abdelwahed, then down at her pieces of cloth. The round buttons down the front of the Aziza's *takshita* strained such that Abdelwahed could see bits of flesh in the gaps. "So how is this new business of yours?" she asked.

"It's slow. I probably should have waited. The war has made it difficult. One company might want me to organize a conference. And then there is a French director who is shooting a movie here and out in the desert. He wants me to be his assistant. And I may have a little role."

"Ay, Errol Flynn! If you need costumes, think of your Aziza."

"I will," he said with a smile. Suzanne was watching him again as he drank from the bottle. "Now I should get something for Zina. Something simple, maybe some stockings like the ones you let me borrow."

Aziza's face became a mask. "I can put them back in their packages."

"Perfect," Abdelwahed said brightly.

Outside he hailed a taxi and told the driver to take him to the Roi de la Bière. An hour remained before he needed to be at the station, and ever since he'd started coming to Casablanca half the month, struggling to launch his advertising and events business, the bar had become his favorite evening stop. He felt guilty for having taken a taxi. The walk wasn't much more than a mile, but he'd wanted that pink combination and had settled for the stockings, so he'd felt permitted an indulgence. In any case, sweet and unspoiled Zina would be pleased with the stockings. He clutched the bag in his hand, overcome with melancholy, dreading another night train. He longed to transport himself back to her and the children in an instant, like a genie in the old stories.

Aziza had unsettled him. Women like her always knew where to place the tip of the knife. Now veiled ones moved down the twilit streets of Habbous, and he thought back to his childhood in Fez, his father and his many veiled women. Amine Chaoui had been a prominent businessman with an authoritarian streak and a taste for the theatrical. They had lived in the large family riad in the El Ayoun quarter, and Amine would arrive for meals on horseback, led into the courtyard by a stable boy who tended the reins. His father had been extraordinarily fat, and the mares suffered beneath him, their hooves slipping precariously on the cobblestones.

Meals were his greatest performances. Numerous concubines brought competing dishes from the kitchen. His Fassi wife was pretty, but the concubines shared his bed. Amine Chaoui had put great stock in his sexual prowess, siring three boys and three girls. Abdelwahed, the youngest, was only five when his father died. After that, his wet nurse, another concubine, had weaned him, and he had started going to the hammam with his sister. Even then he had been acutely aware of women's bodies, their breasts and their sex, so different from his own, such a tantalizing mystery. Once, several years later, a woman had stopped them at the door of the hammam, forbidding him entrance. His sister, furious, had whipped down his pants to show the woman his prick, saying, "Look here! Do you see even one single hair? Now let us pass!" And so they had.

In the steam room, naked women with multiplicitous forms lounged on benches, rubbing their backs with black soap and eyeing each other rapaciously, singling out neighborhood girls with broad hips and pert breasts as marriageable candidates for their sons. All women, Abdelwahed had realized, were beautiful with their clothes off. Skinny or fat, they seemed whole when naked. They had teased him and slapped his bare buttocks. Then his body had begun to change, and he'd never gone back.

After his father died, his uncle had become head of the family and had announced that Abdelwahed would become a maker of baboushes. One of his uncle's friends would take the boy as an apprentice and instruct him in the ways of cutting and sewing leather slippers. But Abdelwahed, for all his social grace, was rebellious at heart, and he'd met a professor at the university named El Qorri, who had taught him to read French literature, simultaneously opening his eyes to the injustices of the French occupation. So he had started writing, and now he didn't even own a pair of baboushes.

"Here we are," the driver said. They were idling on Boulevard de la Gare in front of Chaussures Scali. This was the heart of Frenchtown, and European crowds moved along the arcades.

"How about a little discount?" Abdelwahed asked, flashing a smile into the rearview mirror. "Traffic was heavy tonight."

The driver scoffed, and Abdelwahed handed over the money. He always gave up too quickly, he knew, but then he disliked negotiating with his fellow human beings.

Once inside the cavernous bar, he spotted no acquaintances, so he took a seat near the entrance and ordered a beer. He drank, occasionally reaching into his bag and slipping a hand into the packaging to feel the silk of the stockings. He imagined them sliding up Zina's legs. Perhaps she would tease him. Soon it was time to leave for the station, and still chastened by his taxi ride, he walked.

The train was crowded that night, and he hardly slept as it rattled up the coast to Rabat, then inland towards Meknes until the dark outline of the Atlas Mountains loomed in the night. He felt their presence like a powerful hand on his shoulder. Disembarking at Fez, he walked towards the medina, smelling the jasmine as dawn prepared to fling up its traces.

At the riad he crept through the courtyard, past the bubbling fountain, hoping to slip by any extended family already stirring. Zina would be relieved when he could afford a place of their own in Casablanca. She had been patient, and he knew the wives of his cousins resented her beauty, making her suffer accordingly. He tiptoed into her room, where she still slept, wearing the white nightgown he'd brought back from the theater tour in Tunisia. Salah slept beside her, just a few months old. Finally a son, and he was immeasurably proud, but it hadn't seemed to matter as much as he'd expected.

When it had mattered was at Touria's birth. He hadn't wanted a daughter and had boycotted Zina for weeks before deciding he had no choice but to attempt to meet the extraordinary challenge he'd been presented: a girl. Soon Touria's hair had been cut short like a boy's, and she dressed in pants. As she'd grown older, she'd even accompanied him on theater tours, acting in small roles he often invented for her. Occasionally he was criticized for treating a daughter like a son, but by then he'd taught her that this was how she should be treated.

Gently kissing his wife and son, he moved over to the mat on the floor where Touria slept. Her neck was so thin. She was only eight, but already she moved through the world with such confidence. Beside her outstretched hand was another folded paper airplane, and Abdelwahed's chest flooded with love. Allied planes often passed over the Fez medina, heading from Casablanca to Algiers or Palermo. At the sound of their engines, Touria would scamper out to the courtyard and watch them float across the blue square of sky above. She had learned their names and classifications. He did not know how. And when the skies were calm, she would show her cousins how to make paper airplanes from the pages of school notebooks carefully ripped along the staples at the spine. They sent them whizzing through the air, swerving like fighter jets, or looping slowly to the ground, until the last plane was lost to the courtyard fountain and became a sea monster, or mush.

When he kissed her cheek, her eyes flicked open, and she mirrored his smile. "Let's go up to the roof and see if we can catch a last few stars," he whispered. She nodded, and he took her in his arms. They had a tradition of looking at the stars together, which were brighter here than in Casablanca. She'd been named for a constellation, after all – the Pleiades, the Seven Sisters, Touria – and they could watch the sky for hours.

On the roof he pointed out the Great Bear and Orion, and they traced the shapes of the constellations with their fingers. She could draw her own shapes, he always told her. She could draw lions and monkeys and airplanes. You only needed imagination to see them, and then you just connected the dots.

So they connected the dots, inhabiting two worlds together – the day and the night, the sky and the earth, the modern and the ancient, the male and the female, the French and the Moroccan. This was the gift he'd given his only daughter, or the gift she'd given him.

○

JACQUES LEMAIGRE-DUBREUIL AND JEAN RIGAUD ARRESTED IN PARIS

Lemaigre-Dubreuil, former president of the Taxpayers' Federation, and Jean Rigaud, former director of the newspaper *Le Jour* and former commissioner of Admiral Darlan's imperial committee, were arrested in Paris. They will be prosecuted for violating state security.[10]

---

10   *Le Monde* – 1/5/1945

5

Too many months had passed, but that wasn't what was irritating Mag. The day had passed, and he hadn't said what he'd needed to say.

The finger had healed. The injury had taken him off the job for several weeks, but now most days he hardly noticed it. Meanwhile Mussolini's army had collapsed, and the Allies controlled much of Italy. The real action had moved to Europe, so for months he'd been nothing but a shopkeeper, hustling small profits, whiskey, sometimes even cigarettes. Aziza still kept the profits for him, safe from blackmailers and thieves, but there wasn't much chance of significantly adding to those savings anymore. Bones was flying elsewhere, and Mag had risked too much approaching other pilots. They were heroes, he was nothing. Most of the Navy fliers were working out of Port Lyautey now anyway. Sure, there had been many afternoons in Cam's bedroom, or down on the beach, but a girl like her needed more, and he hated that he had nothing more to give her. To make any money now, you needed to be in Europe. He had contacts there, formerly part of the Casablanca machine, who could get him up and running. So that was something. Something more than fuggin Stec, who was still milking the tit of the U.S. Army. He had given Mag one last option: bring him the girl.

That part he couldn't tell her. He feared she would give herself just to keep him in Casablanca. Either way, she would have to think about it, and he couldn't accept that question in her mind. Better to say goodbye. At least the break would be clean. Then he would go off to

Europe with nine good fingers to fight in the trenches of a dying war. "You'll learn to shoot with your left hand," Stec had said, and maybe he would.

So he was leaving. That was what he'd been meaning to say. But there she was on the rooftop, bundled in a sweater and coat, cooing through the cage at her pigeons, seeming so defenseless against the night. She spoke to the birds, but to him she hadn't spoken in hours.

Maman had invited him for tea. She always wanted to talk about the finger, which he claimed to have lost in an accident. "He was so brave," Camille had said, sitting with perfect posture at the edge of her chair, openly smiling at him now even in front of her mother. They were not a secret, and for Mag this was a strange feeling. He'd always hid the few women he'd known.

Drinking fuggin tea with your left hand was a pain in the ass, and he cursed under his breath, looking down at his trembling cup. Camille had put on a record of this French guitarist called Django Reinhardt who wasn't too bad. Mag had heard it several times before, because apparently this guy had lost some fingers. According to Cam, he was a "true artist", and when she was finally ready to present her onstage gypsy jazz act, it would be at least partially inspired by him.

"This that Django Reinhardt?" Mag muttered. Hell, it took so little to make her happy. "*Oui!*" she cried. "He lost two fingers in a fire, but he is still the greatest guitar player in the world. My performance –"

"He did not *lose* them, *cherie*," Maman interrupted, glancing disapprovingly at Mag. "They were merely *paralyzed*." Camille shook her curls, glowering into her cup while Mag struggled to get his own up to his mouth.

Index fingers didn't matter much, except when it came to triggers and tea.

Finally they'd gone up to the roof to escape her mother. Camille had pretended she wanted to show him the pigeons, but of course the birds were mostly sleeping and wouldn't fly at night. She'd been silent since Django Reinhardt. Mag stood at the edge of the roof looking out at the city, the lights of the port and Frenchtown, and the extinguished zone of the native medina, thousands of dramas there silently screaming in the darkness. The French had made it like a prison again, shutting the gates at night, and as well as Mag now knew Casablanca, he had still never set foot within the medina's walls. It was the place you never went, the place he'd never know.

Now Camille was saying something in the girlish voice she used whenever she was nervous. "The female usually lays two eggs. They hatch in about twenty days." There were tears in her eyes, and she couldn't look at him. "About four months after hatching, the baby birds are ready to fly."

Mag grunted and took a few steps towards her. "My hair is a mess today," she said off to the stars, and he wished he could wrap his arms around her and both disappear.

That afternoon he'd driven her down to Habbous, to Aziza's shop to buy her something nice. The shop wasn't more than a mile away, but she'd never been so far from home, and as they drove she'd watched with growing alarm as the neighborhoods got filthy. He had never really showed her his world before, except maybe that awful day at the fight.

They banged into the shop with a jingle of bells, and

he spoke some rough Moroccan to Aziza, who sat on a stool behind her counter. Money had made her more alluring, maybe, but she was bigger than ever. Although apparently Moroccan men liked that kind of thing. At least that's what Ahmed said. Hear him talk about Aziza, she was a queen. Of course Ahmed didn't have a chance. She might be a queen, but he was still a fuggin lunatic.

Camille seemed unimpressed by the display of kaftans and underwear, humming lightly to herself, avoiding contact. But there were dresses too, French dresses of the finest quality, Mag knew. He insisted she try on a few, as many as she liked, and after nodding at Aziza, he left the ladies to go outside for a smoke.

Sometimes the finger throbbed. He'd learned to hold the cigarette between his second and third fingers, like some French movie star. In Philly, he would be beaten to a pulp for that. But Philly no longer had any part in his plans. He would get something set up in France and return here once the war was done. Stubbing out the cigarette, he went back into the shop.

With the bells, the women awkwardly emerged from the back. Camille wouldn't look at him and clearly wanted to leave. "You find something you like?"

"The ones I liked didn't fit. My hips are wide, and I have such short legs."

"Aziza can do something about that."

"She likes a pretty kaftan," Aziza said directly to Mag, as if Camille was no longer cowering in the corner wrapping her arms around her chest.

"So we take the kaftan," Mag replied, beginning to get annoyed with the whole excursion, but forcing a crooked smile at Camille as he pulled out a five-thousand-franc bill. Aziza looked at it for a long moment, or maybe at him, before saying she'd have to find change in the back office. Cocking her head, she motioned for him to follow. "Come, I wrap this pretty kaftan."

So Mag stepped around the counter and followed her to the office, which he'd visited at least a dozen times. Aziza shut the door behind them. "I don't need your money," she snorted. "But we need to talk."

"Yeah, I know it's been quiet, but my pilots let me down. I thought I had something big, but the bastards didn't give me a choice. Don't tell Camille, but I'm leaving tomorrow for France."

Aziza shook her head. Mag knew she was disappointed, but he still needed her help. "I need you to do me a favor. Maybe you could look out for her while I'm gone? I'll be back, but in the meantime. Use the money I set aside."

"She your girlfriend?" Aziza asked, shoving the kaftan into a box.

Mag grunted. "She's a good kid. Bit of a singer and dancer if you ever hear of someone looking. Maybe she could be a star."

"Promise you talk to her," Aziza hissed. "It's important, you idiot."

Mag scowled and took the box from her.

"You hear what I said?"

"I heard you," Mag replied, feeling the weight of the unwanted kaftan.

"Okay, so you talk to her, and then Mag, my American friend, please do not give any more fingers to the Germans."

And now he was on the roof with Camille, scraping

the toe of his boot against a loose flap of tar paper. Already night, and they still hadn't talked. "We need to talk," he finally said, and she looked at him then. "I wanted you to meet Aziza today because.... I've done some business with Aziza, Cam, and I know she's a good woman. She's tough, but she'll help you out. I mean, they're sending me to Europe, Cam. I'll come back, I'm gonna come back. I swear it to ya. It's just that with the Army I don't have a choice anymore. I tried everything. You gotta believe me. We're leaving tomorrow."

He had expected pain, but the wound was immediate. She crumpled to her knees and wept. He was as miserable as she was beautiful. And he had infected her. Tears smudged her eyes as she groaned up at him: "*Why can't you understand?*" Then she struggled to her feet and hobbled off into the building sobbing.

"Cam! Camille!"

All those miserable nights, but he had never hated himself more than this one. I love you. He hadn't been able to say it, and now as he grimaced out at the world, Casablanca was disappearing beneath him, and he loved her, he loved her, and he'd lost her. He'd lost her without understanding her secret. And now window by window the lights were going out as he stood there watching, until much later he left the roof to descend into this city he'd known, a city that had now almost vanished.

II. PEACE
1948–1952
JOSH SHOEMAKE
F-AIUL
F
THE CASABLANCA QUARTET

THE CASABLANCA QUARTET

II. PEACE

1948–1952

Based on true stories

JOSH SHOEMAKE

Opium Books

WAR

PEACE

**THE ANGLE
OF ATTACK**

1948

Abdelwahed Chaoui

Touria Chaoui

Zina Chaoui

Salah Chaoui

Tony Méléro

Abdelwahed Chaoui

1949

Albert Forestier

Touria Chaoui

Franklin Sydney Felton

Camille Morin

Jacques Lemaigre-Dubreuil

Fadila

Suzanne Benayiche

BLUESHIFT

Touria Chaoui

1951

Tony Méléro

1950

Touria Chaoui

Victor Tessier

Abdelwahed Chaoui

Victor Tessier

Touria Chaoui

Victor Tessier

Suzanne Benayiche

Abdelwahed Chaoui

Victor Tessier

Touria Chaoui

Fadila

Suzanne Benayiche

Touria Chaoui

HANDS

Abdelwahed Chaoui

Tony Méléro

1952

Aziza Benayiche

Touria Chaoui

Hajja Aliya Alaoui

Tommy August

Camille Morin

Lucy August

Victor Tessier

Albert Forestier

Tony Méléro

Albert Forestier

Suzanne Benayiche

Aziza Benayiche

Abdelwahed Chaoui

Suzanne Benayiche

Albert Forestier

Hajja Aliya Alaoui

Touria Chaoui

RESISTANCE

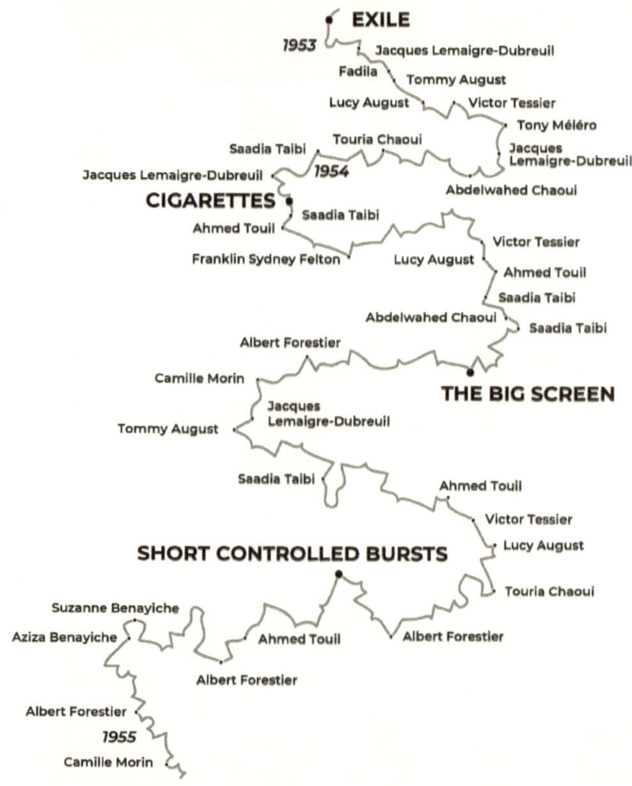

FREEDOM
DJINNS
Lucy August
Tommy August
Victor Tessier
Suzanne Benayiche
Victor Tessier
Touria Chaoui
Hajja Aliya Alaoui
Touria Chaoui
Tony Méléro
Jacques Lemaigre-Dubreuil
INVISIBLE LINES
Touria Chaoui
Aziza Benayiche
Tony Méléro
Saadia Taibi
Hajja Aliya Alaoui
Victor Tessier
Mike "Mag" Magursky
Aziza Benayiche
Ahmed Touil
Touria Chaoui
Mike "Mag" Magursky
Fadila
Tony Méléro
1956
THE BIRDCAGE
Ahmed Touil
Mike "Mag" Magursky
Touria Chaoui
Fadila
Suzanne Benayiche
Tommy August
Aziza Benayiche
Lucy August
Suzanne Benayiche
Tony Méléro
Hajja Aliya Alaoui
Touria Chaoui
Tommy August
INDEPENDENCE DAY
Salah Chaoui
Tony Méléro
Saadia Taibi
Abdelwahed Chaoui
Aziza Benayiche
Fadila
Victor Tessier
Mike "Mag" Magursky

THE ANGLE OF ATTACK
1948–1950

WOMAN STARTS MOROCCO RIOT; 61 LOSE LIVES

SENEGALESE RUN AMOK IN STREETS

CASABLANCA, Morocco – An official announcement said today that 61 persons were killed and 119 were wounded yesterday in a frenzied street battle between Moroccans and black Senegalese riflemen caused by a fight over a woman.

No further incidents were reported after daybreak today, although tension remained high after this latest disturbance in France's troubled overseas lands.

French patrols scoured the countryside for the Senegalese, who fled during the night after firing on a mob of civilians. However, only two Senegalese were missing, either casualties in the fight or fugitives.

One Senegalese Killed

Most of the casualties were Moors, slashed or shot when 50 Senegalese ran amok at the climax of the see-saw battle. Three of the wounded were Frenchmen. The dead included a Senegalese, whose slaying marked the start of the violence, and one of two policemen stabbed when they tried to intervene.

Accounts pieced together today gave this version of the rioting: Two Senegalese soldiers came to blows with a prostitute in the picturesque "reserved quarter" of Douar Ben Msik. A number of Moroccans came to the woman's defense, and the colonial rifleman was killed. The other was chased back to his barracks by a growing crowd of Moors.

Soldiers Seize Rifles

The Senegalese garrison rushed out with knives and bayonets, but were driven back into their camp. They made one more unsuccessful attack and then broke into their magazine room and seized rifles and submachine guns.

This time they came out shooting wildly. French army and police forces succeeded in capturing a few, but most of them temporarily escaped. The Negro troops rallied after dark in a small woods at the outskirts of the city, firing from the cover of trees at all comers. Then they fled into the countryside.

[In Paris, a spokesman for the Moroccan affairs section of the foreign ministry said the outbreak was "a purely local soldier brawl, without political causes or possible consequences." He said it would "certainly not" be necessary to withdraw Senegalese troops now garrisoning Casablanca and other Moroccan towns. The Senegalese are recruited in French West Africa.][11]

○

---

11   *Chicago Tribune* – 04/08/1947

Beyond the apartment door a telephone rang. Abdelwahed was already awake, but now he lifted himself from bed. Zina still slept, and the children's room was silent. The family had recently moved to Casablanca after his appointment as director of a small publicity company, l'Agence Marocaine de Communication. With the post had come a cramped apartment connected to the office at 50 Avenue Poeymirau, a block west of the Stade Philippe. The rooms smelled of dusty agency archives of stacked ledgers and telephone books. Facing two long days, Abdelwahed ignored the phone and stepped into the bathroom.

On the eve of Aid el Kebir, October 13, 1948, he still hadn't bought a sheep to slaughter. In Fez, his uncle had always provided one for the extended family, but alone in Casablanca, the feast was now Abdelwahed's responsibility. But he couldn't worry about sheep that morning. Marcel Cerdan had returned home for a parade to be held the next day in celebration of his welterweight world championship. The date was no accident. With Moroccans off slaughtering sheep, the French would be granted a rare, edited vision of their shining city and its hero, unsullied by its natives. Except for useful natives like Abdelwahed, who had been hired to organize logistics at the stadium, where after the parade Resident General Juin would present a medal to Cerdan. In the bathroom mirror Abdelwahed noticed two creases between his eyebrows. Bringing his face up close to the glass, he smoothed the creases with a well-manicured finger.

Casablanca had become a divided, dangerous place. Moroccans were increasingly targeted by their French protectors. During the previous year's Dakkat Saligan, Senegalese infantry garrisoned south of Bousbir had moved through the slums exterminating one hundred eighty innocent civilians. To the international press the French authorities had repeated a ludicrous story about a Moroccan prostitute. The truth was that the Sultan had been traveling to Tangier's International Zone, where France had no power to censor a planned speech he had announced. The massacre had been meant to stall him in Rabat, but the Sultan had resolutely proceeded north, where for the first time since the dawn of the protectorate, he had publicly demanded independence. Abdelwahed strongly supported the Sultan, but he wondered whether it had been irresponsible to move his family to the city that had become the eye of the storm. Touria was now twelve, and in Moroccan schools girls were not permitted to study any further. Her curiosity was still ferocious, however, and she could not be kept at home with nothing to occupy her mind but books and household chores. She had to be permitted to live with the freedom that Abdelwahed had always insisted upon for himself. Otherwise none of this, nothing the Sultan had said, could possibly matter.

One Sunday evening as the family had strolled along Boulevard de la Gare, they had run into an old Fez acquaintance of Abdelwahed's, Zaïm. Before the war they had spent many hours together discussing nationalist ideas. Now as they embraced and exchanged greetings, Abdelwahed was astonished by how his friend had aged. Deep lines ran from his nose to the corners of his mouth, and wrinkles encased his eyes. "You look extremely well," Zaïm had said. "Making money, *le Français*? Do you even remember the conversations we once had?"

"Every word," Abdelwahed had replied. "And those principles are as important to me now as they were then. The future we planned is one I want for my family."

Zaïm had nodded slowly, looking at Zina, Salah, and Touria, where his eyes stopped. "I remember when she was a baby. You brought her around to the café. Now she's all grown up." Zina's face had fallen, and it was later that evening that they decided to send Touria to Tunis for a while to study stenography. She would stay with friends of Abdelwahed's from his touring days. After that, they would see.

Because once a girl approached puberty, a single remark from a man was all it took to split her life in two, between the time she'd been at liberty to roam the streets, and the time she'd been forced to hide herself indoors in preparation for her final solution, marriage.

○

"They're taking over the city. Have you been out to Carrières Centrales and seen the slums? A hundred thousand of them at least. We should have let those Senegalese monkeys finish the job."

Tony Méléro, Congos, and the Gypsy, three local cops, were drinking coffee at the counter of the Bar de la Gironde. The bar's manager, François Avival, a muscular former boxer with a blunt, shaved head and piercing blue eyes, was a friend of theirs, and they had spent countless hours together at that counter discussing current events. Avival, several years older, liked to think of himself as politically enlightened, and the crew mostly deferred to his opinions. That morning he wore a t-shirt, tight on his biceps and chest. Behind him on the wall hung old newspaper clippings from his amateur fights, photographs of him ducking and jabbing, several medals, and an old pair of boxing gloves. With a practiced wave of his powerful arm, he wiped down the counter while pouring himself a glass of pastis. "I tell you, I'm sick of seeing our city destroyed by these Paris politicians. It's time we took care of our own down here."

The three cops nodded. Out the plate glass windows, traffic moved around Rond-Point de la Gironde, more than usual today. None of the cops was in uniform, having managed to finagle a day off to attend the parade.

Tony folded his newspaper and set it down on the counter. His eyes were drawn again to the elegant Frenchman who sat eating breakfast at a table near the entrance. The man wore a blue silk tie and a pristine white shirt with gleaming gold cufflinks. Gold cufflinks, Tony realized, were what he'd been missing. That was class. He watched as the man spotted an acquaintance across the room and nodded. Another glance from the man to Avival was sufficient to send a drink the acquaintance's way. Then several minutes later, a soft-boiled egg with toast emerged from the kitchen. Avival himself carried it over and set it on the table in front of the man, who murmured something and sat back to watch as Avival clumsily cut the top off the egg. The man then indicated a piece of underbrowned toast, which Avival returned to the kitchen. All total class.

Tony was nineteen and had met Congos and the

Gypsy five years earlier, when his family had moved from Mogador, several hours down the coast, to the working class neighborhood of Derb Talian. As the new boy at school, Tony had been a target, but he had defended himself with a viciousness noted by Congos and the Gypsy, who had previously been the boys you especially didn't want to fight. Together they had roamed the streets, hanging out in the back of the Gypsy's mother's shop, where she groomed dogs, mostly for Jews from the nearby mellah. The floor of the shop was dusted with the short hairs of spaniels and terriers. The hairs floated up, stuck to your clothes, and occasionally found their way into the cups of Jerez brandy the boys poured from the Gypsy's mother's stash. She drank steadily throughout the day, singing flamenco with terrified canines gripped between her thighs.

After high school, Tony had boxed a bit himself, even considering going pro at one point, as Avival had done for a few fights. He had needed a job, however, and his friends were already cops, so they had gotten him recruited. Recently he had returned from three months of police school in Ifrane and was now mostly doing dull traffic beats. You didn't have to be a genius to realize that this wouldn't lead to gold cufflinks.

○

At a table near the bar, Albert Forestier sat drinking his coffee and scribbling in a notebook. Occasionally he glanced over at Avival, who had never paid him any

193

attention, although Albert could recite the details of the man's every fight, round by round, and blushed just ordering a coffee from him. Stuttered, too.

Albert Forestier often had nightmares about the letter C. C-c-c-café. His father, with whom he still lived, had always reassured him that he would outgrow the affliction, and Albert still desperately hoped this was true. His mother, however, had insisted he simply didn't practice enough and had mercilessly drilled him on proper enunciation, at least until she'd gotten bored with it, and then he'd drilled himself for hours alone in his room, stuttering through furiously clenched teeth. But then his mother had run off, it had been several years, and none of it mattered as long as he didn't have to speak, because this was the most exciting day of his life, at least since the day he'd seen Cerdan knock out an American soldier at the Stade Philippe.

Albert was eighteen, and for years he had wanted to be a boxer, but despite the hours he had spent savagely sparring in his striped bathrobe before his bedroom mirror, despite pushups to the point of nausea, his body still rejected muscle, and he was still as spindly as he had been before the sparring and the pushups and the nausea. His imagination, however, was heavyweight, and over time he had learned to call as expertly as any ringside announcer the imaginary fights he inevitably won. In his mind he never stuttered. So one day, confident in this skill, he had walked into the offices of *Maroc-Presse* and had managed to convince Mazzella, the editor, to let him try his hand as a cub reporter at local boxing matches. He knew nothing about the newspaper – whether it was to the right, like *La Vigie*, which La Gironde crew read daily, or to the left, whatever that meant. He had simply passed the offices of *Maroc-Presse* for years on his way home from school.

The first story he filed had covered Avival's last fight one Saturday night at a local boxing club. Mazzella had rejected it. Avival had never been a true contender. But Forestier had continued to write, attending practically every fight in the city, pitching amateur backroom clenches as battles between gladiators, always tossing in a few pugilistic flourishes initially invented for his own fights in the mirror. *Forestier strode like a colossus into the ring.* And today, finally – today of all days – the lead sports reporter had been knocked out by a case of the gout, and Albert Forestier would be covering the parade given in honor of his hero, Marcel Cerdan.

On September 21, in Jersey City, New Jersey, the United States of America, the great man, the colossus, had knocked out middleweight champion Tony Zale in the twelfth round to become champion of the world. Would he appear that day with Edith Piaf, the Little Sparrow? Their affair was the talk of Paris. Probably not, Forestier guessed. Cerdan still had a wife and two children, and Casablanca was his family home. You wanted to keep the wife and mistress separate. That was basic knowledge. *This morning,* he scribbled, *the excitement was visceral in the storied cafés of this throbbing metropolis. Marcel Cerdan had returned like a conquering hero to the site of the first of his many victories, his own birth.* On several occasions Mazzella had suggested that beyond the smattering of insignificant spelling errors, the young reporter might have a tendency to overwrite, but a writer's genius was his style, Albert felt. His bulging eyes, further accentuated by thick spectacles, shone down at his notebook. He was so ready.

But should he order another coffee? A pastis to calm the nerves? Should he lift his arm? Or was it better to go over to the bar and order there, saving Avival the trip? On second thought he wasn't even sure he wanted coffee or pastis. He flipped back through the notes he'd made since dawn. Already two little stars in the margins, he saw with some embarrassment, although detailed recordkeeping was important, both for a reporter and for a man who valued physical fitness. Of course a star signified one session of masturbation pursued to its natural completion.

○

The Moroccan doorman at the Don Quichotte looked Zina over before directing her to the side entrance. Then he noticed Abdelwahed in the crowd and bent to kiss his hand. The children observed this exchange, smiling when it was their turn to be introduced. Inside, the maître d'hôtel led them past the bar and down a curving staircase into the lounge, where a pianist played at the back of a low stage crowded by tables. Only Frenchmen occupied the tables, and Zina, her arm in her husband's, looked up at him with glittering eyes. One table by the stage had been reserved for Monsieur Chaoui.

He loved her. She had no formal education and did not speak a word of French, but she was beautiful, especially so tonight in the pink jacket and skirt he had finally bought at Aziza's, even without the discount she had promised. He could afford it, at least for now. Today had been a good day. Thousands had crowded the streets for a glimpse of the world champion, and the stadium presentation had gone off without a hitch. And now his reward, showing off his family in this place where he, a Moroccan, was respected. Touria and Salah would learn that every door was open to them.

He ordered a beer for himself and Coca-Colas for Zina and the children. A business associate, a swarthy Frenchman who rented limousines, came over to congratulate him on the day's success and obsequiously kissed Zina's hand. Everyone observed. Even the waiters here were French, and of course the girls were too, the most beautiful in the city. Abdelwahed had seen the show at least a dozen times, and he knew Zina would be amused by the sight of them dancing in mere sequins. When the first line came out kicking, she turned to him with mock disapproval, clicking her tongue, but her eyes shone with pleasure, and Abdelwahed eased back into his seat to enjoy the show. The girls danced so close to their table that they could have reached out and touched their bare thighs.

All but one of the dancers could have performed in the finest Parisian music hall. That one, however, moved like a marionette whose strings had been tangled. Perhaps she was an understudy asked to replace a regular wanted elsewhere that busy night. Second from the end, she was several years older than the others, at least twenty-five, and her costume fitted her poorly. The top was too large and kept wanting to slide off. Her arms floated in the air as if she didn't know what else to do with them, but was now too terrified to attempt doing something else. A mole dotted her cheek, and her eyes were moist and desperate.

Did Abdelwahed recognize her? Recently he had helped produce a French film in the desert, *La Septième Porte*, in which he had also arranged a significant role for little Touria, who had shone. Naturally he had put Aziza in charge of costumes, and with her she had brought the French girl, Camille, who was pretty and could supposedly sing or dance – perhaps she could play a harem girl – but on set she had been useless, and off set she had been miserable, so they had been obliged to send her home on a desert bus.

Yes, it was the same girl. She would never be a dancer, and watching her Abdelwahed wondered whether his performance in this place was equally unconvincing.

2

○

Seventeen stories below, sheep grazed in an undeveloped lot. The balcony railing had not yet been poured, and Franklin Felton, breathing heavily, hung back from the edge. With the two elevator shafts still empty, they had taken the stairs up to the unfinished penthouse apartment, which Jacques Lemaigre-Dubreuil had bought in what would be the tallest building in Africa. No man on the continent would sleep further from the earth than Crusoe. Now he gazed out across the city with his jaw set and his eyes inscrutable, breathing as easily as he had on the ground. The old goat had probably been up and down those steps a hundred times to survey his dominion. "So the Liberty Building," Franklin said. "Odd choice of name given current events, don't you think?"

Jacques shot him a dark look. "As you know perfectly

well, below us is the Place de la Révolution Française, so I would imagine the name is meant to signify liberty from dictatorship, from monarchy. Surely as an American you appreciate how France has always fought to defend that."

"Or perhaps the developer meant to evoke the brazen liberty of altitude. Heaven can't be far, right?" Sweat trickled down Franklin's back. He reached around to pinch his shirt away from his body.

"You have the soul of a poet, Franklin."

Poet stung. He hadn't written anything in months. "Of course we all know the result of the Tower of Babel."

"Which is why this country is fortunate to have men like us who speak the same language and will guide it into the future."

Franklin nodded glumly. Lemaigre-Dubreuil would talk for hours to get the last word. If he couldn't win an argument, he outlasted it. For him ideas were like physical things to be wrestled to the ground. Impatient now, Franklin edged out closer towards the void and forced himself to look down. Discarded nails and cigarette packets littered the cement underfoot. The bells around the necks of the distant sheep necks faintly clanged. Several dozen of them picked over isolated patches of grass as a shepherd whistled to stragglers. Further out, a haze enveloped the white city, punctured by the palms lining the Boulevard de Londres all the way up to Parc Murdoch, and the Clinique Mers Sultan, to which he hadn't returned in years. The palms were Washingtonias, native to America, and had recently been planted. He thought of mentioning the symbolism of their provenance, but that would just set Jacques off again.

Directly below was the top of Lemaigre-Dubreuil's green Studebaker. His driver, Ahmed, and the handsome young man he called his assistant, Simon Castet, were leaning against the hood smoking cigarettes. All Franklin knew about Castet was that he had modeled for Dior in Paris, and that he had disliked Franklin, probably because he had been ordered to stay with the car so that Jacques could speak in private to his American friend. The assistant had pouted like a spoiled child.

Franklin assumed that Jacques wanted to discuss the new American radar station southwest at Saddle Rock, to which he had been transferred on detachment from the consulate. He was aware that Lemaigre-Dubreuil had just met with the new Consul-General to address what he viewed as increasing American interference in French territory, and that the two men hadn't hit it off. Not surprising considering it was Crusoe. Perhaps Jacques's assumption was that Franklin would be an easier conversation. So Franklin vowed again to say nothing.

○

After months in a French prison, Jacques had been acquitted of all charges, and the confiscated Casablanca property of Lesieur Oils had been returned to him by order of the Minister of Finance. The ordeal had left him feeling betrayed by many of his old friends at the Quai d'Orsay, but while they had continued to chase their tails in internecine circles, he was already refortifying his power base in the protectorate. Casablanca, the city he loved more than any other, had always been his financial center, but recently he had bought a sprawling villa on the Bouregreg River to be closer to the political capital in Rabat. And now he was writing editorials again for Le Monde, a return to his Paris years, when he had owned a conservative paper there and had warned its readers against the imminent threats to France and its noble history, warnings that had been insufficiently heeded, leading to the shameful capitulation of 1940. Perhaps now the nation was ready to listen to Jacques Lemaigre-Dubreuil.

The arrival of the Americans had complicated the game. Several of his sources even indicated that American arms were being directed to the Moroccan resistance. Perhaps more alarming, the appearance of American bases, including the new radar station and the sprawling air force base under construction to the south at Nouasseur, had given the Sultan a powerful counterbalance to French rule. The Americans were almost universally admired by the locals, despite their unadmirable intentions, which were perfectly obvious to Lemaigre-Dubreuil. Morocco was a lucrative market in a strategic location. And while the United States lectured from a distance, counting its money, France had taken pains to implement a new brand of colonialism based on real cooperation and development. Theirs was a more human protectorate that ruled on behalf of Moroccans, since as a feudal people the natives were still incapable of ruling themselves. Cynical Franklin would disagree, but hopefully Jacques could at least convince him that arming the resistants would be a catastrophic mistake.

"I wanted to speak with you in private, Franklin, firstly because you are a friend, and I trust your counsel, but secondly because I feel your country is leading Morocco down a dangerous path."

○

Franklin smiled. The greatest advantage an American had over Frenchmen was that they invariably underrated one's intelligence. All their revolutions had done nothing to shake their slavish devotion to class. The world's biggest dolt was a genius in Paris if he spoke with a British accent, but speak like an American, and they assumed you lacked schooling, finesse, and several other qualities that only the French could perceive. A lecture on Moroccans from Lemaigre-Dubreuil, who did not even speak proper Arabic – as Franklin did – and did not live among the locals, sharing their customs – as Franklin had for several years – was especially rich. "Oh, Jacques," he said. "I don't know anything about that big political stuff. I'm just a vice-consul."

The Frenchman chuckled. "My dear vice-consul, there are no secrets in Morocco."

"You've got a few," Franklin replied, spittle at the corners of his smile.

"Perhaps," said Jacques. "Secrets are like capital, and I am a businessman. It's always wise to have more in the bank than the competition."

Franklin looked at him crookedly. How transparent was he really to Jacques? Surely the Frenchman had been told that Franklin was CIA, and conceivably he knew about the kif. Could he know about the women? The dreams he had of purity, of his body splayed out in a desert until it was eaten away by the sun and his bones were made white? His creeping sense of failure, which was the biggest secret of all? One big secret like that could make even drinking a glass of orange juice feel like a crime. "I do know," Franklin said stiffly, "that Washington is growing irritated with French meddling in the construction of the bases. We're allies, Jacques. What concern is this of yours anyway?"

"My concern is for the Morocco I love, and the leaders of Istiqlal, with whom your government has maintained ties, are nothing more than unpolished intellectuals harboring some vague ideas about Western democracy and the French Revolution. If you assent to the wishes of their make-believe independence party, this country will again devolve into tribalism and chaos. You cannot continue encouraging their grasping little egos."

"You know very well that we have publicly supported a maintenance of French rule, Jacques, and that our bases here in no way contradict that policy. They target a common enemy, the Soviet Union. They have the atomic bomb. They have taken over Eastern Europe. These bases put Moscow within striking distance of our bombers."

"Will there be bombs here?"

"Come on. I don't know anything about that. I just sit at a desk scanning the skies for radio waves."

"The PCM is plotting now," Jacques said, putting a hand on Franklin's shoulder. "And the communists are even worse than Istiqlal. I have been told that they are receiving aid from the Soviets. Imagine if they got a real foothold here."

"We can't let that happen," Franklin said earnestly, squinting out across the city. Jacques was right, after all, at least about this, and perhaps he would provide information on who the French were watching in the communist underground.

"You're friendly with that Zubov over at the Soviet consulate, aren't you?"

"I wouldn't call him a friend," Franklin replied, barely parting his lips. "He's not to be trusted, and I think he could be a very dangerous man. If we hear anything interesting about him or the Soviets, I will certainly let you know. We need to stand together on this."

Jacques smiled. "It's always such a pleasure to see you, Franklin."

Later that night in his cramped Habbous apartment, with the cacophony of his native neighbors pounding through the walls, Franklin would eat the lamb tagine prepared by his maid and think with astonishment how he had irrevocably become a vice-consul, a diplomat. This was who he was. Previously it had been a game, a part he played for his own amusement as a prelude to poetry and adventure, but now this was actually his life. He was the only person he hadn't meant to become, and the thought filled him with rage. So he lit another pipe.

○

AIR BASES CREATE CASABLANCA BOOM

SKYROCKETING PRICES AND LACK OF LIVING QUARTERS FOLLOW VAST NEW CONSTRUCTION

By B. K. Thorne

CASABLANCA, French Morocco – This storied city, where residents and visitors alike supposedly spend leisurely hours swimming, dancing in the moonlight and sipping champagne at 50 cents a magnum, is a boisterous boom town where the work-week averages sixty to seventy hours and the francs and dollars exchange hands in large quantities.

Casablanca's hundreds of cafés and restaurants are crowded during all the long hours they are open, and a stranger, no matter what he is willing to pay, finds it almost impossible to get a hotel room.

Casablanca's boom began in the spring when it was announced that the United States Air Force was returning to French Morocco and would build new strategic air bases here in addition to operating, temporarily at least, out of Cazès, the city's commercial airport....

What the boom has done to Casablanca is to put its price levels on a par with New York....

Casablanca has a festive air day in and day out. The city's polyglot population fills the streets and cafés until early morning, and everyone seems to have his pockets and purses full of francs. The fakirs

beg more out of habit than anything else and with
little spirit....[12]

---

12   *The New York Times* – 10/23/1951

3

Fadila had inhabited her Bousbir room for over six years, working four to five daily *passes* at one hundred francs apiece and an equal number of weekly *couchers* at four hundred a night. Sometimes she got a twenty-five or thirty-franc tip, but more expensive gifts went to Jean Bart, whose first day loan Fadila still hadn't managed to pay back.

Recently the *couchers* had gotten rarer. Fadila wasn't the type men chose for long nights of affection, especially now that her hair was cut short with a razor, baring the back of her neck, and tattoos covered much of her flesh. The odd ones, the freaks and the perverts, were who she tended to attract, and although they rarely tipped, she had decided that maybe the freaks and perverts were the best. They did not try for love. You could lift your skirt and concentrate on not moving even the tiniest muscle in your face. Stone lips and cheeks and nostrils.

Once or twice in all those thousands of *passes*, maybe for a moment or two, she had glimpsed a flicker of pleasure, but nothing like the pleasure at the end of her pipe. She smoked the contraband kif smuggled down from the Rif by traffickers, not the *kif jiyyed* sold by the state tobacco company, the Régie des Tabacs, in six-gram packets mixed with too much tobacco. She smoked from her clay sebsi with the long walnut stem. Smoke crawled over her arms and legs, retracing the paths she drew across her body, and tracing new paths. To smoke she often skipped the afternoon tagine, their one meal of the day, usually no more than tomatoes, onions, olives, and maybe a sheep's foot. Also she drank beer whenever possible, although not as much as Zohra the Jewess, who could pour a case of twenty bottles down her throat in an hour.

Other than kif, alcohol, and the debt she paid Jean Bart, Fadila's main expense was the notebook she bought in town weekly when the girls were bussed to the clinic to stamp their health certificates. Every week she filled another notebook with drawings of angels – fanged angels, planet angels, angels with green hips. The notebooks she kept hidden beneath her mattress. One time she had shown a few pages to the young French pilot, and then he had brought fresh notebooks when he visited, but he hadn't visited in years. Maybe he had gone to the war and died, or probably he had found other women. So for years of smoking and drawing, smoking and drawing, she had shown almost no one her secret until the drawings had moved off the page and across her body, and tracing the drawings on herself, she had made tattoos of them, permanent angels, painstakingly pricking a needle along the lines after covering the area with crushed bluing. You blotted away the blood with cotton and then rubbed the skin with the inside of the pod of a fresh fava bean. Then after your skin healed, you had a blue tattoo.

People thought Fadila was crazy with her tattoos, but she knew they were beautiful. Recently an older Moroccan named Khalil who occasionally visited had seen the two new upside-down angels on her thighs, their wings extended towards her sex. He went pale and wanted to know what it meant. She swatted away the conversation like flies. To draw the human form was a sin, Khalil insisted. Angels must be even worse.

Was she prepared for hell? Fadila snorted. He removed his pants and told her to lie facedown on the bed so he could see her pretty unblemished buttocks as he took her from behind. Then after he left, she ripped out her best drawings from the notebook and hung them on the wall. Finned angels, twin angels, eyeless angels watched over her from the wall, and she longed for Khalil's return. With her needle she would make him look.

Now the holy month of Ramadan had arrived, and from dusk to dawn even Fadila received more *passes* than she could handle. She swabbed herself out, then another man came. That afternoon as she woke, shouts erupted down in the street, and she went to her window. Especially during Ramadan, when people mostly refrained from daytime cigarettes and alcohol, fights broke out between women over men. They pulled hair, scratched eyes, ripped earrings through lobes, and sometimes even stabbed one another with iron keys they carried on chains around their waists. The police would appear and lead the guilty to the post at the entrance.

Fadila had never been locked up. She feared the men in uniforms and had stopped going into the city on her monthly day's leave. Everything out there she could already imagine, and policemen stalked her on the sidewalks, wanting her body for things she had done. The Jewesses left Bousbir as often as they pleased, uncontrolled by the *patronnes*, but that was because they gave free *passes* to powerful policeman, so the *patronnes* and other policeman left them alone. On Saturdays the Jewesses were also allowed to receive family who brought the dafina from the *Mellah*. More than almost any other smell, Fadila now hated the smell of the *dafina*.

Downstairs Deputy Chief Inspector Marchetti had broken up the fight. He appeared every week to see Zubida, the naked dancer who lowered her snatch onto glass bottles. Marchetti put coins on the mouths of the bottles, and Zubida would gyrate back up from them with the coins inside her like a change purse. Zubida could also smoke a cigarette between her legs, or sometimes a cigar. She burned off her pubic hair with calcium carbide like most of the other women, but Fadila didn't do that, which was fine because at Bousbir bare snatches were going out of fashion in favor of the modern untended European style. Not that Fadila cared. Legs nobody ever shaved.

A knock sounded at the door. Fadila moved from the window and belted her soiled kaftan. European or Jew? Moroccans rarely came before sunset during the holy month. "*Naam?*" The door opened, and Zohra and Suzanne, the new Jewess, walked in. They also worked for Jean Bart but lived in the next house. Neither had ever been in Fadila's room. In Bousbir, Muslims and Jews mostly kept apart. The Jews had better jewelry and clothes and could earn twice as much as a Muslim. They attracted more European clients and were willing to go with Americans, who also tipped more. Once Fadila had gone with an American, but she didn't anymore, because they were circumcised like the Jews, so you never knew. Also there was something hideous about a white man with a penis like that. Moslems were different. They cut it off when boys were ten, and also it was religion, but the Americans and Jews did it to babies.

Zohra and Suzanne glanced around the spare room. Fadila had changed nothing since her arrival, except for the drawings. Zohra huffed down onto the bed, which groaned under her enormous weight. She carried a thousand bottles of beer inside. Suzanne stood beside the bed nervously chewing gum, which also marked her as a Jewess, because they got it from the Americans. Her eyes were pulled to the angels, which she studied for so long that Fadila assumed she liked them, but then Suzanne shook her head and snickered.

Suzanne had a large, firm body, a chubby face, and a broad ass, but unlike most of the other Jewesses, crinkled hair and dark skin. After a month at Bousbir, already on the bus into town she had turned up her flat nose at Fadila. Dark like that, she would have never dared it if she hadn't also been a Jewess. Fadila had wanted to scratch her eyes out, but they all protected one another, and she was alone. Although here they were in her room. She preferred to be alone.

Zohra sighed and pulled a pack of Casa-Sports from between her breasts, lit one and jammed it between two racks of gold teeth. Suzanne was still standing, like a sack of flour that Zohra had set down. Zohra nodded the cigarette at the girl, saying out the corner of her mouth, "Idiot wants a tattoo."

Occasionally Fadila tattooed other girls at ten francs per needle prick. A simple one might take ten pricks, but others could have dozens, and her own had required many hundreds, if not thousands. Her tattoos were special, but many women had basic ones like the vertical line between the lips and the chin, the *siyyala*, or a spot on the cheek, the "fly", and sometimes a "fly" between the eyes, or a ring around a finger, a bracelet around the wrist, the *warda*, or rose. Belly tattoos were also common, especially right above the sex, chains to trap a man, or triangles to ward off the evil eye. Messages too, warnings and reminders, usually in French. Across the chest of a Berber from Beni Mellal, she had tattooed:

PAS DE CANFIANCE
POUR LES HOMMES
DE TELEMSSANE

Don't trost men from Telemssane.

Or on the arm of another:

PATCHANCE
MAROC

Batluck Morocco.

"What do you want?" Fadila asked. Suzanne was too shy to speak. From the bed Zohra clucked and held out a scrap of paper that read *VIVE LAMOR.* "What does it say?" Fadila asked.

"*Vive l'amour,*" Suzanne murmured, and pulled her kaftan off her shoulder, exposing one large breast.

○

○

In late May, sixteen-year-old Suzanne Benayiche had gone to the municipal swimming pool with a girlfriend from the neighborhood. Sitting on the concrete platform at the south end of the pool, they had kicked their feet in the water, gasping at the cold drops that spattered their legs and arms. The sun was hot, but not the water, pumped in daily from the ocean. The salt flavored your lips. Suzanne looked out across hundreds of bobbing heads towards the opposite end of the pool. She couldn't even see that far. They said it was the biggest swimming pool in the world.

Her mother had always forbidden her to come to the *piscine*, but at that point Suzanne hadn't been home to her mother in two days. With the money she had stolen from the register on her last visit to the shop, she and Meriem had bought bathing suits, chocolate bars, and cigarettes. Some boys had treated them to sandwiches for lunch. Meriem had promised it would be easy.

Now a skinny boy in oversized trunks rocketed out of the mouth of the spiral slide, resurfacing nearby with a grin for the girls. "I think he likes you," Meriem said. Suzanne splashed her with a sweeping kick, and Meriem squealed. Anyway, she didn't believe it. Boys always made fun of her dark skin, which she hated. Monkey, they called her. Once she had tried to scratch it off with her fingernails, but it hadn't faded, only bled. Her mother was to blame, her pale mother, making a baby with a black man. Suzanne's father was not something they had ever discussed, but he wouldn't be coming back, and Suzanne wore the shame. For that she would never forgive her mother Aziza.

Maybe Meriem was right. The boy kept looking. All day the boys had been looking. Her new breasts and hips, which had come quicker to her than to other girls, had made her feel misshapen and unbalanced, but today the boys had been buying her Coca-Colas. Three handsome Marrakshis in their twenties had invited them for a stroll on the rocks at Sidi Belyout, but Meriem had waved them off, murmuring afterwards, "Those Marrakshis have no money."

They strolled for a while, boys calling out to them, back-flipping off concrete ledges. Suzanne studied Meriem out of the corner of her eye. Her arms floated out by her sides, and her feet walked a straight line so that her hips wiggled. Suzanne attempted the same but kept losing her balance, so then she just walked normally and vowed to practice once they got back to Meriem's place, which she shared with her brother. Meriem knew so much. She had nice things and dressed like a lady. They had only been friends for a few months, but already Meriem was more like family than her mother had ever been. She put her mother out of her mind. Suzanne was never going home.

Over by the changing cabins, Meriem recognized someone laid out on a lounge chair in black pants and a black shirt. As they came closer, Suzanne realized it wasn't a man. "*Labas?*" Meriem sat at the woman's feet. Suzanne remained standing, feeling awkward now, naked, without Meriem by her side. The woman was six feet tall, with short hair and a hard face. Like a man she looked Suzanne up and down, then reached to take her hand. "You're beautiful," she said. Suzanne felt her face grow hot again.

"Jean Bart is like a mother to me," Meriem said. "She can take care of you too."

"You are a queen," the strange woman said, "and deserve to be treated like one. So what is your name, my queen?"

○

The girl Suzanne wanted the tattoo across the ribs at the side of her breast. She sat on a stool with her hands clasped atop her head, the rings on her chubby fingers scraping against one another. Fadila worked beside her on her knees, focused on her needle. Zohra had brought them tea. There was always tea. Every woman under Jean Bart needed to sell five trays per week at two hundred francs per tray. Before any talk of prices or sex, you would offer tea, and if you didn't sell your weekly thousand francs, you paid the *patronne* the difference out of your pocket. Any sales over a thousand francs were shared, and Suzanne had developed such a knack for getting men to want tea that she often earned an extra thousand francs per week.

So Suzanne had money. Fadila had seen it. Downstairs was a wooden box divided into compartments. Each woman had a slot in the box, and after a *pass*, she would slip the money through the slot. Then every Monday all the women gathered to open the box, paying Jean Bart her cut for rent, food, and protection, then keeping the rest. Suzanne often had more than ten thousand francs left over. Fadila looked at the girl's smooth, firm breast and its large, dark nipple. A fly landed there, and the girl's arm twitched. "Don't move," Fadila whispered, watching the fly pick up its legs and step across the skin, transparent wings pinned against its furry body. Slight goosebumps appeared on Suzanne's breast. Wisps of smoke trailed up from her Favorite, stuck between full, painted lips. Maybe Fadila should charge her more. The lines were straight, and she had even managed to turn the O of LAMOR into what was becoming a heart beneath the blood pellets.

After the last leg of the R, Fadila rubbed the skin with the bean pod, rose from her knees, and smiled. Nobody in Bousbir could make such a perfect tattoo. Probably nobody else in all of Casablanca. Suzanne stood to show the final result to Zohra, who grunted. Fadila wanted them gone now, with all their fancy jewelry. She wanted to sit by the window alone with her pipe, and so she decided to charge them only the standard rate. Thirty-five pricks of the needle meant three hundred fifty francs.

Zohra chuckled. Her belly shook, and her gold teeth flashed. Lifting her hand, she twisted it beside her ear and snorted. "You're crazy," she said, rising from the bed and nodding at Suzanne. "Give her two hundred. She can be happy with that."

Fadila was stunned. "I told you the price," she said to Suzanne. "You don't like it?" Suzanne reached into her pocket, pulled out a two-hundred-franc note, and held it out with her flat nose in the air.

That's when Fadila exploded. She leapt on Suzanne, spat on her cheek, pinched her exposed nipple between her knuckles. Suzanne screamed and smashed an arm into Fadila's ear, drawing blood. Then Fadila kicked the Jewess in the shin with the hard top of her foot and pulled with all of her weight at a gold ring lodged on the girl's finger. Now Zohra was lumbering across the room, snorting and bellowing, but Fadila kept pulling at that fat finger as tears streamed down her face. She would pull off that finger. With a knife, she would have cut them all off. But finally the ring came free over the knuckle, and shaking with rage Fadila fell back against the wall with the gold clenched in her fist.

Just at that moment Jean Bart barged in. The women froze. Tears sprung to Suzanne's eyes. "Thief! Thief!" Zohra barked, pointing at Fadila, who in one swift motion popped the ring into her mouth and swallowed.

Jean Bart and the Jewesses stared in disbelief. They stared until gunshots outside broke the silence.

○

When Tony Méléro showed up on the scene with Congos and the Gypsy, Deputy Chief Inspector Marchetti was already dead. The bastards hadn't even had the respect to cover the body. Just a bunch of dumb natives standing around looking at a dead French policeman, none of them appearing too upset about it. The killer was probably still among them, and that thought made Tony furious. "Who did this?" he shouted at the onlookers. "You saw it! Nobody thought to call the police? Nobody?!" Several dozen Moroccans looked down at the ground.

Poor Marchetti had been set to retire the next week. He had been doing his last rounds at Bousbir, probably intending a last visit to that dancer who had always been his favorite. Marchetti had never done anyone any harm, and he was entitled to a bit of fun. But these Moroccan animals had murdered him in cold blood, for no reason at all. Tony and his friends had been walking down Route de Medouina when they'd heard the shots, but by then it had been too late.

He looked around at the filthy cowards on that dusty street and set his jaw. They would find the man who had done this. Then they would find the man who had given him the gun, and then the terrorists who had helped him escape, and then those who were hiding him now. Justice would prevail.

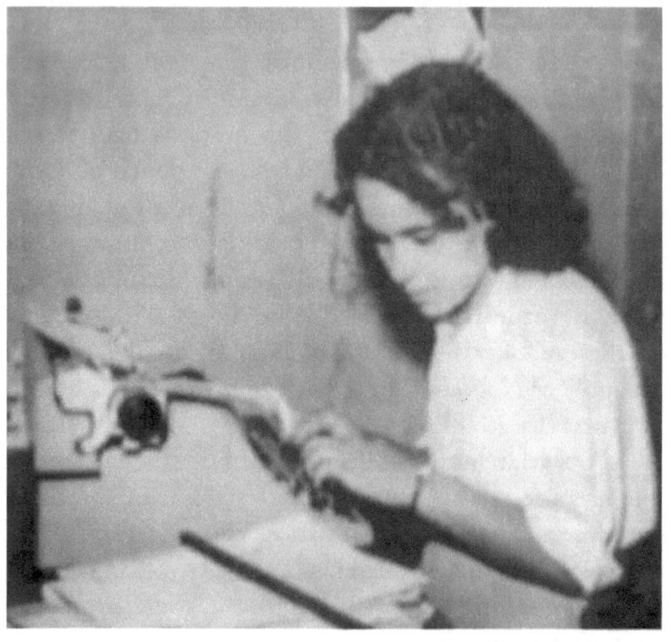

○

4

Touria had returned home from Tunisia with a diploma in stenography, but she was still only thirteen, too young to work yet too old to move freely through the streets. She read constantly and helped Zina around the house, but the work wasn't enough for the two of them. Abdelwahed had always pushed his daughter towards independence, but now that she was becoming a woman, that independence, and her confidence, were dwindling. He hadn't planned for this, and tossing and turning in bed at night, he never reached any answers, except the one he had arrived at thirteen years earlier: he would do everything in his power to help realize his daughter's dreams.

Touria's biggest dream had always been to fly. Abdelwahed had never taken this too seriously. He had assumed that dream was impossible. But seeing his daughter imprisoned in his own house made *impossible* seem like a good option.

At Tit Mellil, ten miles east of the city, was a flight school. She had mentioned it often. The airfield had been built by the French after the war to help replace the bases now run by the Americans. They trained fighter pilots there, including those in the French Acrobatic Patrol. Why couldn't she enroll? Touria asked the question one afternoon in the fall of 1950. Abdelwahed sighed and took her hand. Over the past year her eyes had grown more turbulent as his had grown more reflective. He knew that even if he could miraculously find some way to pay for the lessons, there was no chance a Moroccan civilian would ever be allowed to enroll in a French flight school. Especially not a thirteen-year-old girl.

Zaïm, the Zaïm who had triggered his daughter's exile, had once told him that history was the story of those who rehearsed the most. And Abdelwahed, an old translator of Molière, a wearer of silk stockings, knew from stage experience that a performance could become truth. So as he sat and looked into his daughter's fiery eyes, he asked himself how Moroccans, or she, could ever become free if they could not at least pretend to be free. So he spoke to a neighbor named Hashmi, a taxi driver with a Volkswagen Coccinelle, who drove them out to the base one afternoon so that they could pretend to enroll Touria in flight school. Because at least they could pretend, which felt better than doing nothing at all.

"Let me do the talking," he said as they drove through the airfield's stone gates. Touria had been up at dawn, chattering ever since. He turned and winked at her in the back seat, raising the corner of his thin mustache. He could not let her see how nervous he was. Prejudice was a constant of his daily existence, and he had mostly learned to ignore it, but he dreaded subjecting his daughter to what would surely be an avalanche of ridicule heaped upon her thin shoulders. A low plane passed overhead, and she called out: "A Cessna, *Ba!* I bet that's what I'll fly first." Abdelwahed nodded. She had never even been in a plane. They had taken the train to Tunis.

Hashmi pulled up to a small white building with a blue door, which was attached to a large hangar with a pitched roof. Next to the door a French flag flapped on a pole angled into the wall. He parked the Coccinelle next to two large Citroëns with military plates, and they got out. Abdelwahed had worn his finest suit – pinstriped, with a handkerchief in the front pocket – and Touria a white shirt and overalls. He took one last look at her beaming face before pushing through the blue door.

Inside three uniformed Frenchmen sat at three metal desks. One read a newspaper, another appeared to be dozing, his head thrown back at an odd angle, and the third was scribbling notes with aggressive little strokes of his entire arm. None of them gave any indication that they had noticed the appearance of Abdelwahed and Touria. "Bonjour," Abdelwahed said to the scribbler, who was nearest the entrance. The scribbler did not look up. Abdelwahed smiled out at the room as if at a dubious theater audience and projected: "*Bonjour!*"

The scribbler huffed and looked up. "Hey, Michel, Philippe," he said, "look at this one." Laughter machine-gunned through his teeth. "Look at that suit! Very impressive, *monsieur*, although entirely unnecessary. Do you have any experience with custodial work? We have quite a few applicants, but I'll take down your name and identity number, and you can call us next week."

"He probably wants a job for the girl too," said the sleeper, who was now half awake. "Maybe we could find a, ah, position for her."

"I wouldn't have thought she was your type," said the one with the newspaper. All three men burst into laughter. Abdelwahed felt Touria go rigid beside him.

"My name is Abdelwahed Chaoui," he said, still smiling, "and this is my daughter Touria. We have come to enroll her in flight school."

This resulted in a moment of total silence, as if time had been stopped and anything was possible. Then the three men doubled over and brayed like donkeys. Nothing had ever been this funny in the history of French civilization. "She wants to go up in an airplane, does she?" gasped the scribbler. "She wants to fly like a little birdie?"

"Yes," Abdelwahed said. "She does." He reached down to Touria's hand, but she wouldn't let him take it. She stood like a soldier at attention, her eyes absorbing every instant. A drop of sweat ran down his forehead, and he felt it crawl through the hairs of an eyebrow. This was no performance. This was the same old world.

Then a door at the back of the room jerked open, and a fat man in a more decorated uniform appeared, accompanied by a handsome pilot who looked even colder and crueler than the others. He was tall, his back as rigid as Touria's. "What's going on here?" the fat man demanded.

The others bit off their laughter. "*Directeur Martin*," the sleeper began with great difficulty, "this little Fatima pretends she can, ah, enroll in flight school and become a pilot." The director's mouth creaked open into a smile, releasing the others' laughter again. They were three balloons whose holes had been unknotted. Meanwhile the taller pilot remained like a statue carved with sharp knives.

"I can pay the tuition, *Monsieur le Directeur*," Abdelwahed said. In truth he couldn't even pay Hashmi the taxi fare. He wanted to gouge out their eyes. Life imprisonment, execution, was preferable to exposing his daughter to this. "Is there a rule that forbids her from enrolling?"

Touria took a half-step forward then and raised her chin, her fear neatly contained in a new place she had discovered inside. "*Monsieur le Directeur*," she said in perfect French. "I have studied aviation ever since I was born, and I will be your finest student."

The laughter died. There are some situations so improbable that they do not require a rule. There are no rules preventing elephants from surfing. Chimpanzees are not expressly forbidden to board trolley cars. "But she will never survive a week in this program," the sleeper stammered to the director, who several times began to speak, clouds gathering behind his eyes. The others watched with growing confusion until finally he turned to the tall pilot and sighed: "Arrange a trial lesson for our little Fatima. We shall see what she knows about aviation. No special allowances, you understand."

"*Merci, Monsieur le Directeur!*" Touria cried, as if none of the previous unpleasantness had occurred. "My name is Touria." The others looked down at their desks, playing with pencils and paper clips. As Abdelwahed's chest filled with lightness, his heart sunk. No special allowances. Even if Touria somehow made it through this trial lesson, she would be constantly ridiculed by sniggering fools, and the cold one who would teach her scared him the most. Only a man like that could break his daughter's spirit.

The cold one then took a clipboard from the front desk and handed it to her. "I am Lieutenant Tessier. Put down your name, your age, your identity number, and your address, and I will see you here next Thursday."

Outside by the Coccinelle, Touria rushed into her father's arms, suddenly seeming so young. Ecstatically she whispered the names of airplanes into his ear. *Piper, Dassault, Curtiss, Boeing.* He corralled her into the car, and she repeated the names to Hashmi, who smiled into the rearview mirror. "I will drive her to the lessons," he announced. "I do not want money. She will do honor to her family, to her neighborhood, and to the Moroccan people."

Then they drove out through the stone gates again. Touria stuck an arm out the window into the slipstream, rotating her flat hand so that her arm swooped up and down like wings. She grinned at Hashmi and her smiling father and edged her palm up and down so that even her smallest gesture was multiplied. She knew, as any pilot should, that the positioning of her tiny palm was called the Angle of Attack.

BLUESHIFT
1951

NOUASSEUR – A MASSIVE ANT COLONY WORKING DAY AND NIGHT

By William Le Fur

Outside the construction site of the main American air base at Nouasseur, in the suburbs of Casablanca, a massive encampment of wooden barracks has been built…. Almost everything is being produced in workshops onsite: not only the buildings themselves (temporary and permanent), but furniture and equipment for staff offices – twenty-three buildings designed for 1,500 workers. One large hangar is occupied entirely by paint. Enormous iron forges make countless fittings and repair the many machines working on the base.

The American Village of Nouasseur

The residential area meant for military personnel, technicians, and their families, the "American Village" of Nouasseur, will include a first phase of three hundred homes, of which fifteen are already built…. Children in cowboy outfits play out in front of them. This will be a real city of its own…. Besides housing, plans include churches, shops, a library, a school (which is complete and already welcoming children), private clubs, sports complexes, etc….

A Giant Ant Colony

Upon arriving at Nouasseur one has the impression of seeing a vast bare terrain home to a few *douars* – native villages – from which distant dust clouds rise among large cranes. But come closer, and a scene of intense activity is revealed: monstrous earthmoving machines scrape the ground at astonishing speed, raising suffocating dust....

Dominated by cranes, giant anthills appear in the deafening roar made by dozens of machines, whose tires are sometimes two meters high – tractors and excavators serviced by the constant coming and going of huge trucks. Floodlights illuminate the construction sites so that work can continue day and night....

A large area near the main road remains flat, but it is no less battered by the machines. Perhaps it is meant for underground depots, bunkers for personnel or ammunition.

Population 17,500

The Moroccan coast is being transformed by the hundreds of cars marked U.S.C.E. and brightly painted trucks – red, blue, yellow – filling the roads at all hours; by American military personnel visiting its cities, and especially by civilians who have come from the U.S. to work on the base, and who initially shocked with their long-visored fitted caps, their baggy and aggressively colored floral shirts, their proudly displayed tattoos....

According to the agreements signed between Washington and Paris, across the five U.S. airfields in Morocco, there will be 6,500 American military personnel (plus 3,500 at Port Lyautey for the Navy), 3,000 technicians (1,500 at Port Lyautey). Including families, this will mean a total presence of about 13,000 American citizens (17,500 with Port Lyautey)....[13]

○

"They call this a baptism by air," said Lieutenant Noguera, the moon-faced pilot who had been assigned Touria's first test flight. "Once you take off, you'll be reborn."

"I don't want to be reborn," Touria said. Two lines appeared between her eyebrows, echoing the two between her father's. "I'm only thirteen."

On a balmy November morning, Hashmi had driven them out to the airfield, where in the office of Directeur Martin, Abdelwahed had slid an envelope across the desk. "The first four lessons," he said. "I will bring the next four in a month."

The director pulled out the cash and counted the bills. His face twitched when he had finished. "Very well," he had said. "Lieutenant Noguera will take her up, but if he judges her unfit for our program, the money cannot be refunded." Abdelwahed nodded, a faint smile on his lips.

---

13   *Le Monde* – 10/19/1951

Then Noguera had appeared and jovially shook their hands. He was in his late twenties, poorly shaven, already balding, and seemed amused by anything he set eyes upon, his lips constantly parting into a slack-mouthed smile. His hands hovered by his shoulders as he spoke, their stubby fingers tickling the air. His uniform was sloppy, his pants wrinkled, his jacket stained.

"Shall we, Touria?" Noguera said gaily. "Very nice to meet you, Monsieur Chaoui. I shall have her back to you in an hour at most. No loopy loops today, I promise." Then they stepped out into the sunlight together. Abdelwahed waved, but Touria was already firing questions at the delighted Frenchman whose fingers tickled the air.

"You, young lady, are the first Moroccan ever to experience a lesson here," he said as they walked across the shimmering tarmac. And since as far as he knew, the country's only flight schools were at Tit Mellil and Rabat, he doubted that any Moroccan had ever obtained a private pilot's license. In any case, it was all very exciting, and he hoped the flight – her baptism by air, so to speak – would live up to expectations. "As you may be aware, Mademoiselle Chaoui, many historians believe that the first man ever to fly was an Arab. Abbas ibn Firnas. He lived in Córdoba during the ninth century, when the caliphate extended across North Africa and up through Spain and Portugal."

"How did he fly, Abbas ibn Firnas? Did he make an airplane?"

"Not exactly. Funny fellow, our Monsieur Firnas, quite brilliant for his time. He covered himself in feathers. Glued them right to his skin as if feathers are what make a bird fly. Can you imagine? Then he fashioned a couple of wings, which he attached to his arms before climbing up a hill and jumping. And he flew, Mademoiselle Chaoui. He most certainly did! They say he flew for quite a distance, but that when he fell, he broke his back. Although he had provided himself with feathers, he had forgotten that a bird needs a tail to land. A bird needs a tail, Touria! Never forget it! But don't worry. Our little Cessna not only has a tail, it even has wheels. *Voilà!*"

Before them on the tarmac sat a Cessna 170. Its nose was red, and a single red stripe ran horizontally along its fuselage. They circled the plane, the lieutenant pointing out each part and its purpose: the rudder, which allowed you to point your nose left or right; the elevator flaps on either side of the horizontal stabilizer – "*Voici* our tail, Mademoiselle Chaoui." – which pointed the nose up or down and controlled the angle of attack; the wings, jutting out from the top of the cockpit, each supported by a strut angling down to the body; the flaps, at the back edges of the wings, which you adjusted by turning the control column, banking the plane left or right; and then of course our shiny propeller, driven by a 145 horsepower engine.

"You will be piloting us today," Noguera announced as he opened the pilot's door and boosted her up into the seat. "I am merely your co-pilot." As he walked around to the opposite door, she marveled at the dozens of dials, buttons, and switches crowding the instrument panel. For the first time that day she doubted herself. How would she ever learn where all those needles should point? Would they spin like propellers and send her crashing to the earth like poor Abbas ibn Firnas? *Allah give me strength*, she murmured.

Noguera had taken his seat beside her. He flipped a switch, and a radio crackled. On a clipboard he showed her a list of flight preparations to be checked off. Gripping the control column, still studying the dials, she understood little of what he said. He laughed. "Don't worry, captain. Today you won't need to do anything until we get up into the air, and then I'll still be in control. I won't let us crash."

He started the engine, and the propeller jerked, then spun into a blur as he edged the throttle up until the tachometer read 1000 RPM. The roar made conversation impossible. He showed her how to put on her headset. The roar was instantly muffled, and she heard his voice inside her head. *Are you there, Touria Chaoui?*

"I'm here."

The control tower was talking. The words sounded like a foreign language. She had always imagined, like Abbas ibn Firnas, that flight would feel free and unfettered, like becoming a bird, but the knowledge required to fly now seemed to triple the force of gravity. The control tower gave permission to taxi. Noguera pulled back the throttle and released the brakes, checked them once again, then eased forward the throttle. They rolled towards the runway. Heart pounding in her headset, she glanced over towards Hashmi's Coccinelle, but she didn't dare look long enough to find her father.

The nose of the plane was now aligned with the runway centerline, and Noguera went down the checklist. Touria nodded at each incomprehensible phrase. "Is your door locked? Seatbelt fastened? Feathers glued?" She nodded, her knuckles white on the controls. Then

Noguera pushed in the throttle, and when the engine had roared to full power, he released the brakes. Speed came quickly, pressing her against the seat.

Trees whipped past. They moved fast down the runway, but not as fast as she had expected. Having imagined a rock from a slingshot, she missed the moment she first left the ground. Then she saw that the propeller had nosed up over the horizon line. She looked out her side window. The runway quickly receded. "Welcome to the sky, Mademoiselle Chaoui," Noguera said in her head. "Introduce yourself to the clouds."

Salaam alaikum, clouds.

"You're flying it now." She snapped back to attention, hands tighter on the controls. Was she really flying it? How could she know? What about the dials, the pedals, the throttle he had pushed, or pulled? "Gently pull back on the control column." She did, ever so slightly, which was as much as she dared. The nose aimed up, and they flew higher. "Now push it in a bit. Don't be nervous." She eased the column forward, and the plane descended. Choked laughter burst from her mouth, and on her own she eased the nose back level. "That's it. You're a natural, Touria. Now take us wherever you'd like to fly. Nice and easy, turn us left or right. You choose."

Exhilarated, she banked right. The landscape turned beneath them, and she needed more eyes to see. Tiny roads, tiny trains, tiny soccer matches on tiny dirt fields beside tiny villages.

"So what do you think?" Noguera asked.

"It's just like I imagined it," she said.

Once a week Hashmi drove her out to Tit Mellil for her lesson. Word spread about the Moroccan girl who could fly a French plane. The Chaouis were hardly aware of this, but late one evening, at the end of his walk home from work, Abdelwahed was approached by an associate of Mohamed Zerktouni. Zerktouni was a charismatic twenty-four-year-old former soccer player who had established his extensive underground network by organizing the annual Casablanca *Coupe des Quartiers* soccer tournament and was now head of the Istiqlal Party's Logistics and Holiday Decorations Commission. His associate was about nineteen and smiled too much. Pilot lessons were expensive, the boy pointed out, his voice cracking. Abdelwahed nodded, irritably glancing around to gauge whether they were observed. So the Istiqlal Party wanted to help pay for those lessons, the associate continued. Touria could be a powerful symbol for the independence movement.

Abdelwahed wanted to strangle the kid. Instead he replied that he supported Istiqlal, and longed for the return of Allal al-Fassi from exile in Cairo, but his daughter was no symbol. She was a fourteen-year-old girl. And although he appreciated the support of the party, he could not accept their money. Even then he was annoyed with himself. Why was he treating this boy like an elder?

"Then we'll be in touch," the boy said.

"Please do not ever come to my house again," Abdelwahed said. The associate smiled and sauntered back off down the sidewalk.

He could last another month or two. Allah would provide.

○

The other pilots hated her, refused even to look at her, as if her existence put into question the most basic principles of aeronautical science. Directeur Martin was waiting for her to slip up, or for some technicality to materialize. It wasn't difficult to read his mind. Clearly the school needed a more comprehensive rule book. You couldn't have little Fatimas from all over the countryside turning up to become pilots. And he couldn't become known as the man who had permitted a schoolgirl to become a national symbol.

Every week her course started with a classroom briefing, where more complex concepts of aerodynamics and the use of the flight instruments were explained on the blackboard. Afterwards was an accompanied flight, with her assuming more responsibilities each week. Her two instructors were Lieutenants Noguera and Tessier. She had grown to love Noguera, whom she felt wished her success. Tessier, however, treated her like an unwelcome distraction. He rarely said more to her than what was required. But on their second or third lesson together, when she had asked about flying during the war, he had told her about Königsberg.

He had only earned his wings late in the war. Then he had been posted to the Normandie-Niemen

Regiment of the Free French Air Force under the First Air Army of the Soviet Union. In 1945, they were sent to Königsberg on the Baltic Sea, which had been razed by British bombers months earlier. Refugees were flooding out of the city in advance of the Red Army, but Hitler had ordered his generals to fight, and whole swaths of fleeing citizens were dying of disease and starvation on the roadsides. Seven thousand Polish Jews were rounded up from camps and sent on a death march to Sambia. Tessier saw it all beneath him, columns of ants, smashed ants, singed trees and rubble, flattened houses along smudged streets. Their siege lasted three months. He was shot down in March, two months before the end of the war in Europe. For days he had walked through corpses and endless chains of prisoners until he was safe behind Soviet lines. Over forty thousand civilians had been killed at Königsberg, and still every day he wished that he had not crashed and seen that horror up close. Every night he dreamed of Königsberg.

Touria did not even dare look at him then. For weeks she saw dead people beneath her when she flew and wished she hadn't asked. His tone had been flat, with little hint of emotion. The story had seemed like a warning. She didn't understand Lieutenant Tessier.

Aimed down, you need more power; aimed up, you need less. In the air he was more controlling than Noguera, directing her every gesture. *Push your right rudder pedal with your right foot. Make it trim. Forward with the control column. Increase the throttle. Now ease the column back.* He didn't explain. He expected her to understand. And she did, although occasionally he got impatient, and her hands would sense that his had taken the controls. His hands would be moving hers, as if a *djinn* had possessed her body. Sometimes then, as he took them through a tricky turn, she would sneak a glimpse at his face. He and Noguera were opposites. Tessier looked like a pilot from the movies, with pale gray eyes, sharp cheekbones, and the scar on his forehead angled up from his thin eyebrow. If you looked at him closely, his face was slightly asymmetrical. Each eye saw a different half of him, it seemed, and she couldn't quite bring the two together. Although sometimes she didn't notice the disjunction at all. Once, just once, she had seen him smile while talking to Noguera about a stunt they had performed. He had lifted only one corner of his mouth, as if joy was a physical effort. The expression could have been mistaken for a snarl. "We make art that doesn't exist," he had said one day about his acrobatic flights with Noguera. "Like giant invisible paintbrushes. Flying is art that vanishes." Then sometimes when they were alone and he wordlessly assumed the controls, he would whistle pieces of jagged music, and she liked him better when he whistled.

One day after returning home from her lesson, her mother remarked that she was especially talkative that afternoon. Lieutenant Tessier didn't like her, she was saying, not at all, she really didn't think so, but Lieutenant Noguera was kind, and he let her fly the plane now all by herself, and next week he had promised to let her fly out over the ocean. She spoke with such animation that her curls danced on her head. For the first time in her life, Touria was growing out her hair.

A heavy knock at the door cut her off. They knew the sound. Rifle butts, police. Abdelwahed rushed into the front room. "Go into the bedroom and shut the door," he hissed.

But Touria refused to hide, so *Zina* stayed too. Abdelwahed gritted his teeth, stepped towards the door, and opened it. Two cops barged in brandishing rifles and shoved past him. They did not speak. They looked the women up and down, then moved from room to room, smudging their muddy boots on the floor. Eventually they returned to the entry. One noticed the portrait of the Sultan that Abdelwahed had kept on the wall in defiance of the unwritten regulations.

"What is that portrait?" one cop barked. Touria watched mutely. This was her fault, she suddenly understood. She looked at her father, wound so tight. She had not meant to do this to him, or to her mother, but now she didn't know what else to do. She alone was causing this, and with horror she realized that she had become something separate from them. She ran up to her room.

"It's personal," Abdelwahed replied. A policeman grunted and ripped the portrait from the wall, and they left with it under his arm.

That night Abdelwahed sat up for hours watching the place the portrait had hung. His debts were mounting. Several Moroccan clients had loaned him money for the lessons, and although Islam forbade collecting interest, they were collecting a pound of flesh, running him ragged with endless favors. Salah was also a concern. One afternoon he had come home from his Moroccan school with cuts on the soles of his feet. His time in the classroom was spent memorizing the Koran, and when he forgot a line his teachers beat his soles with a stick, a common practice called the *falaqua*. Salah was six years old. Abdelwahed realized that he would have to put him in the French school, but that would be another risk, not to mention an expense, and Abdelwahed was exhausted by risks and expenses. The boy, extraordinarily sensitive, would not have it easy. He was not the student his sister had been, but he had shown exceptional talent for drawing that might be developed. He must have his chance too, and Abdelwahed realized that he could no longer think of his own career as a separate pursuit. He would work harder for his family, who needed him more than he had ever needed fame or glory or Molière. He stared at the blank rectangle on the wall and sighed.

Around midnight another knock came – not a rifle butt, so he presumed it was friendly and opened the door. Mohamed Zerktouni's Istiqlal associate stood out in the shadows. Again Abdelwahed sighed. The idea of inviting the associate into his home was loathsome, but he couldn't be seen outside with him either. "I told you not to come here," he said, waving the boy into the house and quickly shutting the door.

"We want to help." The boy glanced around the room. He was too at ease, Abdelwahed thought, just like the policemen. "Your daughter may not be a symbol, but she is an example."

"Have a seat."

"I'll stand." The boy smiled and paced about the room. "Please accept our assistance. Whether we like it or not, we are all becoming part of the resistance. Soon none of us will have any choice in the matter."

Abdelwahed looked down at his shined leather shoes, which seemed so ridiculous, another man's feet, and nodded.

2

Suzanne sang to herself when she brushed her hair. These days she had it straightened at a fancy hairdresser in town, and the brushing was superfluous. Her hair was as smooth and shiny as satin, and for the first time in her life she was pleased to look at herself in the mirror. Everybody said she looked like Maria Montez in *Siren of Atlantis*, which pleased Suzanne immensely. Who cared if the hairdresser cost twelve hundred francs a month. The men who had wanted discounts when she looked like a Negro now let her name her price.

An American had taught her the trick with the lemons. He had laughed when she took the tip so seriously. The great love of his life had been black, he said. Clearly there was something wrong with the man. He also spoke Arabic. But he paid like all the others and drank tea before and after, which was when he told her about the lemons. Since then she had been halving the fruits and scrubbing her skin with them, leaving bits of pulp behind, juice trickling down her legs through her toes. She was a lighter shade now than before the American, just like Maria Montez.

Another man had recognized her as her mother's daughter and had started to jabber. Aziza had opened a new shop, apparently, a fine one in Frenchtown with a section for men. An extraordinary woman, Aziza. Would she please send his regards? Suzanne had wriggled out of her kaftan then simply to shut him up, and her breasts always did it. The new shop was less than a mile away, but this was another world, like Atlantis, and she was the queen.

242

Sometimes, though, even in the mirror she felt terribly alone, and then she would pace the floor singing, or stick her head out the window for hours, watching the street opera. The *sous-maîtresse* was constantly telling her to shut it, she'd catch cold. The *sous-maîtresse* was too old to sell her own body, and Suzanne knew she spied for Jean Bart, counting her *passes* to ensure she never cheated the box, but Zohra had taught her to tip the *sous-maîtresse* at the end of each month, and now the old woman sometimes brought special clients up the back staircase and split the money. So Suzanne couldn't be bossed around anymore and kept her window open except on the very coldest nights. Otherwise she felt as if she was suffocating in that room.

There were enemies too, especially that crazy Fadila, who had swallowed the ring Suzanne had taken from her mother's jewelry box. One time Suzanne had confronted the bitch in line for the showers, which they were obliged to take on Mondays and Thursdays. Fadila had flipped out. The ring was still in her belly, she'd screamed, it had never come out, and then the others had stepped in before Suzanne could kill her. In the showers you saw all this bitch's scary tattoos. Sometimes seeing them made Suzanne wish she had never gotten one of her own, although she still believed in love. *Vive l'amour.*

3

On the rooftop of the aerodrome, where the city could not dim the stars, Victor stood with his back to his telescope studying the light patterns made by his spectroscope, which was connected to the telescope at an angle. For weeks he had not been drinking, managing to avoid women too. At night he had remained at the airfield, wanting to change his patterns. Touria didn't count as a woman. She'd been on his mind, and he had considered the possibility that her enthusiasm was the cause of his return to astronomy for the first time since boarding school.

The spectroscope he had bought in Paris in the days after the war. Surviving Königsberg had made him want to take up the youthful hobby again, and for a few months he had watched the stars, taking careful notes. The spectroscope was built with a collimator that split a star's light into parallel rays, projecting them onto a detector, which formed a visible spectrum he could study to understand more about celestial bodies. Over the past weeks he had occasionally found himself still on the rooftop at dawn, still moving between telescope and spectroscope without even shivering. Sleep had always felt like defeat to Victor, and he was weary of the small compromises that slowly separated a man from himself. Better sleeplessness. He took careful notes, writing by the glow of his cigarette and the light of the stars themselves. What he discovered about them seemed immeasurably important, even if others were looking further with more advanced telescopes. But most of astronomy's discoveries had come from men standing alone in the night.

Blue on the spectroscope meant a hot star, and red a cold. Through the spectroscope you could find differences in surface temperatures, and each of a star's elements had its characteristic colors. Carbon shifted towards the oranges, nitrogen towards bright blues, oxygen towards purples. It still seemed incredible to him that one could divine the composition of an object trillions of miles away. He tended to know less about the women he took to his bed. He was glad to be free of them for a while.

Color could also indicate a star's motion, which was otherwise imperceptible to the eye. The spectral lines of some stars shifted towards the longer wavelengths at the red end of the spectrum. Redshift, this was called, and it indicated that a star was moving away from the observer. Most stars were redshifted, because the universe was expanding, flying off in pieces towards the unknown. Some stars showed blueshift, however, lost stars fighting back against the expanding swarm. Perhaps they would one day hit the earth, or perhaps they had already crashed into other stars. All Victor could see was a moment that had occurred a long time in the past. Existing catastrophes were still unknown to the present. History could not yet be observed. He had always suspected that this odd timeshift might also exist within himself. Some previous cataclysm within him was still undiscovered. Once it arrived, however, and burst into his present, he would be transformed.

The spectral lines of Polaris were especially interesting, because they showed both redshift and blueshift, which had led to the discovery that Polaris was in fact a binary star, two stars bound by gravity, spinning both towards and away from the earth, shifting blue then red. He stepped away from the equipment and rubbed his eyes. Maybe he was kidding himself. Maybe there were no more discoveries. Maybe all stars became the same, like women and second bottles of wine. He should stop for the night.

Down on the tarmac planes slept, their skins pale and soft in the yellow light of the hangar spotlights. Victor took a deep breath. The world spun beneath him, and he thought of Touria again, impetuous girl. They had connected despite his first misgivings, although neither had fully relaxed into the connection, and still they circled each other like binary stars, coming and going in opposite directions. Initially he hadn't respected her childish dream, but then he'd seen how the others hated her, resenting her independence, and he could not help but align himself with anyone who could so unfailingly draw hatred. Outcasts possessed a vision, one that tended to destroy them in the end, but that didn't matter, and in her he saw the sort of idealism that had once colored his own life blue.

○

○

Together they walked towards the Cessna. Touria's hair blew in the wind, and she kept pushing it back. Who would have guessed that hair could become such a distraction? How did other women do it?

Her relationship with Lieutenant Tessier was now comfortable, or at least professional. Rarely did they need to exchange words, and although the silence had made her uneasy at first, she had found the calm to inhabit it. As the date of her final test approached, the other pilots, except for Noguera, hated her even more conspicuously. Directeur Martin kept closer watch too. But at least Tessier seemed to have faith in her now, although he never said it.

"What do I do?"

"You know what to do."

The slipstream would yaw the plane when you changed airspeed, so you had to apply right rudder to maintain the slip ball in the middle. You had to go sideways to go straight. That's how Tessier put it. He was the only person in her life who wasn't somehow worried about her.

Sometimes he also talked about the stars. She knew that in Berber her name meant "daughters of the night", and that another name for the daughters was the Pleiades, a constellation also called the Seven Sisters. He told her that their father Atlas had been forced to carry the heavens on his shoulders. His daughters were so beautiful that Orion had hunted them, and so Zeus, the Greek god of gods, had transformed the sisters into stars to keep them safe. But Orion still chased them across the night sky, and so now the Pleiades – Touria – disappeared from the sky from March until September.

That day of the star conversation she insisted on driving Hashmi's taxi home. She knew how to fly a plane. Surely she could drive a Coccinelle. Hashmi shook his head and reluctantly swapped seats. Never say a word to Abdelwahed. She was a crazy girl, driving too fast with her hair tossed by the wind.

4

For weeks Fadila had mashed her stool in the pot. At first she chopped it up with a knife, repulsed by the sight and smell of it, but then she worried that she might be missing the gold ring, and the filth no longer seemed so repulsive when she squeezed it between her fingers. Even then, however, the ring had not appeared. So she had decided she was crazy, and had never swallowed the ring, but then Suzanne had attacked her in the showers, and the blood on her lips told her the ring must be inside her like a baby.

Walking aimlessly through Frenchtown that day, she wondered about the ring. Somewhere inside her gold was hidden. Her body was as much of a mystery as the city in which she was now lost. There were parts of herself she couldn't find, or didn't know existed.

Years had passed since she'd used her monthly pass to leave the walls of Bousbir for a day, but men had exhausted her body, which craved an escape. Now she regretted it. Casablanca had become unrecognizable, and people stared at her as if she had fangs and was meant to crawl on the ground. She avoided their eyes. Her eyes were too powerful. If she stared hard enough at anyone, even someone across the street, he would feel her eyes and stop, turn. Everyone, not just men.

Strange world. Where were all these people going, and why did they hate her? Hate her, she didn't care. Place de France was crammed with honking cars and elbows. The chaos frightened her, and in the crush of bodies she felt as if she might be pulled into a thousand pieces, bits of her flesh and bones scattered out across

249

the Place where she would never find them, assuming she still existed.

At the bus station she forced herself to smile at a man, but he glanced away. Then another, a Frenchman, but he scurried past, a rabbit with big ears. She frowned and walked up the boulevard towards the shore. For half a block she decided to shut her eyes and stumbled past bodies, wondering if one hit her head-on whether its flesh would move right through hers. Maybe she was transparent like an angel. She kept her eyes shut then and concentrated on signaling to the angels.

As tattoos had covered more of her body, fewer clients visited her room, even if she believed she became more beautiful with every prick of the needle. There were dots beneath her eyes now, a line down her chin, stars on her knuckles. Foreigners were beneath her, she still believed, but Moroccans almost never wanted her. Marked by sin, she had no choice but to accept the foreign freaks. There was the scary Russian, for example, who paid just to talk over tea. He spoke perfect Arabic too, so she suspected he was possessed by a djinn, but still sometimes she wondered why he didn't want her. He would study her tattoos, moving close to peer at them through his spectacles, like the doctor at the clinic, but otherwise her body held no interest to him. He seemed to be searching her skin for clues, and sometimes she couldn't hide her laughter. The Russian really was crazy.

Jean Bart occasionally beat her for wasting time on lunatics. She was a prostitute and would never be more, so why did she destroy her body like this? Fights, and three times she'd fallen pregnant, mostly unfuckable once she'd started showing. Thankfully each time she'd lost the baby. Otherwise how would she ever pay her debts?

Instead of continuing towards the ocean, she turned left into the mellah. When the streets narrowed, she recognized them again, the low doors, the windows high on white façades, the hammam where the Jews had cooked the *dafina*. The streets were a familiar dream, like the golden ring inside her. On their own, her feet had been following a path through the dream, but now they stopped as if at a border. She violently shook her head. Wake up. In front of her was the house of the Jews where she had once lived. Three steps forward. The house did not vanish. A cart of spiny cactus fruit trundled past behind a festering donkey, squeezing her closer to the door. She pictured the thin cousin named Abel, bushy eyebrows and never smiling. She knocked at the door with the stars on her knuckles.

The wheels of the cart creaked around the corner. Still her hand hovered in the air. A surge of energy shot through her legs. She would run, but then the door scraped open a sliver, revealing an ancient headscarved Moroccan. Fadila heard a sound like her voice asking about the Jewish family.

The woman answered that a year earlier they had gone to the camps with the others before finding a boat to Israel. All of them? Fadila asked about Abel, and then the woman called her a whore and told her to scram, slamming the door. Fadila banged her fists against it, but it stayed shut, and then she staggered up a street that was no longer so familiar.

She wanted to smoke then, but the effort it would take to find good kif was inconceivable, and she didn't have any money anyway. Wandering through the reeking Seagull Souk, where the fishermen lived in crumbling shacks, the fishermen's wives looked out from open doorways with extinguished eyes. At Sidi Belyout, the jagged rocks slanted out of the ocean as if the earth had once been turned at a different angle and everybody was now sideways.

Eventually she found herself at the gates of the municipal swimming pool. She thought of diving in, but she knew that as soon as some of her flesh was bared, she would clear out the pool like a piece of floating shit. Looking out past the vast, placid rectangle to the frothy waves of the Atlantic, she thought of all the men who had pretended to love her, and all those who had beaten her. Their faces blurred together as her own spread into a sickly smile. There was nothing beyond the ocean. There was only this, over and over again. She turned away and walked south towards Bousbir, because she was done with the city and there was nothing else.

But there were the fancy shops on Boulevard de Paris selling tailored clothes, French pastries, and leather shoes. She hated such things now because she no longer dreamed of them, although one shop did catch her attention. In its windows were framed paintings, on the walls inside too. She had never seen such a shop before. Inside, a French couple studied the paintings, as if they could be bought like kaftans or fruits. To Fadila the pictures were uninteresting. They only showed the world – women washing clothes in a river, the lighthouse at El Hank, the clock tower of the Hôtel de Ville. These things anyone could see for herself, so why look at them twice? Her angels were better pictures, she knew, and she turned up her nose and walked on. The wings on her thighs were more beautiful than anything about the Hôtel de Ville.

Down the street a Berber woman in a straw hat decorated with colorful wool tassels sold oranges from a pallet hanging from a leather strap around her neck. This was a perfect test. Fadila stopped and stared into the woman, holding her breath. She made her eyes into oranges, and her body flowed through her eyes. She stared and stared, angrier with each passing instant, staring with all her might until the Berber woman shifted her weight, and one of the fruits was dislodged. Once Eventually she found herself at the gates of the municipal swimming pool. She thought of diving in, but she knew that as soon as some of her flesh was bared, she would clear out the pool like a piece of floating shit. Looking out past the vast, placid rectangle to the frothy waves of the Atlantic, she thought of all the men who had pretended to love her, and all those who had beaten her. Their faces blurred together as her own spread into a sickly smile. There was nothing beyond the ocean. There was only this, over and over again. She turned away and walked south towards Bousbir, because she was done with the city and there was nothing else.

But there were the fancy shops on Boulevard de Paris selling tailored clothes, French pastries, and leather shoes. She hated such things now because she no longer dreamed of them, although one shop did catch her attention. In its windows were framed paintings, on the walls inside too. She had never seen such a shop before. Inside, a French couple studied the paintings, as if they could be bought like kaftans or fruits. To Fadila the pictures were uninteresting. They only showed the world – women washing clothes in a river, the lighthouse at El Hank, the clock tower of the Hôtel de Ville. These things anyone could see for herself, so why look at them twice? Her angels were better pictures, she knew, and she turned up her nose and walked on. The wings on her thighs were more beautiful than anything about the Hôtel de Ville.

Down the street a Berber woman in a straw hat decorated with colorful wool tassels sold oranges from a pallet hanging from a leather strap around her neck. This was a perfect test. Fadila stopped and stared into the woman, holding her breath. She made her eyes into oranges, and her body flowed through her eyes. She stared and stared, angrier with each passing instant, staring with all her might until the Berber woman shifted her weight, and one of the fruits was dislodged. Once it hit the sidewalk, it rolled towards the gutter. This seemed to take years. Then after years Fadila darted past the Berber woman, snatched up the orange, and flew down the sidewalk with it clasped in her hand. The blow from behind never came, and near the Central Market she ducked into a narrow passageway filled with garbage and discarded chicken parts. Slumping against the sticky wall, she frantically peeled the orange, digging her nails into its flesh. This orange had always been hers, and she had found it with her magic powers. Alone in the reeking passageway, she dug her teeth into its flesh, and with its juice down her chin, she joyfully anticipated the day when she would learn to concentrate so hard that Fadila the whore would possess the power to transform herself into the world's most wonderful creature, an angel. Her flesh would come alive, and her heart would turn to gold.

○

Jean Bart, Suzanne, and Zohra were smoking cigarettes on the steps at the house's entrance. Suzanne now chewed gum whenever she smoked her Favorites. She called it a menthol. On the steps the women had built a fire for tea in a clay brazier, but the fire was too big, flames leaping between them, black smoke belching into the air. Fadila stepped around the smoke. Somewhat ashamed of having returned three hours before curfew, she had hoped to avoid Jean Bart. She had hoped to hide in her room with a pipe before the night banged at her door.

"You see," Jean Bart said, blocking her path. "You belong here. Start acting like it." Fadila stared hard up at the woman's chiseled face until the *patronne* snorted and stepped aside.

In her room she sighed and kicked off her baboushes. Her head pounded, and she moved towards the bed, but stopped almost immediately. Something was wrong. The bed looked like hers, but her pictures were gone. Frantic, she rushed over to the wall. Had she entered the wrong room? But her fingers quickly found the holes made by the pins she had used to hang the pictures.

Tears sprung to her eyes. She stormed downstairs with bare feet. Shoving the women aside, she kicked over the brazier and stomped the flames until nothing remained beneath her feet but the charred pieces of her old notebooks. Weeping, she attempted to work some kind of magic, staring through tears at the ashes. Suzanne embraced the other two women. "*Vive l'amour,*" Zohra chuckled, stroking Suzanne's perfect hair. Fadila stared hard at Suzanne, but the magic was gone.

She turned and ran barefoot down the main street of Bousbir. She flew out the gate and across Route de Medouina, her bedroom feet already bleeding, but that wasn't the principal pain. She would run into the sea. She would fling herself from windows, but she was already lost, screaming and berserk, a prisoner of the city. Before she ever escaped, she knew they would catch her, but because she had nothing, she would run.

5

Touria had found a flight suit her size through a friend of her father's, and on the morning of October 17, 1951, she put it on and looked at herself in the mirror. Previously her appearance had felt superfluous, but was it possible that she was pretty? Maybe not with those dark circles under her eyes, the mark of several nights spent too excited for sleep. But she was almost fifteen. She had been taking lessons at Tit Mellil for a year. And today she would become a pilot.

After breakfast the family loaded into Hashmi's Coccinelle, dressed in their finest, Abdelwahed in a suit, Zina in her pink dress, and even Salah in a little blue blazer. Touria sat in the back and stared out the window. For months now she had been flying solo, first in brief circuits around the runway, taking off, circling, landing, putting the nose on the horizon right before the wheels touched down, each time perfecting her control until she could land as lightly as a leaf.

Near the outskirts of the city, the temperature dropped. The wind was pulling in dark clouds from the ocean, buffeting the Coccinelle. After a calm summer, Touria had never flown in anything resembling storm conditions. She wondered if the test would be delayed, and her stomach clenched.

Lieutenant Tessier had drilled her to fly using only the controls, in case she ever experienced poor visibility. He had jerked the steering column whenever she glanced up through the windshield. Eventually she had glanced up on purpose, confident she could handle his every challenge, and also wanting to annoy him. She was ready, he had decided, and then she had told him about the final weeks of stenography school in Tunis, when the professor had tied blindfolds over the eyes of the girls to break the habit of sight typing. She remembered the click-clacking of the rows of typewriters, an intricate roar in a darkness so loud she had felt she was swimming through it, stroking with her fingers through a depthless sea. During the exercise she had always acutely felt the presence of the professor pacing the aisles. Her skin had tingled whenever he passed behind her desk, but soon she could also locate him in any other spot in the room. All alone then in Tunis, everything had struck her more vividly, especially when they wore the blindfolds. Now the air outside was even colder. She rolled up the window and shut her eyes.

As they pulled into the airfield, the sky looked ready to crack open. The French flag snapped violently on its pole. The family pushed through the door into the office, which was deserted except for Lieutenant Noguera, who leapt up from a desk, papers scattering in the wind until the door slammed shut. He shook the hands of Abdelwahed and Salah and bowed to Zina. Then he took Touria's arm and pulled her aside. "Directeur Martin has refused to postpone the test," he murmured, his chubby fingers squeezing her arm. "It is the last way he can stop you. You cannot do it, Touria. It is too dangerous. Even I would not fly in this weather."

Before she could reply, the director burst from his office, closely followed by Lieutenant Tessier. "Monsieur Chaoui, Mademoiselle Chaoui," the director said, then disdainfully at Zina and Salah: "I assume the rest of the souk will be arriving shortly." Touria studied Tessier's face, but it was a mask. "The weather is unfortunate," the director continued, "but we cannot move the exam date. Institutional policy, I am afraid, recently put into place by our rules and procedures committee. I have no control over the matter. So it is up to you, Mademoiselle Chaoui. Yes or no. Pass or fail."

"It is too dangerous," Noguera said again with uncharacteristic force, his face red, his hands clenched. Touria turned away from Noguera to study Tessier, desperately hoping for a crack in the mask. There was none. "What do you think?" she finally asked.

"Pass or fail," Tessier murmured through lips barely parted. Abdelwahed went pale then, even paler than Touria. But her decision had been made.

○

Alone she approached the Cessna, seeming smaller beneath a sky so heavy it looked as if it might fall. She had become a young woman, Abdelwahed realized as he watched her walk from the edge of the tarmac, leaning into the wind. She circled the plane, then climbed into the cockpit and adjusted her headset. A test administrator, a pilot they didn't know, had grudgingly joined her. Beside the Chaouis on the tarmac stood Lieutenant Tessier and Directeur Martin. The weather was now genuinely frightening, great black cloud masses collapsing into one another. The director sighed and put his hands in his pockets, behind his back, on his hips.

The Cessna taxied to the end of the runway.

Abdelwahed desperately wished that he could be connected to his daughter via radio, but only his own thoughts chattered in his head. The little plane jolted forward then, and picked up speed. Soon it had lifted off the ground with a wobble, and he watched with Zina's hand in his as their daughter was immediately swallowed by a cloud. The drone of the engine faded, and then there was nothing but that terrible sky. The weight of the earth seemed intolerable then. They believed in her, but belief had never seemed so insufficient.

○

Touria had turned out of the crosswind, but the takeoff had been terrifying, smacking her so hard off her line that she had feared the plane would flip over onto its back like a beetle. Now she needed to rise out of the clouds and get her sight again, because cold panic told her the plane wasn't level, and that she was already spiraling blindly out of control. She ignored the test administrator, who remained silent anyway. She used only the controls, as Tessier had taught her. For a moment, just a moment, she imagined crashing and being liberated of this fear. Abandoning herself to speed, to chaos and the explosion. For a moment that seemed the ultimate bliss. But then she pulled up into the sunlight and saw that she was level. She had managed it all perfectly.

Never had she flown so high, and it was cold up there. She flew higher. Now she would have to execute a spin, to force a loss of control and whirl down through the air before guiding the plane out of danger again. She wanted to be high enough not to spin into the clouds. She needed to see everything.

○

Abdelwahed dropped his eyes from the clouds and glared at the director, who was also fuming. None of this had been meant to go this far. They waited, pacing. Noguera was so miserable that he had folded a test form into a paper airplane and had escaped into tossing it back and forth with Salah, who scampered across the tarmac whenever the plane got snatched into the distance by the wind.

Ten minutes later Noguera stopped mid-toss, holding the battered plane. He had heard something, maybe, no louder than a buzzing fly. The fractured group scanned the sky, each desperate to end the waiting.

Then the little Cessna appeared, and Zina wailed with joy, holding her husband tight. The director cleared his throat. "Please!" he cried. "The test is not yet over." So in silence the Chaouis watched the plane circle down, holding their breaths as it bounced through the wind, descending quickly until it was aligned with the runway and glided towards the earth again.

The landing was perfect. They burst into cheers, except for the director, who stormed back into his office. And then Abdelwahed took off running towards his daughter's plane, Salah behind him, and when Touria hopped down from the cockpit, grinning exultantly, he was there to take her in his arms, his daughter, his life, his greatest achievement. She was a pilot.

○

○

The next days passed quickly. The story of Touria Chaoui appeared in newspapers all over the world, even in Morocco, where the press was tightly controlled by the French. She was the first Moroccan, male or female, to obtain a civil pilot's license, and the first aviatrix in the whole of North Africa. Casablanca hailed her as a hero. The apartment filled with visitors offering congratulations.

Touria responded conscientiously to the attention, as if this were just another test to be passed, ignoring the cold she had caught above the clouds, which had now developed into a hacking cough. Several days later she and Abdelwahed were received at the palace. Together the Sultan and the pilot grinned for the cameras, the Sultan in his brown djellabah, Touria in a dark tie, white shirt, pants, and double-breasted pilot's jacket, wings pinned to her right breast, her arms filled with flowers. In the photos that were published the next day, some saw more than a celebration of one girl's accomplishment. Some saw a savvy Sultan who understood what a powerful symbol of independence this fourteen-year-old girl had become.

In the early days of November, Touria's cough worsened. Abdelwahed and Zina took her to Doctor Chenbou at the Hospital Colombani, fearing tuberculosis. The doctor put Touria on a heavy dose of Rimifon and announced that it would be a miracle if she lived ten days.

For three straight nights Abdelwahed and Zina separately dreamed that their daughter was dead. Then on the fourth day there was a call from the palace. The Sultan had been informed of Touria's condition and insisted on flying her in his private plane to a sanatorium at Sancellemoz in the Haute-Savoye region of France. Morocco needed Touria Chaoui alive, and so for the next six months she sat on her snow-swept balcony, cheeks growing fat beneath the white summit of Mont Blanc. She was up among the clouds, but she'd been up there before.

○

HANDS
1952

Tony Méléro sat in the office of Captain Fillette of the SDECE at the Résidence Générale in Rabat. After receiving the call at the police station that muggy morning in June 1952, he had driven up the coastal road from Casablanca in his black Peugeot 203, mind hitched to the dotted center line. This road led from past to future, and discipline would be rewarded. Captain Fillette had instructed him to appear out of uniform, and his old dark suit was a size too small, pinching his shoulders and thighs, which was unforgiveable, but he was determined to let that be the day's only oversight. His white shirt was clean but regrettably unadorned by cufflinks. Hardly an oversight, but obviously an area needing improvement.

Tony was twenty-three and handsome, with an appearance lacking any incongruity. No chaos disturbed his blue eyes. In his three years on the police force, his superiors had praised him as serious, reliable, and polite. His friends in the department were mostly unmanageable hooligans, but Tony seemed to relish orders, and could be effectively brutal when appropriate. The watchers in Rabat had recognized this rare combination, and now face-to-face with the crisply uniformed captain in the cool and windowless office, Tony would not have described himself as nervous. He had trained his mind to erase such thoughts, and his body to maintain perfect posture. Instead he would have said that no man had ever loved France as much as Tony Méléro.

"I've had my eye on you," Captain Fillette was

saying. The lone object on the desk between them was a paper clip. Tony assumed this was significant, but he was trying to ignore the thought. "Since you left the police academy at Ifrane, I have been assembling a dossier on you, your family and friends, your habits. You spend too much time chasing women, but at least you're not a fag."

Tony set his jaw and stared at an invisible spot on the captain's flat forehead, just above the round glasses that seemed screwed into his skeletal face. Not having expected the captain to mention women first, he nonetheless admitted to himself that he was a bit of a lady killer. There had been that Marie, whom he had taken to the beach at the end of May. Poor Marie, who abruptly inhaled each time she said *oui* and had lost her house key in the sand. Then the Moroccan on the windy ramparts of Mogador over the Christmas break, salt spray stinging his eyes as she put a hand on his cheek. True, she had probably wanted money. In any case, he never saw a woman more than once or twice, because then she would start to make demands, and for Tony there was no more edifying pleasure than being alone in his room at night with his only book, the one he believed every civilized man should possess, a poetry compilation entitled *Souvenirs poétiques de l'école romantique, 1825 à 1840*. He had found it in his apartment when moving several years earlier. Most of the poems he had not yet read, because the book tended to fall open to the same worn page featuring Henri de Lacretelle, who in Tony's opinion was France's greatest poet, definitely better than Lamartine, who followed him alphabetically. This was his only criticism of the otherwise excellent compilation. De Lacretelle was criminally underrepresented, with only one long poem, *The Bells*.

> O bell! vibrate yourself with beauty's breath.
> So, delirious instrument,
> Broken just by touching,
> The bell became a lyre,
> And to its song I slept.

"You're in top shape," Captain Fillette continued, "but with your friends you start too many fights. None of that is important to me now. We need to prepare for difficult days in Morocco, and I'm wagering you're just the sort of man required."

"Why me?" Tony asked huskily. In his ears his voice sounded disgustingly flirtatious, like Marie asking if she was pretty. Marie hadn't been all that pretty, and Tony was wholly sure of himself, so it wasn't the same thing.

"I can't stand fanatics, schemers, or liars. I need trained men with solid beliefs, and also I think you'll be discreet. And yes, you'll probably have to kill a few people." Tony nodded sharply. Anyone besides the experienced captain of the Action Service of the French foreign intelligence service would have assumed that the young policeman had already notched multiple kills. "Don't think killing will be easy," Fillette continued. "Possibly it will be helpful for you to tell yourself that you are merely an arm."

"I am merely an arm," Tony repeated, mentally checking his posture again. He was a hammer, a knife. He could also be an arm.

"Or perhaps we should say a hand, a right hand in the service of France."

He could be a hand.

"Also, you won't earn a single additional franc. You will retain your policeman's salary. What is it, four hundred per month?"

"Precisely, sir," Tony said, staring at the invisible spot on the captain's forehead. This useful trick he had discovered in a self-improvement guide bought at the newsstand on Avenue de la République. Congos and the Gypsy had later discovered the guide in his glovebox and had mocked him for it, tossing it back and forth to read passages aloud, but look where he was now. He loved those two like brothers, but they simply weren't on his level. They were too content with what is called the *status quo*, from the Latin. The guide had contained dozens of motivational quotations from some of the world's greatest literature, but of course you couldn't begin to explain that to Congos or the Gypsy.

"All of this will remain between us," Captain Fillette was saying. "That includes friends and family. Total secrecy. You're talented, Méléro. You can't let yourself be compromised. From this day forward, you are a new man."

"I understand completely, sir," he said, tamping down his smile as best he could. "And I won't let you down."

The captain then described the different sections of the service. "There is Intelligence, headed by a man you will never meet and whom I will call Pascal. He collects and coordinates detailed information on your targets. Then there is Security, headed by a man we'll call Claude. He studies the point of attack, and during the action he secures the area, creating diversions if necessary, all at a distance. And then there is Action itself, your domain. Each mission will be communicated to you at the last possible instant, at which point you will be given information from Intelligence in order to design the action. Even then, however, you will each remain in your compartments. With you in your compartment will be a team of two to three men, depending on the action. They will find you in advance of your first action, which will take place next week. All I will say about it for now is that I think you will be pleased. We have located the financiers of the terrorists who killed Deputy Chief Inspector Marchetti at Bousbir."

"Sir, I have longed to take our vengeance on that nest of vultures," Tony replied, straining mightily to hide his ecstasy. Of course that bit about the vultures was a paraphrase of de Lacretelle.

"That will be all for now," said the captain, perfunctorily shaking Tony's hand. The young man then strode boldly out of the room, and what might have been a smile appeared on the thin lips of Captain Fillette, which was an alias for Jacques Morlane, which was an alias for Henri Fille-Lambie. That was probably as far as it went.

○

Tony drove in a trance, whipping past a dilapidated truck rumbling along with a cargo of watermelons stacked to twice its height. The truck briefly veered onto the shoulder, dislodging a watermelon, which hit the asphalt with a gruesome splat. *Vibrate yourself with beauty's breath*, Tony murmured. *Vibrate yourself. Vibrate yourself.* Feeling ruthless and reborn, he entered the city through Roches Noires, ignoring the slums and the sun swelling towards the horizon off Boulevard du Commandant Fages. Approaching the police station, he reluctantly slowed at a red light and glanced around at the chaotic city, where he had honestly never felt at home, but whose chaos he would now reorder. Across the intersection, two cops frisked a Moroccan against a wall. Nothing unusual. After sunset, the medina and outlying Moroccan neighborhoods had been put under curfew, and the police could justifiably stop and arrest natives still out on the streets. Tony had frisked dozens of them. The task demoralized him and seemed less fit for trained policemen than for the street sweepers who whisked endless cigarette butts along the city's gutters. All anyone was asking the Moroccans to do was follow a few basic rules designed to ensure everyone's security, theirs included, but they couldn't seem to grasp even the simplest instructions. Sweep, sweep. Thankfully Tony's mission had been upgraded.

The light turned green, and he accelerated through the intersection, keeping an eye on the cops. He wasn't especially surprised when they turned out to be Congos and the Gypsy, who arrested more curfew violators than any other two cops in the city. Given that most of the Moroccans they frisked avoided arrest by paying some form of "toll" – cash, pussy, occasionally whiskey – Tony's two friends did little else during working hours. Then in the evenings out of uniform they liked to shake down shop owners, with Tony sometimes backing them up. Every once in a while you would encounter some sniveling merchant running guns for the resistance from the back of his shop, and then Tony felt redeemed.

Swerving onto the sidewalk, he hopped out of the Peugeot, clapping slowly at the familiar performance. The Gypsy had pinned the Moroccan to the wall while Congos hissed into the idiot's ear. Their faces were contorted and ghoulish, at least until they saw Tony and dropped the charade, happily calling out his name as Congos kicked the Moroccan free down the sidewalk. Their motorbike had broken down, and they had been killing time while figuring out what to do next. "Now you can give us a ride," Congos said, rolling the bike around to the back of the Peugeot.

"Not a chance," Tony said. "I just washed it this morning." He hadn't mentioned the Rabat trip and hoped they wouldn't ask where he'd been and why he wasn't in uniform. Which was partially why he watched in silence as they lifted the bike to slot it into the trunk. "It's too big," he finally said. "It'll never fit."

"Funny," Congos gasped, straining under the bike's weight. "That's what your mother said last night." Weakened by mad laughter, the Gypsy dropped his end of the bike, and he and Congos started shouting at one another. Tony gritted his teeth and glumly shook his head. Don't encourage them. You can't descend to their level. Headquarters was less than a mile away, and they could roll the damned bike there themselves. But Congos had already heaved out the spare tire from the trunk and was rolling it over to the curb.

"What do you think you're doing?" Tony snapped.

"We won't forget the tire," Congos grumbled, attacking a smear of grease on the sleeve of his uniform.

He and the Gypsy lifted the bike again and maneuvered it into the trunk, although one wheel still hung out and the door wouldn't shut. Tony regretted stopping but remained silent as they clambered into the car, Congos in front, the Gypsy in back with the filthy spare tire dragged up onto the clean seat beside him. Congos reached out to turn on the radio, but Tony snapped it off. "*Mon dieu*," Congos said, turning to wink at the Gypsy. "Somebody's got her period."

"Oh, shut the hell up, both of you," Tony shouted, and they did.

Several blocks later they pulled up alongside a green Morris Minor. What drew their collective attention was that the Morris was driven by a pretty Moroccan girl. You didn't see that every day. Tony cruised along beside her for a while until Congos asked: "Isn't that the crazy pilot girl? Now they've given her a driver's license? Next those clowns in Paris will decide to name her Resident General."

"Let's pull her over," said the Gypsy, tapping Tony on the shoulder.

"Leave her alone," Tony sighed. "Don't you think we've got better things to do?"

"Come on," Congos begged. "It'll be fun! Then we promise we'll clean the car once the bike's out."

Tony sighed and honked the horn. The girl glanced over, and Congos called out through his open window: "Police! Pull over!" The girl shook her head as if she hadn't understood, then slowly braked to the side of the road. Tony pulled around her, and the other two burst out of the car like shorn dogs out of the Gypsy's mother's shop.

"Where did you get this car?" Congos was asking

when Tony sauntered up. His head was down by the girl's window. She was still in the car. The Gypsy nudged Tony in the ribs with an elbow. *Watch this.* "Is it stolen?" Then in Moroccan: "We all speak Arabic if you don't understand French."

"I speak French," the girl calmly said. "And the car is not stolen. It is mine, given to me by my father, Abdelwahed Chaoui."

"Get your papers and step out of the car," said the Gypsy, popping his head through the window beside Congos's. After a moment they stepped back to let the girl emerge with the papers. She was prettier than the newspaper photos, Tony thought, with curly hair down to her shoulders, full lips, and disturbingly calm eyes with dark rings beneath. She wore a light sweater and pleated pants and looked directly at him, perhaps assuming his suit gave him power over the others. He glanced away. There was no talking sense to Congos, especially once he got started, and also the girl was an embarrassment to French Morocco. For all he knew, the story about her father was a lie and the car was in fact stolen.

The Gypsy stared at the papers for a long moment, then said to Congos: "Better check if she's armed."

Sadly then, as if begrudging her for putting him in such a situation, Congos reached out to frisk the girl. "Hands out, please." Only then did Tony see a hint of fear crease her forehead, but she held out her arms.

Congos started patting, slowly moving down the sides of the girl's body before lingering at the flesh of her small breasts. The girl remained motionless. Her eyes switched off.

"Anything?" the Gypsy asked anxiously.

"Not yet," Congos said, moving closer to the girl as his hands slid down around her waist and over her hips. He dropped to his knees and patted up her right leg, his ear cocked at her belly like a safe cracker straining to hear the click of tumblers. Tony turned away and paced. Congos's hands moved quickly past the girl's knees then slowly along her thighs.

"Anything?" asked the Gypsy, feigning deep concern.

Congos shook his head. "But I could be missing something," he murmured, his right hand still between the girl's legs. "Maybe you should check." The girl looked down on him then with pure hatred, her arms still straight out by her sides. The Gypsy could no longer keep a straight face. "Flap them, and maybe you can fly," he giggled.

Congos clucked like a chicken as he lifted himself up out of his crouch. *Bawk bawk bawk.* "She's that pilot girl, isn't she? Imagine that! What's her name? It's on the tip of my tongue…."

The Gypsy looked down at the papers. "Touria Chaoui," the girl said, emphatically dropping her arms.

"Did I tell her to drop her arms?" Congos asked.

"You didn't tell her anything," the Gypsy tittered. "I want her to flap those arms and show how a little Moroccan girl flies."

"You're in serious trouble," Congos said, now pressing his body to hers. "You shouldn't be out alone past curfew. How old is she?"

Behind him the Gypsy looked down at the papers. "Sixteen," Touria said into Congos's face.

"Got a mouth on her too! Listen, Mademoiselle Chaoui, we're going to have to impound this car until we've fully investigated your situation. Get in. You will drive us to the station." *See*, said the look he shot Tony. *Problem solved.* Tony shook his head. The bike was still in his car, and he would inevitably have to deal with it.

The girl, however, wasn't about to get back into her car with Congos and the Gypsy. She reached in to pull the keys out of the ignition, then held them out to the two flabbergasted cops.

"Come on," Tony said after a long moment. The insolent girl probably deserved to spend a couple of hours in a cell with them, but her fame made him hesitant. He couldn't get involved in a situation that might bring attention to himself, jeopardizing the trust of Captain Fillette. "Let's get out of here. We'll drop the bike off at the station, and then I'm buying drinks at La Gironde."

Reluctantly, Congos and the Gypsy turned away from the girl and climbed back into the Peugeot. Tony pulled off again, watching in his rearview mirror as she opened the door of the Morris and slumped down into it. He watched for several blocks, and the Morris did not move. With every passing second he grew angrier at Congos and the Gypsy. He loved them, sure, but why was he still hanging around with them? All they could ever see was what was directly in front of their own faces. They could never conceive of the larger picture as Tony did. He wondered if they had always been like this. Had he changed, or had they? Why was he wasting his time? He thought of the exhilaration he had felt in Captain Fillette's office at being *recognized*, for once, by a man he truly admired. By the time they reached the station, he was regretting the offer of drinks. He wanted to be alone, but they would never understand that either.

"I've got a couple things to do first," he said once they had hauled the bike out of the car. "I'll meet you over there."

○

A stylish Moroccan woman in a short plaid skirt sat on a stool rolling a silk stocking up her thigh when Tony walked into the shop on Rue Nolly. The bells jingled. The woman, perhaps thirty-five, registered his presence with an unconcerned glance and rolled the stocking higher. Squiggly lines ran up the silk like snakes. Tony figured the woman was a rich wife from an old Casablanca or Rabat family. Hovering at the entrance, he forced himself to stare at the exposed leg, wanting revenge for the woman's disdain. To a woman like that, he was trash. It didn't matter that he was French. Women like that had the confidence of centuries. The blood of the prophet ran in their veins, or at least that's what they believed. Moroccan men would only stab you in the back, but their women would stab you in the front and hold your eyes as they twisted the blade. First the haughty aviatrix, and now this long-legged hatred. The women were the dangerous ones. Tony congratulated himself on the observation and filed it away for mention to Captain Fillette. Impress him with your initiative. Perhaps the Intelligence section should be paying closer attention to wives, daughters, and sisters. Not that Intelligence was Tony's compartment, of course, but perhaps the Action section should be paying closer attention as well. Just a suggestion. Sir.

"If you'll give us a moment, *monsieur.*" The fat proprietress had emerged from the back of the shop with her arms full of luxurious stockings. Tony nodded and stepped back out onto the sidewalk, lighting a cigarette. People spoke of Aziza's on Rue Nolly. He had passed the shop often, and in the windows were always beautiful shirts, piles of them. He kept track of the best places. That was how you knew what you wanted when you reached a point where you could have it. And today he'd reached that point. If not a tailored suit, then at least a new shirt with cufflinks. For months he had even been dreaming of glittering cufflinks.

He paced, refusing to look through the window, furious he hadn't said something elegant and cutting. Or charming, even flattering, something to make the woman wonder about him. But she could never know the truth. None of them could ever know the truth. He would move through the night like a black panther. Or a hand. But even that fact didn't diminish his anger at the woman, and he smoked quickly, puffing out lines of de Lacretelle: *A woman, you know, a stem full of mystery. The flowers of her goodness should scent the earth!*

A Citroën 15 screeched up to the curb, startling him from his thoughts. Four men in flashy suits – checks and stripes – piled out. The smallest man looked familiar, and the others deferred to him. They wore holsters beneath their jackets, Tony noticed, but they weren't police. Hiding his face behind his cigarette, he felt his heart beating in his fingers. His cigarette twitched. The rumors were that Jo Renucci had come to town.

A feared boss in the Marseille Gang, Renucci had

recently had five tons of cigarettes seized in Tangier. His fortune had been made in "trafficking blondes", but in recent years the Gang had been moving into heroin, whose raw materials came from Indochina through Marseille, where the morphine was refined and shipped on to the United States. The CIA and SDECE knew about the trafficking but looked the other way, because the Gang was committed to preventing French communists from controlling the Port of Marseille.

The rumors were that Renucci was in hiding. Nobody knew from whom. Some claimed he was running guns again, so strapped for cash that he was even selling to violent resistance groups like the Black Crescent, who were aligned with the Moroccan communists. Tony wasn't convinced. Captain Fillette surely had men watching all persons of interest, and in Morocco nobody could keep a secret. That was the advantage. The problem was that everybody also lied. In any case, Renucci wasn't exactly hiding. As the four men approached Tony, their hands moved almost imperceptibly towards their thick waists. It had to be Renucci. He noticed Tony and stopped. The others closed ranks. "Bonjour kid," the gangster said.

"Bonjour." Tony failed to locate an invisible spot on the gangster's forehead. He was wearing his own gun, of course, but the bodyguards would have noticed that.

"You like girls? Huh? You like to have a good time?"

"Yes sir," Tony murmured. The bodyguards chuckled.

"Then starting Friday night, this is the place to be." Confused, Tony glanced from one face to the next. "Right here, kid!" Renucci cried, pointing up at a new sign next door to the clothing shop. In pink neon, blinding in the dusk, one word: *Paradise.*

"I appreciate the invitation," Tony said.

"The name's Jo," the gangster said, extending a hand. Tony glanced down at it and noticed the man was wearing cufflinks. "We'll have drinks. I'll introduce you to people."

Then the four men entered Paradise, Tony stubbed his cigarette out beneath his heel and strode back into the shop, saying, "A white cotton shirt, one hundred percent Egyptian, or at least Brazilian, and a pair of your finest cufflinks."

The long-legged Moroccan had disappeared. Probably snuck out when he was talking to Renucci, scared to face him again.

"Of course," Aziza purred. "An elegant man deserves the best."

Tony nodded. At least the fat proprietress showed him some respect. She asked for his size and vanished into the back. The place was fancy, and he was pleased. It was large and well organized, not like those cheap Moroccan places with stuff piled everywhere. Women's clothes down the left side, men down the right. He fingered a tan linen suit hanging on a rack. Pretty good quality.

The proprietress reappeared with a white shirt and a wooden box. He took the shirt. It was just a shirt, but it was beautiful and expensive, and people would know, or if they didn't know, they would sense it. Then he looked into the box, where dozens of cufflinks were pinned into felt slits. His eyes immediately picked out two in the shape of a bell. "Do you have them in gold?"

"I'm afraid not."

"Silver will be fine."

His jacket came off then, and he unbuttoned his old shirt, which he was surprised to find damp with sweat. He peeled it off, down to the undershirt. Let her get a good look. Then she handed over the fresh shirt, which fit perfectly. Holding out his wrists to her, he frowned as she arranged the cufflinks. The price was higher than he could have imagined, but he was elated and didn't mind. Afterwards he told her to keep the old shirt, do whatever she liked with it, because he would be wearing the new shirt right out of the store.

○

2

Lucy was ticked that he wasn't going to make it to the Kiddie Karnival. "You promised, Tommy August!" she cried from the kitchen. The screen door slapped shut behind him. The things he had always loved most about Lucy, like the dramatic Texas drawl, were also the things that made him want to strangle her sometimes. She knew damned well he couldn't control when General Jackson called a meeting. He realized she'd spent weeks planning the Kiddie Karnival. Hell, it was all she'd been talking about. And of course he wanted to be there more than anything, for Jimmy and Mary especially. And yes, he knew the past couple of months had been stressful for his wife. She hadn't wanted to be apart from him anymore. *One war's too many for me, Tommy August.* So she had come out sooner than most of the other wives, and he saw that she was starved for company. Lucy rarely complained, however, and after getting the house in shape, she had kept busy with all sorts of creative projects, showing the gumption that was something else he loved about her until it made him want to strangle her.

The Cadillac was an oven. He should have kept the windows cracked, but the leather got dusty when those desert winds blew in. The car had come on the boat with Lucy and the kids, a black 1952 Eldorado Series 62 Convertible Coupe, $7750 and worth every penny. He checked his tie in the mirror, attempting to put Lucy out of his mind. These days in meetings he was usually the only civilian, which still felt strange. The tie looked fine. He turned the key, switched the fan up to full blast, and reversed out of the driveway onto Echo Court.

The Augusts' house was one of few in the neighborhood already completed. The others had fallen behind schedule, like most everything else at the base since the Nouasseur had opened. First, the runways had been poured with substandard concrete, and sections of them were now useless during the winter rainy season. Congress had investigated, construction stopped, including on the water tower, which had meant no running water. You couldn't use the sidewalks. They led nowhere. Electricity had been cut at nightfall, and base personnel had tromped through the mud and darkness to their Dallas huts, which leaked. As head contractor on site for the Atlas Corporation, Tommy had probably been the least popular man on base. Several of his superiors had been fired for graft, but General Jackson's faith in him had never wavered, and now all across the base, crews of Moroccans under his command were putting up new buildings from sunup to sundown. Even if they continued to meet their new deadlines, however, Tommy would still be an outsider at best among this crowd, especially as a Navy man, and he dreaded any call to meet with the general and his staff.

He was no longer a flier. Technically he was no longer even Navy. By the end of the war, after thirty-eight missions flown over North Africa, Southeast Asia, and Okinawa, he had left the Red Rippers with the rank of captain. A career in the Navy had been on offer, but as much as he loved flying, he had declined it, because he had still dreamed of becoming a composer.

Lucy had encouraged him to follow his dream. From the base in Norfolk, where she had spent the war with Jimmy, they moved to Chicago, Oak Lawn, where they could occupy the second floor of Tommy's childhood home. His father had died during his last tour, and his mother was glad for the company. She and Lucy spent the days together with three-year-old Jimmy, and soon Mary, born in 1946. Meanwhile Tommy paced the floors of his father's dusty old office, confounded by his inability to find any note belonging next to any other. Occasionally he shuffled out to the upright piano in the parlor and held a few chords while staring up at the two photographs on the wall. Tommy in uniform, so serious, staring down the future. And his parents on their wedding day, laughing in a crowd outside the University Club. Then, mumbling to himself, he would shuffle back to the office and shut the door. Unaccustomed to dark thoughts, and alarmed by this feeling of impotence, he found himself escaping into memories of the war – the cool isolation of the cockpit, but also Morocco, and those vivid days when he had been lost to the world, a prisoner of his fantastical Spahis with their turbans and bandoliers. At the time the experience had been hellish. But nothing had felt more vivid since. When at dinner sweet Lucy asked him how his day had been, his response was always the same: "I'm making progress."

But he was already twenty-seven and wasn't making progress, not in any sense. For a man whose life had never missed a beat, this was disorienting. *I have a wife and children to feed*, he started repeating to himself, until it almost became a melody. And then to everyone's surprise, he took a part-time job with his brother Ron, a general contractor with whom he'd never been close. To Lucy, who still had dreams of cocktail parties on the arm of a famous composer, and also wanted Tommy to be happy, he pretended that the work with Ron was deadening, and sometimes hearing himself talk to her when they were finally alone in bed, he believed it himself. Deadening. The truth, however, was that he enjoyed the camaraderie of construction sites, the physical activity, the challenge of organizing supplies and men. He even enjoyed Ron. Part-time became full-time, and after work they would sit in the empty offices and drink whiskey, making projections and laughing at crises averted. Ron was nothing special. He was brash and hungry for money. He couldn't have told the difference between Bach and Schoenberg and had always regarded Tommy's talent as a sort of handicap, an unnatural goal for a man who looked more like a quarterback, but their moments together soon became Tommy's favorite part of the day. Four years passed. He wrote very little, just a few snippets which he struggled to fit into any larger musical structure. The snippets were no more substantial than memories. Palm trees, flags, the scent of jasmine. Not music, more like longing.

When an old Navy friend told him about the opening with the Atlas Corporation, he hadn't hesitated. By then Lucy was also eager for a change, and the salary would enable him to practice the skills he'd learned in Chicago while also charting a more artistic course for him and his family in exotic Morocco.

Nouasseur was Air Force, under the newly formed Strategic Air Command, which controlled U.S. nuclear strike forces, including bombers and reconnaissance aircraft, and also ran the base at Ben Guerir. The USAF was at Sidi Slimane, and the Navy was up the coast at Port Lyautey. Tension was high between the two services, which had fought in Congress for control of America's nuclear arsenal. The Air Force had won that battle, and although Tommy still resented the decision, he had learned not to mention to Air Force pilots the storied history of the Red Rippers. The Air Force guys liked to believe they were at the forefront of the new Cold War against the Soviets, and guys like Tommy were living in the past. So he just did his job, despite odds stacked against him that would have frustrated even Ron, and he kept his memories to himself, even in Morocco.

Turning right off Custer Boulevard onto Arnold Avenue, he waved to Ricky Snodgrass in his green Ford, likely heading over to the Logistics Plans Office, where he was responsible for the acquisition and distribution of base supplies and the maintenance of aircraft and equipment. Saturday morning they had played nine holes together. The grass on the flat muddy fairways was finally starting to appear. "Day and night I plan for how to repair our bombers in the event of an attack," Ricky had sighed as they walked towards the clubhouse. He was single, sleep-deprived, and had four-putted the ninth. Even when Bob Hope and Debbie Reynolds had come to perform, Ricky had been stuck in his office.

"And what everybody knows but won't say is that the work's completely pointless. War breaks out, we'll likely cross the nuclear threshold within a day, and we'll be gone before we've started. For over a year now I've been researching and drafting our SAC support plan. Is it a good plan? We'll never know."

Tommy had laughed, but he disliked that kind of talk. You had to stay positive, he believed, and keep seeing the bigger picture. He pulled into the Officer's Club parking lot, rolled up the windows of the Cadillac, and stepped out into the sun. What was so urgent about this meeting anyway? He didn't want to know.

In the general's large office a dozen uniformed men had assembled. Tommy smiled affably and ran a hand over his scalp, searching for a friendly face. The Air Force guys tended to let their hair grow longer, as if the power of flight gave them special dispensations. Tommy still shaved his close in the Navy style, something else that set him apart, he knew, but then he'd flown more missions than most of these guys – in the U.S. Navy's toughest flying squadron – and he didn't intend to forget it.

Several of the officers he didn't recognize. Either they'd driven from the other bases or had flown from further afield. Standing in the corner were also two French officers. This was unusual, but also a relief, because for once the meeting wasn't likely to be focused on the failings of the Atlas Corporation, represented by yours truly. No, something else was going on. Only one other civilian was present, a cagey-looking American in a rumpled jacket. Tommy moved around the conference table, nodding and smiling, until one of the French officers drew his attention. Handsome and aloof, the officer was chatting in low tones to his compatriot. Tommy glanced away to collect himself. He felt dizzy, as if time was collapsing. Then he smiled and glanced back at the man. "Vic?" The Frenchman turned. "It's Tommy August! Your old American pen pal!"

Vic's eyes flickered before his thin lips turned up at the corners. "Hello Tommy," he said, shaking hands. "I didn't recognize you out of uniform."

Tommy chuckled, not wanting to let go of the kid's hand. Although not such a kid anymore. He could hardly believe it. Now almost ten years to the day. "Well let's be honest," he finally replied. "Besides the civilian clothes, I've got a little less up top and a little more around the middle. What are you doing here? You became a pilot! I knew you would."

Vic briefly outlined his career. Six months after Operation Torch, he had joined the Armée de l'Air, and after training he had been sent to Germany with the Normandie-Niemen Regiment, fighting under Soviet command. Now he was stationed back in Casablanca, mostly at the Tit Mellil airfield.

"I guess you're happy to be home." Tommy still grinned, marveling at what Vic had become. Once upon a time he'd just been a wide-eyed kid with some dirty postcards. But he had remained unusually present in Tommy's mind through the intervening years. Of course they were both older now, but that only made their seven-year difference seem more negligible, and Vic had clearly turned out all right. Maybe they could be friends. He seemed a bit stiff, maybe, not as sociable as he'd once been, but Tommy knew how war could do that to a man. In Chicago he'd experienced a bit of that darkness himself.

"Well I've admittedly been back for about a year now," Tommy went on. "I wanted to look you up, but I didn't know where to start and figured you were probably long gone anyway. And here you are! What brings two French officers out to the American suburbs?"

But General Jackson had called the meeting to order, and the reunion was put on hold.

After some introductions, Colonel Leblanc, Vic's superior, spoke, his English extremely formal. The French, who officially shared the base, had concerns that the Americans were not being entirely forthright about their military intentions in Morocco. Ever since the 1942 landings, their American friends had been significantly more popular among the local population than the French, for the obvious reasons, but was it also possible that they were encouraging this popularity at the expense of French interests? There had been secret meetings with the Sultan conducted without the permission of the Resident General, and then there were the humanitarian projects, noble endeavors to be sure, but once again conducted without permission.

Tommy had taken a blank page from his briefcase in order to jot down notes but still couldn't for the life of him figure why he'd been asked to attend such a meeting. His eyes wandered up to the ceiling, where there appeared to be a water stain just above the general's desk. Cripes. Of all places to find another leak.

The conversation continued. The words "mutual cooperation" were uttered at least a dozen times. Tommy wrote "mutual cooperation" beneath "leak" on the paper in front of him but otherwise paid little attention. Eventually the sloppy American civilian – CIA, Tommy figured – interrupted: "The Soviets are a shared enemy, *messieurs*, and the purpose of these bases is to give us the mutual capacity to confront that enemy in the event of a nuclear escalation. Our cooperation has positioned us to gather unprecedented intelligence, and at the request of Washington, I have been overseeing recent construction of the radar and communications station ten miles north of here at Saddle Rock, manned by the 736th AC&W squadron."

"Thank you, Mister Felton," the general barked, livid at the interruption.

"Saddle Rock?" Tommy murmured, disengaging his eyes from the water stain. "That's where Breezy and I rendezvoused, and then I went down." The general shot him a withering look, and Tommy clamped his mouth shut. He hadn't meant to speak aloud. These days he often felt disconnected. Now in the prime of his life, nothing seemed to matter as much as it had that day over Saddle Rock. He looked down at his sheet of paper. Still feeling the general's eyes, he furrowed his brow and scribbled his name across the page. Tommy August.

"We would like to know more about your actual capabilities here at the base." Colonel Leblanc took a map from his case and unfolded it across the table. "For example, what is this mechanical bull?"

There was some low chuckling from the Americans. Colonel Leblanc went pale. "The mechanical bull," General Jackson replied with utmost seriousness, "is an oil drum suspended via four ropes tied to the top of four wooden poles. One man rides the drum as if it is a bull, while others shake the ropes attempting to dismount him. It is in no way classified, and after this meeting, if you like, I would be happy to escort you over there so that you can test your skills. Personally I've never been able to stay on the damned thing for more than ten seconds. No doubt you will do better, Colonel."

Tommy grinned along with the others. The general was a good guy. Heck, they'd been together since the beginning at Nouasseur and were now practically friends. Tommy glanced over at Vic. The kid's expression had hardly changed, and reminded Tommy of his own serious portrait above the piano in Chicago. Meanwhile Colonel Leblanc was respectfully declining the general's mechanical bull offer while stabbing his index finger at the map. "And this area here, *par exemple*? There is nothing on the map, and yet driving in today I could not help but notice a large building with false windows. What is this building, *par exemple*?"

"That's just an ordnance dump, gentlemen," the general replied, glancing at Tommy, who now understood why he'd been invited to the meeting. "And any further questions about the configuration of the base can be addressed to our head contractor, Tommy August."

Tommy nodded. "Happy to take you through it any time," he added, "but as for that particular building, as the general said, it's just an ordnance dump. We simply neglected to include it in the original plans."

The French colonel slowly nodded, folded up his map, and the meeting was soon adjourned.

Afterwards Tommy and Vic walked out to the parking lot together. He should come around to the house sometime, Tommy said, and meet Lucy and the kids. Vic nodded vaguely as if he hadn't understood. Had he lost some of his English?

"So how about you?" Tommy continued. "Wife? Kids?"

"No," Vic said. They had reached his car, an old, dented Peugeot. To Tommy's disappointment, Vic didn't linger. He shook Tommy's hand and got into the car, but then the engine wouldn't turn. Through the open window Vic cursed to himself in French. Tommy smiled. "Don't worry, *mon ami*. I happen to know my way around an engine. One of the benefits of the job, you could say. Pop the hood."

The hood clunked open, and Tommy propped it up. The engine was old, but he couldn't spot any obvious problems, except that the battery leads were somewhat rusted. He jiggled them back and forth. "Try it again." Vic turned the key, and the engine started. Grinning, Tommy slammed shut the hood and walked around to Vic's window. "You should probably get that battery checked. Might be leaking acid. And I'm serious about coming around to the house. Lucy's heard all about you."

Vic nodded and stuck out his hand again. "Thank

you," he mumbled. "And the composing? Are you writing music?"

"Not in a long while," Tommy said, still smiling, "but I'm glad you remembered."

"Well, thanks for your help, Lieutenant August."

"Captain, actually, but that's ancient history. It's Tommy between friends." Vic nodded, shifted the Peugeot into reverse, and drove off towards the base entrance. Tommy watched until he disappeared and then stood there for a while longer, gazing off at what they had called the ordnance dump.

3

NORTH AFRICA: TO CREATE MARTYRS

It was Sunday in Manhattan, and the diplomats of the United Nations had postponed for a day their discussion of France's troubles with her rebellious North African protectorates, Morocco and Tunisia. But fanaticism knows no holidays, and in North Africa itself, Arab nationalists, urged on by the Communists, were busy seeking ways to exploit the latest incident.

Few of the 500,000 Arabs and 120,000 Frenchmen in Morocco's teeming, gaudy boomtown Casablanca, some 1,000 miles from the scene of the murder, had even heard of the victim, Tunisian Labor Leader Farhat Hached (*TIME*, Dec. 15). Yet Casablanca's Nationalist daily *El Alam* that day urged all Moroccan workers to mourn his death in a general strike....

Can Town. [I]n the vast jungle of tin-roofed hovels known locally as Bidonville (Can Town), an angry mob was forming.... Glib agitators harangued little knots of Arabs while others began hiding stones under their burnooses. From shack after shack came the ominous scrape of crude knives being honed.

At 10 that night, a shower of stones fell on the roof of an isolated police station just across the dung-strewn road from Can Town, and within seconds the police were inundated by Arab rioters. "They appeared as if by magic," said one of the eight policemen on duty, "out of the ground, from holes in the wall. It was unbelievable. One minute the street was deserted. The next minute it was filled with a horde of madmen screaming for blood." The police fired at short range killing some 20 Arabs.

A Quick Look. Next morning the peaceful clop-clop of fiacres on the Boulevard du Quatrième Zouaves was interrupted by the rumble of trucks filled with Berber troops and the quick march of the blue-black Senegalese riflemen. They were met by a mob of some 10,000 screaming Arabs armed with sticks, stones and anything else that could pierce or bludgeon. Hard-bitten French Commandant Louis Durand three times commanded the mob to halt. As the Arabs continued to surge forward, Durand gave the order; the crack of rifle fire split the air and an estimated 40 Arabs dropped. The rest dispersed to carry on the fight from rooftops and doorways. French observation planes circled overhead to keep track of other mobs snaking angrily through the city....

Shoehorns & Scimitars. At the end of the two days of rioting, some 3,000 Arabs were rounded up in the same union hall where the trouble began. As the police forced them into a sullen huddle, the hall was filled with the clatter of weapons – clasp knives, ice picks, scimitars, poniards, shoehorns, hatchets, fire tongs and brass knuckles – falling to the floor. Net score after two troubled days: 1,000 arrests; 100 or more Arab dead, 60 known wounded and probably many more cared for by their people; five European civilians dead and 13 wounded; three soldiers dead and 43 wounded....

What was the point of the slaughter? One arrested Arab Nationalist explained: "It was the best way to create incidents so that we could offer martyrs to the United Nations."

At week's end in Manhattan, France's friend, the U.S., which had alternately blown hot & cold on Arab nationalist aspirations, joined the majority at U.N. in deciding (by a vote of 27 to 24 in the case of Tunisia) to let the French settle their problems in North Africa without interference.[14]

○

A wounded sun set over a city still weeping for its dead. The air was as cold as a corpse. At the epicenter of it all was your intrepid reporter, who for days had waded through the bloody streets, expecting at any moment to be knifed, betrayed by his stubborn insistence on bringing you, dear readers, the story of three horrific days. The experience had left him battered and bruised, both physically and spiritually. Whither Casablanca?

Albert Forestier put down his pen and glanced around La Gironde for inspiration. *Stubborn* or *passionate?* Mazzella, his editor at *Maroc-Presse*, had not officially asked him to cover the riots, but this was the kind of story that could really establish a young reporter. Perhaps Albert had not directly observed any of the rioting, and was neither battered nor bruised (although perhaps spiritually?), but surely the newspaper's front

______
14   *Time* – 12/22/1952

page could benefit from the vivid, literary style he had brought to the undercards of local amateur boxing matches. So far, however, Mazzella had disagreed, with inexplicable vehemence, and Forestier had grown increasingly frustrated, until in recent days he had decided to make an exciting change in his life.

So why was he still writing the story? Perhaps because he was a born writer, as simple as that. Behind the bar Avival had been holding forth on the day's news, and Forestier had been eavesdropping from a nearby table. The talk was of the riots in the Carrières Centrales slums: "At least after all that we finally had the good sense to ban Istiqlal and the Parti Communiste Marocain. But the Sultan's still here. Can somebody explain that to me? Anybody?"

And the revolution in Egypt: "The Brits made the mistake we can't afford to make here. Those animals in the Muslim Brotherhood will destroy that country. Just watch."

And the election of Eisenhower: "Better than Stevenson, but I'll never forgive him for attacking us here."

And the expanding war in Indochina: "France must defend its territories. Let's just hope those spineless politicians in Paris don't forget it."

All excellent points, Forestier thought. He considered going over to join the conversation. Avival and his crew seemed to respect him now, but maybe he wasn't quite yet inner circle. Turning toward the large windows out to the street, he snuck a long look at Avival's latest girl, who had been working at the bar for a few months and was now sweeping the sidewalk. Her black dress swayed, her large breasts too. Avival was always commenting on them, and in response she'd just smile, maybe a little sadly, as if her breasts had nothing to do with the rest of her. Forestier wouldn't have minded getting a good look at them. Sweet girl. A little worn out, maybe – she was already thirty – although back in her prime, Avival said, she had danced at the Don Quichotte. Sang pretty well, too. Albert had heard her. After breakfast every day, she would collect uneaten baguette bits and go outside to feed the sparrows from her hand. Sometimes she sang, and even talked to them as if they could understand. A sensitive woman, Camille. Avival was lucky to have her.

Albert looked back down at his notebook and flipped over to where he'd put the papers from the army recruitment office. In another month the La Gironde gang would still be sitting here discussing the newspapers, but he would be off in Indochina actually making the news. Soon enough they would be reading about him. *Local hero leads successful raid on Vietminh.* "Look at this," Avival would say. "It's our Forestier. They've already made him a lieutenant. He was always a dark horse, that one." As of yet Albert had told no one, not even his father or Mazzella, but the papers were signed, and he only needed to turn them in. He would do it that evening, he decided, before the office closed. Maybe he would have another drink before going. In any case, Casablanca had gotten too small for Albert Forestier.

○

Tony took another sip of whiskey. Congos clapped him on the back, but he hardly noticed. Although he had vowed to avoid La Gironde, this evening he had needed a drink. And then Avival had read out the part about the Red Hand. The Red Hand had shot Farhat Hached, or whatever his name was, and Tony's mind whirled as his excitement mounted. Everything added up. *The Red Hand.* He was a member of the elite Red Hand, and they were operating in Tunisia as well. Captain Fillette hadn't called it that explicitly, but he had kept mentioning how Tony would be a *hand*, hadn't he? Honestly it made perfect sense. And now that they had taken care of that communist traitor in Tunisia, it was Tony's turn.

"Pour us another, Avival," Congos said. Tony surfaced from his thoughts to put a hand over his glass. "Where's the girl?" Avival barked.

Tony checked his watch. "Hey," Congos cried, grabbing Tony's wrist. "Look at pretty boy with his fancy cufflinks. When did you get those, pretty boy?"

Tony pulled his wrist free. "While you were off knocking over fruit stalls and feeling up three-hundred-pound Berbers." As the others laughed, Tony checked his watch again.

The girl came in from outside then and poured another round. Avival knew how to handle his women. Treat her with respect, but never let her forget you're boss. She looked up at Tony, but he shook his head. "Pretty boy's saving his money for silk underwear," Congos said. The girl held his eyes for a moment, it seemed to Tony, as the others laughed. She was pretty, with that mop of curly hair and the dark spot on her cheek like the American actress Marilyn Monroe. Probably she liked him a little bit, but she was Avival's girl, and even if Tony figured he could handle the ex-boxer, Avival would kill her if she got caught. She looked as if she never forgot it.

"Look at this," Avival was saying, his head buried deep in the newspaper. Whenever he got agitated, he would beat the paper down flat against the bar and read with an index finger underlining the words. Returning on a Douglas DC-4 from a family trip to Malaga, the story reported, the celebrated young Moroccan aviatrix, Touria Chaoui, had caused quite a stir when she had boarded in full pilot's uniform. Mocked by the crew, who had wondered aloud whether the girl suffered from "an excess of elegance", once airborne Miss Chaoui had demanded to be shown into the cockpit, where she had remained for the duration of the flight. Upon landing in Tetuan, the pilot had emerged with Miss Chaoui. "Ladies and gentlemen," he had announced, "it is my honor to inform you that our flight today was piloted by this young lady."

The men groaned. "Nationalist propaganda," Avival muttered. "Anyone who publishes this rot should be put in jail."

"A buddy of mine works out at the Tit Mellil airfield," Congos said, "and he swears she never actually earned the license. They invented the whole story."

"I heard she was spreading her legs for one of her French instructors," said the Gypsy.

"We're clear for takeoff!" Congos cried, humping his stool.

"My god," Avival said, shaking his head. "Bousbir's not enough for them? Now the whores are working the airfields?" The others chuckled.

A new voice chimed in: "I heard that for t-t-two hundred francs she'll spin your p-p-propeller until you t-t-take off."

The room went silent. The men turned to look at Forestier, that reporter kid who was always hanging around. Avival still wasn't laughing, so nobody else did either. "I believe it, boys," Avival finally said, "because if anybody knows about spinning a man's propeller, it's this miserable little faggot."

Forestier flushed and stammered like a drowning man. "I have a s-s-story to write," he said, and laughter chased him out the door into the night.

Tony smiled as Forestier fled, but without much pleasure. He had bigger things on his mind, and his eyes kept flicking from his watch to the door. About five minutes later a small man in a motorcycle helmet and dark goggles appeared. He did not enter the bar. He merely nodded. So that must be Rémy.

○

The target was wearing yellow slippers and a green djellabah, said Battuta, the supposedly blind marabout who panhandled outside Bousbir. Of course Battuta didn't use the word *target*, but the man in question was said to be sleeping in the cavernous garage of Société des Transports Bradley, across the Route de Medouina. Tony placed a coin in the marabout's palm. The old man popped the coin into his mouth and chewed, his face ecstatic. For the first time Tony doubted the setup, but

Rémy was already striding back to the bike.

Rémy had not spoken a word since they had met, nor had he taken off his helmet or goggles. Outside La Gironde, he had led Tony into an alleyway, where the bike had been parked. From a leather saddlebag he had drawn out two woolen djellabahs with hoods. They had proceeded to slip them on, raising the hoods, Rémy's right over his helmet. As they mounted the bike, the grip of Tony's 7.65mm Herstal dug into his stomach. Rémy drove fast, south down Route de Medouina, expertly darting through traffic. His skill calmed Tony's nerves.

Captain Fillette had announced the action over the telephone. He was not in Rabat, but traveling, he couldn't say where. Tunisia? Rémy would lead Tony to the target, whom Intelligence had confirmed was Marchetti's killer. This man's death would send a message to his terrorist organization, which they suspected was partially financed by prominent fabric wholesaler Tahar Sebti. As Tony hung up the phone, he felt like a bullet just fired from a gun. Now he would rocket through the city, whipping around corners, sailing over sleeping innocents, until he found the target's heart. The thought calmed him.

Traffic streamed along the Route de Medouina, leaving a red glow in its wake. Rémy puttered up to the side of the garage and turned to Tony with his goggle eyes. Each reflected the yellow orb of a streetlamp. "I wait here." His voice was flat and cool. "If someone's coming, I will call out for *Abdulatif.*" Tony nodded and slipped his hands through the open djellabah pockets. He slid the pistol from his waistband and screwed the silencer to the barrel. Then he swung down off the bike and strode towards the garage, where one of the bay doors was open to the night. He held a deep breath, then slowly let it out.

The darkness inside lacked any texture, and Tony stood motionless until his eyes drew out a few surrounding contours. There were trucks, many of them, several busses. The transport company repaired them here, and a few of the vehicles were partially dissected across the floor. Tony moved further into the darkness. He could not be afraid. The present was infinite and captured all his attention. He moved slowly, the soles of his shoes sticking slightly to the oily cement floor. Beneath the trucks and along the walls, bums slept in contorted positions. In the cabins of some trucks, stranded drivers slept. Almost all wore djellabahs against the cold. Tony stared into the darkness, which was still too deep for colors.

A bum coughed and gurgled. Somebody else muttered through sleep. Even the slightest sounds echoed off these corrugated metal walls. Tony remained acutely aware of his footsteps, fitting them into the faint undertone of the surrounding shadow life, stepping through shifting zones of pungent smells: gasoline, grease, solder, sweat. Moving down the rows of trucks, he inspected each sleeper, softly kneeling, sometimes raising himself up to peer through a cabin window. There were maybe green djellabahs, several of them, and yellow baboushes, but not yet both on the same man. Meticulously he inspected each truck, then circled the room's perimeter again. The target was missing.

Had the marabout lied? Or had he tipped off the target? Tony crouched beside a bus debating his next move when a voice called out, "Ay, Abdulatif!" He gripped the pistol, clicked off the safety, and slowly rose to full height before creeping around the vehicle for a clear line of sight towards the entrance, which framed a gray square of night beyond. Within the frame appeared an orange speck of light. Somebody smoking a cigarette. Tony froze. He couldn't see the face or much of anything else about the man. After a minute the orange speck arced through the air, and the man appeared to vanish. Tony waited another minute before moving again.

One last check of the garage. He was determined to make his first report to Captain Fillette a successful one. Truck, bus, bus, truck. Again he carefully inspected each one. Creeping along the back wall of the garage, he came to a rusted-out American military truck. Nobody slept beneath it, and the cabin was empty. He moved around towards the back, and in the bed of the truck, he saw a blanket move. Slowly, delicately, like a father checking on a sleeping infant, he reached out and took the edge of the blanket in his hand, gently pulling it towards him. A head was revealed, a green djellabah. The bastard had found an old mattress. Probably he'd been staying there for weeks, even months. Tony silently cursed. How many people would have had to keep the man's secret, willingly harboring a terrorist? As the blanket slid down, the body did not stir. Not that it mattered now. Already Tony had moved around at an angle for a clean shot at the man's head. Finally he flipped the blanket off his legs. On the man's feet were a pair of soiled yellow baboushes. Tony counted three of his own heartbeats then pulled the trigger twice in quick succession. The sound the shots made was no louder than two taps on the side of a tin gasoline can.

Then he moved deliberately back through the garage. No one appeared to have noticed the shots, and even if they had, there was nothing much to see: just a man in a djellabah killing another man in a djellabah. He slipped the Herstal back through the djellabah pocket and into his waistband before emerging out on the sidewalk. Rémy had not moved. Tony nodded, took another deep breath, and jumped on the back of the bike.

Headlights swarmed past, and cold wind washed his face. Beneath the djellabah he clasped his hands together. They did not tremble. All the people on the sidewalks would never know, but Casablanca was a safer place that night. Sleep a little easier. As the bike turned onto Boulevard de Lorraine, one pedestrian in particular caught his eye. That sniveling idiot Forestier, it looked like. That sickly little stutterer hurrying down the sidewalk as if someone was tailing him but he was too timid to break into a run. Tony smiled. Killing a man wasn't hard, provided you knew exactly why you were doing it.

○

The nervous Frenchman with buggy eyes wouldn't stop talking. "Yes, I'm g-g-going off to w-w-war. I just went over and handed in my papers. The officer on duty was th-th-thrilled. He said a man like m-m-me will see action right away. At first I was w-w-worried they would be closed, but th-th-they knew I was coming, and I have a f-f-feeling they stayed open for me."

At first she had wanted to laugh at the way his lips got stuck on certain words, but now she was bored with it and softly sang along to her new radio as he talked. One of her regulars had given her the radio, and she never turned it off, even when sleeping. How could she get this over quick? She had never seen the Frenchman before, and he obviously wasn't used to women. She was already practically naked, having undone her kaftan almost all the way down the front, but he avoided looking anywhere near the gap. She poured him another glass of tea. "*Merci*, Suzanne," he said, as if she had done him some big favor. This was already the second pot, and it was going to cost him.

"Let me show you my tattoo," she said with a leer, shrugging a shoulder free of the kaftan to expose a breast. The man seemed shocked and timidly sipped his tea. She lasciviously took the breast in her hand, rubbing her nipple with her thumb while watching him for a reaction. She read it out to him: "*Vive l'amour.*"

"What a b-b-beautiful sentiment," he said into his glass. So she stripped the kaftan off her other shoulder and let it fall to the ground. Nothing. Completely naked, she petulantly picked up a French society magazine from a chair and flopped onto the bed. Swiping through pages, she found the photographs of Georges Marchal. Now that was a man. Georges Marchal wouldn't have sat there drinking tea. Suzanne sighed. The star had just married the actress Dany Robin. Pale skin and blonde hair. Probably that was why the skinny Frenchman didn't want her. She got up, walked over to him, and pried the glass from his hand.

○

U.S. RUSHES BASES IN MOROCCO AREA DOLLAR WASTE DISREGARDED IN TERMS OF SPEEDY EFFICIENCY

By C.L. Sulzberger

NOUASSEUR AIR BASE, Morocco – In the event of a third world war, it would now be possible for the heaviest United States bombers to pulverize Soviet industrial centers from newly established bases in Greenland, the United Kingdom and French Morocco.

Of these three complexes, that being erected here is the largest. In compliance with United States Air Forces directives, its building is being supervised by the Army Corps of Engineers and actually handled by a special combine of five United States construction companies.

This is the largest individual undertaking that the Corps of Engineers has ever been in charge of. It involves the creation of five separate airfields, all with runways more than two miles long....[15]

---

15   *The New York Times* – 02/08/1952

4

"It's extraordinary," Abdelwahed cried, gazing around the new shop on Rue Nolly. Aziza eyed him suspiciously. Such a performer. She hadn't seen him in forever. But she was glad to see him, even if she wouldn't show it, and yes, the new shop was extraordinary. In business, at least, she had been a success. Mag's money had helped a bit, but mostly she'd earned it all herself. "To what do I owe the honor of a visit from *le beau français?*"

"I don't know if that's still a compliment." He flashed his movie star smile and stepped over to take her hand. She wondered where he was buying his suits. This one was nice, checked blue, a white handkerchief in the breast pocket. "I heard about your success, naturally, and found myself in the neighborhood. I've missed you, Aziza."

"And how are Zina and the children?" The question was now sincere, and no longer a subtle flirtation. For some time she had been acutely aware of no longer existing as a woman. Every day she welcomed women into her shop, and they trusted her to make them beautiful, but she never made herself beautiful anymore, nor was she sure she would ever want to again. Being a woman like that had only ever brought her pain. "Touria? I read everything about her. I save all the newspaper clippings." And she did, obsessively scouring the papers for news, filling folders with the clippings, sometimes spreading them on her desk in the evenings to read again. Her own daughter had been gone for two years.

"So, you're looking for something for Zina?" she continued. Her smile felt forced. "Or maybe for yourself?

I have a men's section now, you see. Although I always preferred you in a dress and silk stockings."

He chuckled. "No, I just had some time to kill. Touria and Zina are over at the palace visiting the Sultan."

She nodded. "I saw the photographs last year when you both visited him, after she got her license."

"A remarkable man. And of course I'm grateful for the interest he's taken in Touria."

Aziza felt a stray thread of anger inside and looked Abdelwahed in the eyes. He glanced away.

"Touria understands the dangers of her position," he said after a moment, "but like you, Aziza, she's an independent woman, and won't be told what to do. I can only pray that Allah protects her. How about Suzanne? She must be almost eighteen. How is she?"

Aziza thought of ignoring the question. "I haven't seen her in two years," she said coldly. "My daughter went off with some bad girls and never came back. Just like her father."

"I'm sorry," Abdelwahed murmured, obviously uncomfortable, but let him be the uncomfortable one for once. "If she's her mother's daughter, and I know she is, then I'm sure you have nothing to worry about."

But of course she had so much to worry about. Had she been a bad mother? The question preoccupied her more than any other. "Now, were you looking for something in particular? I just received some beautiful silk ties."

Abdelwahed smiled and glanced around the shop again, lingering on a purple kaftan with gold embroidery. "I'd better not," he said. "Money's rather tight at the moment…. I'm afraid this is somewhat embarrassing, but I was actually wondering whether I could borrow a few thousand francs just to get through end of the month."

She watched him for a long moment, not without pleasure, but the satisfaction of being freed from his spell also broke her heart. "Times are tough for everyone," she said. "You know I would help you if I could."

○

Not in a taxi. Aziza didn't want to be forced to say the name. In twenty years, she hadn't said the name, hadn't even thought it. But now she couldn't think of anything else. *Bousbir.* Taking a deep breath, she crossed the street in her most respectable kaftan. In the mirror she had even tried on a headscarf, quickly rejecting it as ridiculous. Around her neck was the same hand of Fatima that she'd worn for years, the one that had been meant to protect her from the evil eye.

Walking south through the dusk on Rue Pascal, a thousand times she almost turned back. She did not need to feel like this anymore. She had wanted to forget the past, but the past was where she believed her daughter lived. Months ago a customer had claimed to have spotted Suzanne at Bousbir. Aziza had immediately buried this piece of information alongside the name of the place. But her encounter with Abdelwahed had uncovered it, and now she needed to look.

At the gates she steered away from old Battuta, still in the filthy robes doing the blind man act. By now he had chewed enough francs to buy himself a house on Anfa hill. Aziza and her friends had always stopped to whisper filthy propositions into his ear on the days they got passes to go to the beach. This had always cured Battuta of his malady long enough to look them over. They had all been so young, and she wondered what had ever become of those girls. Some might still be working, she realized, into their forties now. The ones who had managed to save money might have become *patronnes*.

The main street she had expected to look different, but what had changed was her, and the street was still the same. Several drunken men approached her, immediately backing away from her fearsome scowl. Intimidation, at least, she had perfected. A few meters further along she thought she heard someone calling for Aziza, but she ignored the sound. Suzanne would have called her *mother*, if she still called her anything at all. There was still a chance.

"Aziza!" A creaky voice. She felt a bony hand at her elbow and turned. The hollow-cheeked face was familiar, if wrinkled by time, but she could not remember the name. All the names she had willed herself to forget.

The old *sous-maîtresse* had been ancient even in Aziza's days, too old for *passes*, but skilled at advertising the beauty and talents of girls who tipped for each new client she presented. "What a pleasure to see you, Aziza. How long has it been?"

Embarrassed by the familiarity, Aziza moved to pull her elbow free of the woman's grasp. But this was why she had come, so she forced herself to speak: "A long time. I'm glad to see you're in good health. Maybe you can help me. I – I am looking for my daughter Suzanne.

Perhaps you know her."

"Let's have tea and catch up," said the old crone too loudly, her grip tightening as she glanced down at Aziza's fine leather shoes. Other women watched them now from the entrances of houses. Aziza stiffened, but let the old *sous-maîtresse* pull her off down the street. "I don't want tea," she muttered, but the *sous-maîtresse* didn't respond.

Men looked her up and down as if she were on offer. They eyed her gold as if it made her more beautiful, and some whispered towards the *sous-maîtresse*, knowing she found delicacies. Aziza made her face into a mask. *Suzanne*, she had to remind herself, over and over again. Never had she felt so humiliated, even when she'd lived at Bousbir doing unimaginable things.

"You've had your fun," she hissed at the *sous-maîtresse*. "Now get me out of here." Another block, and then finally the old woman pulled her into a dingy passageway between two houses. Around the back of a house, with no one else in sight, she nodded at a low wooden door, her grin now missing a few teeth. Aziza felt sick. She moved towards the door, but the *sous-maîtresse* snarled, tapping a thin bare foot on the ground.

"Oh, what is it you want?" Aziza cried.

"Whatever you like," the woman said. Exasperated, Aziza reached for her purse, carelessly pulled out a hundred francs, then hesitated a moment and pulled out another hundred. "This stays between us," she said, handing over the bills.

"Suzanne gets twice as much," the woman said sourly. "Times have changed, my dear." Furious, Aziza thrust out another two hundred francs, and the *sous-*

maîtresse slipped the money into the folds of her haik before disappearing the way they'd come. Aziza stood before the door with a pounding heart, damp with misery although the night had grown cold. With her money she had paid like a man for her own daughter.

Past the doorway she followed a staircase up towards the sound of a radio. With each step her body felt heavier. At the top of the staircase was another door. Now she could almost make out the song on the radio, beneath the sound of a woman speaking in sweet, low tones. She did not hesitate then. She pushed open the door.

On the bed a skinny Frenchman wearing only socks was panting on top of a naked Suzanne. One of her daughter's arms was wrapped around the back of the man's head, so that his face was smothered between her breasts. She smoked a cigarette while droning bedroom French: "*Ooh cheri, c'est bon. Oui. C'est tellement bon.*"

Turning her head to exhale, Suzanne saw her mother. There was no time to react. Aziza launched herself towards the bed, wrestled the astonished Frenchman up into the air and dumped him on the floor, where he lay stunned and squirming. Suzanne defiantly put the cigarette to her mouth, not bothering to cover herself. Something French was tattooed across the body that Aziza had produced from her own cursed womb. Aziza felt the Frenchman scampering across the floor by her feet. She flung herself onto the bed and slapped her daughter twice, screaming, "Shame! Shame!" She beat her, scratched, as Suzanne clumsily fended her off. "Quiet, Mother! Not so loud!" The girl's face was contorted by fear, or hatred.

The main door banged open and women rushed

in screaming. Aziza drew away from the bed, and they covered Suzanne with a sheet, livid at the intruder, whose identity they hadn't guessed. Nobody had mothers here, and probably Suzanne had never mentioned Aziza, who stumbled back into a corner, crippled by rage. In a mirror she glimpsed the naked Frenchman in his socks, still cowering on the floor.

Suzanne lay on the bed and wept. The others forced Aziza and the Frenchman through the back door. Aziza stumbled down the staircase, throbbing with shame. Outside in the cold night she discovered the Frenchman again. He stood before her clutching a shirt to his waist, saying, "Your d-d-daughter is very b-b-beautiful, madame."

5

MOROCCAN SULTAN WANTS FRENCH OUT
SAYS THEY KEEP PROTECTORATE IN 'BABY CLOTHES' THOUGH IT HAS COME OF AGE

RABAT, French Morocco – Sultan Sidi Mohammed Ben Youssef, nominal ruler of this French protectorate, said today that while he was "profoundly touched" by the friendship of French officials, he wished they would go home.

In a "speech from the throne" on his twenty-fifth anniversary as Sultan, he compared the 40-year-old treaty under which France governs Morocco to "baby clothes" and said that "great tension" had been created by the French refusal to let his country figuratively wear long pants.

…his words were broadcast to Arabs from one end of strife-torn French North Africa to the other. The speech was considered certain to reinforce the nationalist case in coming United Nations debates.[16]

○

Zina followed Touria into the reception hall, looking especially beautiful in a new French dress. Touria wore her pilot's uniform and wasn't too concerned about

---

16   *United Press* – 11/18/1952

beauty. Her mother was nervous, Touria knew, having never met the Sultan. He sat across the room on a sort of throne, although maybe it was just a fancy chair, receiving a line of women who wished to kiss his hand. This was an annual tradition, the palace reception for prominent Moroccan women, mostly the wives and sisters of wealthy men, active in a variety of non-profit associations. The Sultan looked jovial and relaxed, although Touria knew from her father about the Fête du Trône speech he had made the day before, which had called for independence. The Sultan was a very brave man.

On tables across one side of the room were cookies, tea, and even Coca-Cola. Zina took Touria's hand, and for a while they stood alone in the crowd. Many women seemed to recognize her. They whispered and watched but didn't approach. Then eventually an attractive woman, about thirty-five and also unveiled, shook loose from the observers. She wore a stylish suit and silk stockings, squiggly lines up them like snakes. The woman presented herself – Hajja Aliya Alaoui, president of The Future of the Moroccan Girl, whose mission it was to teach underprivileged Moroccan girls practical skills, including reading and writing. At this point several other women approached, all association members, mostly wearing headscarves, among them Hajja Hiba, Hajja Aliya's younger sister, also very beautiful. They spoke in French, and so Zina understood little apart from her daughter's responses, which remained in Arabic, until Hajja Aliya looked sweetly at Zina and said, "Yes, better to speak in Arabic. And this must be your lovely mother."

Hajja Aliya had been impatient to meet the famous Touria Chaoui, she said, hoping the young pilot might someday do them the honor of joining the association board. The commitment would be negligible, she promised with a little light laughter. Touria's mere presence would be such an enormous benefit, not to mention an inspiration to those poor girls.

Touria's cheeks flushed. A *board member*. She had been longing for a new challenge. She was not like other girls her age and had been struggling to find a worthy cause to which to devote her attention. Sometimes she still felt as if she hadn't accomplished anything at all. Just a few newspaper stories, and little more. Her mother squeezed her hand.

Hajja Aliya knew what it was like to have an exceptional child, she told Zina. Her son, Haj Driss, was a few years older than Touria, and she believed he would also do great things for the country. But women needed to look out for one another, didn't Zina agree? Zina could only nod. Hajja, Haj. These names signified that the sisters had made the pilgrimage to Mecca. Hajja Aliya was probably even descended from the prophet.

Touria watched her mother closely. Still not entirely comfortable around adults, she sensed that Hajja Aliya might be saying something slightly different from the words she actually spoke, but the association itself sounded interesting, and she looked forward to learning more about it. Now, however, conversations across the room were trailing off. The Sultan, Allah protect him and his family, had risen. And when Touria turned, she found him beaming right at her, his arms spread wide.

"Touria!" he boomed.

"Come on, *Mouin*," she whispered to her mother "You have to meet the Sultan." Then she scampered over to him and was enveloped in a royal bear hug.

And as her mother watched the others watching Touria, she felt the same fear as on that stormy October morning when her daughter's little Cessna had disappeared into the clouds.

SELECTED BIBLIOGRAPHY

Michel Abitbol, *Histoire du Maroc*, Perrin, 2009.

Michel Abitbol, *Les Juifs d'Afrique du Nord sous Vichy*, Riveneuve Éditions, 2008.

Charles-Robert Ageron, *La décolonisation française*, Armand Colin, 1994.

Rick Atkinson, *An Army at Dawn: The War in North Africa, 1942–1943, Volume One of the Liberation Trilogy*, Henry Holt and Co., 2002.

Alison Baker, *Voices of Resistance: Oral Histories of Moroccan Women*, State University of New York Press, 1998.

Jean-Claude Baker, *Josephine: The Hungry Heart*, Random House, 2003.

Leon Borden Blair, *Western Window of the Arab world*, University of Texas Press, 1970.

Nadir Bouzar, *L'Armée de Libération Nationale Marocaine: Retour sans visa (journal d'un résistant maghrébin)*, Publisud, 2002.

Tim Brady, *Twelve Desperate Miles: The Epic World War II Voyage of the SS Contessa*, Crown, 2012.

François Broche, *L'assassinat de Lemaigre-Dubreuil: Casablanca, le 11 juin 1955*, Balland, 1977.

Paul Brown, *The Whorehouse of the World: Tales of Wartime Italy – Casablanca, Algiers and Sicily*, AuthorHouse, 2004.

Jean-Louis Cohen and Monique Eleb, *Casablanca, mythes et figures d'une aventure urbaine*, Hazan, 2004.

Carleton Stevens Coon, *A North Africa Story: The Anthropologist as OSS Agent 1941–1943*, Gambit Publications, 1980.

Guy Delanoë, *Le retour du Roi et l'indépendance retrouvée, Tome 3*, L'Harmattan, 1991.

Guy Delanoë, *Lyautey, Juin, Mohamed V, Fin d'un protectorat, Tome 1*, L'Harmattan, 1988.

Carlo d'Este, *Patton, A Genius for War*, Harper-Collins, 1995.

Gilbert Grandval, *Ma mission au Maroc*, Plon, 1956.

Luella Jemima Hall, *The United States and Morocco, 1776–1956*, Scarecrow, 1971.

James J. Heaphey, *Legerdemain: The President's Secret Plan, the Bomb, And What the French Never Knew*, History Publishing Co., 2007.

William A. Hoisington, Jr., *The Assassination of Jacques Lemaigre-Dubreuil: A Frenchman between France and North Africa*, Routledge, 2011.

Abdellatif Laabi, *The Bottom of the Jar*, Archipelago, 2013.

John W. Lambert, *Wildcats over Casablanca*, Phalanx, 1992.

Rom Landau, *Moroccan Drama*, Robert Hale, 1956.

Christine Lévisse-Touzé, *L'Afrique du Nord dans la guerre, 1939–1945*, Albin Michel, 1998.

Jean Mathieu and P.H. Maury, *Bousbir: La prostitution à Casablanca*, Paris Méditerranée, 2003.

Antoine Méléro, *La main rouge: L'armée secrète de la République*, Éditions du Rocher, 1997.

Marc Méraud, *Histoire des A.I.: Le service des Affaires indigènes*, Public-réalisations, 1990.

Susan Gilson Miller, *A History of Modern Morocco*, Cambridge University Press, 2013.

Jacques Mordal, *La bataille de Casablanca*, Plon, 1952.

Robert Murphy, *Diplomat Among Warriors*, Doubleday, 1964.

Kenneth M. Pendar, *Adventures in Diplomacy: Our French Dilemma*, Simon Publications, 2003.

C.R. Pennell, *Morocco since 1830: A History*, NYU Press, 2001.

Douglas Porch, *The French Secret Service*, Farrar-Straus-Giroux, 1995.

Elliott Roosevelt, *As He Saw It*, Greenwood Press, 1974.

Beatrice Russell, *Living in State*, D. McKay, 1959.

Richard Harris Smith, *OSS: The Secret History of America's First Central Intelligence Agency*, University of California Press, 1972.

Georges Spillmann, *Du protectorat à l'indépendance, Maroc 1912–1955*, Plon, 1967.

Lucian K. Truscott, *Command Missions*, Presidio Press, 1990.

Hal Vaughan, *FDR's 12 Apostles: The Spies Who Paved the Way for the Invasion of North Africa*, Lyons Press, 2006.

PHOTO CREDITS

Chaoui family archives (used with permission): p. 218, 245, 260, 262
Collection of the author: p. 5, 87, 96, 117, 138, 197, 212
Nelson C. Brown High School - Nouasseur, Morocco – www.nouasseur.com: p. 281

9 798988 840254 1